SWORD
OF THE
GLADIATRIX

FAITH L. JUSTICE

RAGGEDY MOON BOOKS

Sword of the Gladiatrix

2015
Raggedy Moon Books
raggedymoonbooks.com

Cover image licensed from iStockphoto.com
Cover design by Todd Engle
toddengle-englecreative.com

Print ISBN-13: 978-0692386491
Print ISBN-10: 0692386491

*To Hope and Robyn
who continue to fight the good fight.*

By Faith L. Justice

Novels:

Selene of Alexandria

Twilight Empress: A Novel of Imperial Rome
(coming in 2015)

Non-fiction:

Hypatia: Her Life and Times

Short Story Collections:

Time Again and Other Fantastic Stories

Slow Death and Other Dark Tales

The Reluctant Husband and Other Historical Tales
(coming in 2015)

Acknowledgments

I CONSULTED A HUNDRED OR MORE BOOKS, dozens of people, a couple of top flight museums; personally tramped the streets of Rome and Pompeii; sat in Roman amphitheaters; and gazed at the ancient graffiti advertising gladiator games during the course of writing this book. Among the books I found most helpful were: *The Kingdom of Kush* by Derek A. Welsby, *Boudica: Iron Age Warrior Queen* by Richard Hingley and Christina Unwin, *Nero: The End of a Dynasty* by Miriam T. Griffin, *Pompeii: A Guide to the Ancient City* by Salvatore Nappo, *Roman Sports and Spectacles: A Sourcebook* by Anne Mahoney, *Invisible Romans* by Robert Knapp, *Spectacles of Death in Ancient Rome* by Donald G. Kyle, *Isis in the Ancient World* by R. E. Witt, and *The Gods of the Celts* by Miranda Green. You can find a much more comprehensive bibliography on my website.

I am forever grateful to members of my writer's group *Circles in the Hair* for reading and critiquing the first couple of drafts of this book. Their encouragement and advice was invaluable. Many thanks to my beta readers Alisha, Hope, and Laura who gave freely of their time and feedback. As always, I cannot give enough credit to my husband Gordon Rothman and daughter Hannah Rothman for their unique contributions to the book and their never-wavering support. Did I mention the cats? They didn't do much except sit on the keyboard and sleep on my piles of notes…but they were cute doing it

*But who has never seen a woman behind her defiant shield
repeatedly striking at the exercise pole with her sword?
A helmeted woman like that thinks she can do anything.*
—Satyricon *by Juvenal*

Characters in Order of Appearance

Afra—Roman name meaning "Woman of Africa," Kushite name Amanirenas—huntress from Kingdom of Kush, gladiatrix, fights as *myrmilla*

Cinnia—young British woman of the Iceni tribe, gladiatrix, fights as Thracian

Decimus Cornial Asina—Roman general sent to Kush

Kashta—chief advisor to the Kushite King and Pye's father

Piye—Kasta's son, Asata's husband, Afra's brother-in-law

Amanitenmemide—*Qore* (king) of Kush

Amanikhatashan—*Kandake* (queen) of Kush

Suetonius Paulinus—Roman Governor of the province of Britannia

Lucius Marcius—Roman trader

Asata—Afra's step-sister, married to Piye

Oriana—Dumnor's wife, Cinnia's sister-in-law

Melva—Oriana's younger sister

Dumnor—Cinnia's brother

Boudica—Iceni Queen

Prasutagus—Iceni King

Brianna—Boudica's older daughter (actual name unknown)

Maeve—Boudica's younger daughter (actual name unknown)

Catus Decianus—Procurator of Rome, Province of Britannia

Quintus Petilius Cerialis Caesius Rufus—general in charge of the IXth Legion

Mesbat—Asata's mother, Afra's step-mother

Clio—snake handler/dancer, Lucius Marcius' wife

Rufus—a friend of Lucius Marcius

Paetus—*doctore*, gladiator trainer

Varro—brothel owner

Caecus—brothel doorkeeper

Bassa—Roman matron, prisoner

Corva—old woman herbalist, prisoner

Celer—lame boy, prisoner

Priscus—poet, prisoner

Sextus Licinius Murena—Pompeii magistrate

Calvus—gladiator recruiter

Silo—*lanista*, gladiator school owner

Julia—Roman gladiatrix, fights as *retiaria*

Gerta—German gladiatrix, fights as *secutor*

Portia—Roman gladiatrix, fights as *myrmilla*

Barba—*doctore*, gladiator trainer

Fullo—*ludus* slave in charge of supplies

Naso—beast handler

Capeio—*doctore*, gladiator trainer

Nero Claudius Caesar Augustus Germanicus—Emperor of Rome AD 54-68

Poppaea Sabina—Augusta, Nero's second wife

SWORD
OF THE
GLADIATRIX

FAITH L. JUSTICE

PROLOGUE

A FRA! AFRA!" THE CROWD IN THE AMPHITHEATER CHANTS MY NAME, calling me forward to kill or be killed for their amusement. The Romans call me Afra—"woman of Africa"—because they don't care to wrap their tongues around my real name. Or perhaps the fact that I am named after Amanirenas the one-eyed warrior queen, who wiped out the Roman garrison at Aswan two generations ago, gives them pause. It matters little now.

A slave wraps my lower legs with felted wool and straps a gilded greave to my left shin, because I fight as *myrmilla*. He smells of sour sweat, as do I. I've already fought once today, tested fate, and won. The gold sand that Nero favors in the arena still crusts my hair and rasps the skin under my sweat-soaked breast band. I will go again before the ravenous crowds to satisfy their bloodlust. For what? An emperor's whim? The crowd's passing fancy? A sacrifice to their gods?

I swallow the bitter gall that surges into my mouth.

Across the room, another slave straps armor on Cinnia, my beloved. She looks at me with pride in her eyes and a brief smile on her lips. We said our goodbyes last night, clasped breast to breast, thigh to thigh, a stolen moment before being sent to our lonely cells. My heart beats an irregular rhythm.

My love. Light to my dark. Fire to my ice.

Cinnia is goddess-given to me; from a land of mists and forests, so different from my country of desert and blistering sun. Without her, I would be dead. Without me, so would she. We have suffered, struggled, lived, and loved. Now we go out upon the sands of the great arena to die. One by her lover's hands, the other by her own.

It is not the life or death I chose for myself, but it is the one the gods gave me.

CHAPTER ONE

Kingdom of Kush, in the sixth year of Nero's reign (60 CE)

AFRA WATCHED WITH HER FELLOW KUSHITES, as the small contingent of Roman soldiers escorted General Decimus Cornial Asina through the streets and plazas of the Kush capital of Meroe. The setting sun washed the city in bloody light—an ill omen. As their guide from the Egyptian border, she should have tried to delay the Romans till morning, a more auspicious time for new beginnings.

She shook her head. *Leave the auguring to the priests. Only they can determine the will of the gods, what is auspicious, what is ill-omened. Besides, the General had been most insistent on setting the pace. Any ill-luck is his own.*

The blare of curved horns—what the Romans call *buccinae*—announced the Roman presence at the palace. Bright limestone steps led up to a colonnade sheltering a massive wooden door, flanked by monumental stone carvings of the king on one side and the queen on the other; both smiting their enemies with flails and spears. The red sun reflected off the soldiers' burnished breastplates and sharp spears.

Kashta, the king's chief advisor, and his own entourage of aides and guards, met the delegation with their own fine show of trumpets and drums. Among them, Afra spotted Piye, Kashta's son and her step-sister's husband, dressed in shimmering striped robes. His hooked nose curved over a cruel mouth.

Her stomach roiled and her lips unconsciously curled into a snarl.

Gods curse him!

A final flourish of trumpets called her attention back to the ceremony. The chief advisor raised his hands for silence. "My Lord Amanitenmemide, *Qore* of the Kushites, born of the gods, and his wife *Kandake* Amanikhatashan, Mother of the next *Qore*, bids the representative of Nero, Imperator of the Romans, welcome to their lands."

General Asina gave the briefest of bows. Afra knew he would take the King's absence as a slight on his honor. Her people knew the absence of the queen was just as great an insult. Perhaps it was meant to be. If so, it was a dangerous game to bait these Romans.

Asina intoned in his stentorian voice, "Imperator Nero Claudius Caesar Augustus Germanicus, *Pontifex Maximus*, *Pater Patriae* and four times Consul of the People of Rome sends his greetings."

Kashta did not bend his neck. "My *Qore* has had accommodations prepared for you, but asks your pardon for his absence. He has duties in the temple of Amun and will greet you properly at a feast in your honor after you have rested and refreshed yourselves." Asina gave him a stiff nod and ordered his men to camp outside the walls. An honor guard accompanied him to his more comfortable accommodations.

The Romans marched off and the crowd dispersed, muttering. One young man spat in the street as the Romans left it. Three women with kohl-rimmed eyes watched the soldiers retreat; speculative smiles on their faces. Afra shrugged as the women drifted down the street in the Roman's wake. Everyone had to eat. If not for her hunting skills, it might be she following the Romans to their beds. The thought made her shudder.

Thank you Mother Isis, Queen of all Gods, Goddesses, and Women for saving me from that fate.

Afra walked across the plaza fronting the palace and the brightly painted Temple of Amun, wondering if she dared visit her step-sister before retiring for the night. She lived for Asata's smiles and loving embraces, but it was dangerous meeting too often. Her rumbling stomach and a whiff of rancid odor decided for her. Dinner, then a wash.

She didn't make it to her room.

One of the queen's servants caught up to her, panting. "Huntress, the *Kandake* wishes to talk to you."

Afra indicated her sweat-stained linen clothes, worn sandals, and dusty hair. "Now? It's been a long journey escorting the Romans from Hierasykaminos. I don't wish to offend the *Kandake* with my stink."

The slave sniffed and raised the corner of his mouth. "She says at once."

AFRA ENTERED *KANDAKE* AMANIKHATASHAN'S private receiving chamber through a small back entrance used for servants and others with more clandestine charges. Afra had used that entrance more than once doing the queen's bidding. The room opened on an interior courtyard which, during the day, provided bright light and cooling breezes. Now the room glowed in the soft light of oil lamps hung from the ceiling. Coals in a brass brazier chased off the night chill and gave flickering life to the frescos of Nile plants and animals on the wall. The queen entered and Afra abased herself on the soft wool carpet.

"Rise and be seated. Take some refreshment." In the tradition of Kushite queens, Amanikhatashan was an immense woman—shorter than Afra by a head, but three times her girth. Her dusky skin glistened with oil; her ears, hands, and arms glittered with gold ornaments. A gold pectoral decorated with blue faience rested on the substantial bosom of her white linen gown. She had not finished her preparations for the Roman banquet. The queen's shaved head awaited the elaborate wig and headdress reminiscent of the ancient Egyptians her ancestors had once ruled.

Afra perched on a chair decorated with blue-green cushions made of a smooth material that felt like water gliding over her fingers—silk it was called, from lands beyond the east sea. She reached for a blue glass goblet filled with cool wine but left the plate of sliced melon untouched.

The queen settled on a more substantial couch and clasped her hands in her lap. Afra lowered her eyes and awaited the queen's pleasure.

Finally the queen nodded. "My daughter, you have been a good and faithful servant since you came to me two years ago. Your hunting skills are renowned and you have completed every…delicate…task set to you with diligence and discretion."

Afra bowed her head in acknowledgment. She had seen but eighteen summers when her step-mother drove her from home, calling her abomination. These last two years, serving her queen, allowed her hope of a future with Asata.

The queen sampled the wine and looked at Afra over the rim of her goblet. "What did you learn on the trek?"

"A little, *Kandake*. I'm still learning their language." She smiled. "The General's name, Asina, means female ass. For some reason the Romans delight in having insulting names."

"Now I will have difficulty speaking to the man without seeing a braying donkey." The queen's eyes sparkled then sharpened. "But I need to know more than their penchant for silly names. Why this expedition? Why now? Relations are good with Rome. Trade is profitable."

"The soldiers are sharp-eyed; the traders anxious. Asina talks of a journey to discover the origins of the Mother Nile. All seem curious about the source of our gold and ivory."

"Rome expands like a desert storm, gobbling up all the lands on their borders. They fill our northern horizon and menace us with destruction." The queen leaned back into her cushions, frowning. "If they see any benefit to adding our land to theirs, they will crush us."

"Can we not defend ourselves? Frighten them with a show of strength? The Romans in the garrisons on the border are few. I heard of rebellion on their other frontiers."

"Kashta and others would like to think so, but…" The queen shook her head and sipped her wine. "What the Romans want, the Romans get—eventually. Even your namesake struck only a temporary blow. She destroyed a garrison and took the bronze head of Augustus as a trophy, but the Romans returned in force and destroyed her capital Napata. We must offer neither defiance nor thought of treasure."

They sat in silence for a few moments until the queen lifted her head and said with a bitter smile, "We must convince them Kush has nothing that cannot be gotten easier elsewhere."

Afra saw the sense in the queen's instincts. She had seen the discipline of the soldiers on the border and listened carefully to the stories of conquest they boasted of. It rankled her soul to offer no resistance, but she trusted the queen understood the extent of the Roman threat. Afra was a hunter. She recognized the predator in the Roman attitude, but had no way to gauge the larger danger to her country. That task lay with the *Qore* and *Kandake*, who had other spies among the Romans and traders.

"The Romans wish to continue south. You are right. They seek the source of our riches under the guise of this quest to find the source of our Mother River." The queen handed Afra a leather bag filled with clinking coins. "You know the lands to the south best. Take the Romans through the most desolate wastes to the Great Swamp. Your task is not only to guide the men, but also guide their thoughts away from conquest. This is a subtle task. Do you think you can do it?"

"I will do my utmost."

"That is all I ask." The queen smiled. "I will plant one or two others in the expedition with the same message. If you succeed, there will be a greater reward."

"Thank you, *Kandake*." Afra bowed deeply.

On her way out of the palace she hefted the bag of coins. Yes, she would soon have enough to pay back her step-sister's bride price and take her away from Piye. *Asata, my gentle love…sister with the voice of a song bird.* She winced at the memory of the last time they had met: Asata sobbing in her arms, eye swollen shut, lips bruised. *When I return.*

Chapter Two

Roman Province of Britannia, 60 CE

CINNIA KEPT A FIRELESS VIGIL on a ridge above the Roman army camped on the shore across from the Sacred Isle of the Druids—what the Romans called Mona. She breathed into her cupped hands to warm them. Why were they here? She thought the new Roman Governor Paulinus fought the rebel Silures in the hills to the southwest. Besides, it was late fall, time for warriors to retire to their winter quarters. Her people, the Iceni, were allies of Rome. She should be able to walk up to the camp and ask questions, but something told her to hide. If the Romans were on the march, no one was safe, much less a young native woman. She had heard stories…

Her empty stomach distracted her thoughts. Cinnia was nearly out of journey bread. She'd eaten the last of the dried meat two days ago. She had planned to be on the Sacred Isle by now, feasting with her father. Her brother's wife had given birth to a healthy son—her father's first grandchild and she brought the news. But that was just an excuse for her to visit her father after a long absence.

Father. She could almost feel his strong arms lifting her up, see his crooked smile and green eyes sparkling with humor, smell the wood smoke in his hair. She shook off the dream state and concentrated on the Romans. She couldn't afford to be stumbled over, but sometimes the waking dreams were hard to disperse. She did not want to wander in that other world too long. Her brother showed no aptitude—in spite of springing from a long line of druids and bards—for other world walking. But perhaps his son would...in time.

Since her mother had died of a fever seven years ago, her father had taken Cinnia on most of his wanderings. She learned the songs, folk lore, and minor rituals at his knee. Her heart rejoiced in the roaming bardic life, but she knew her fate was to be married. Her tall form and curly blond hair attracted attention when they travelled. When Cinnia turned sixteen last year, her father left her with her brother and his wife and came to Mona to complete his Druidic training.

Burrowing under a pile of oak leaves, and wrapped in her faded green and brown checked cloak, Cinnia watched the Romans patrolling the shore; no craft was in sight except their heavily guarded flat-bottomed boats. The currents were treacherous in the strait even when the tide was out, providing further protection to the Druid sanctuary. She could see campfires across the narrow stretch of water. Druids? Bards? Warriors? She debated trying to make her way across the water and joining her people. She was strong and, like most Iceni, perfectly capable of defending herself. But she was not of the warrior class. She carried but a single weapon, a knife with a carved bone hilt—a gift from her father—used for cutting meat and other camp tasks. Cinnia could do nothing but watch and wait. Maybe the Romans would move on. Surely if they *did* attack, her gods would protect their most holy site.

By dusk, Cinnia had tired of watching the Romans. They scurried like ants around the tidy camp, hiding behind a protective ditch and palisade. Inside were neat rows of tents and fires providing hot food. Her stomach growled. Cinnia pulled out the last of her journey bread and moistened it with water. She drank sparingly, not wanting to leave her vantage point to relieve herself. She burrowed further under the leaves for warmth, plumped her pack and fell into a fitful sleep.

*****

Cinnia woke to a great din from across the straits and crawled to her observation point. Clouds rolled across the skies; dark and threatening rain. Wind whipped white caps on the water as the tide receded. The harsh sound of the *carnyx*, the tribal war horn, drifted across the water. She couldn't hear the shouts of individual warriors as they clashed their swords against their shields, but they came to her as a dull roar. The white forms of naked women danced among the warriors, shrieking and brandishing torches, spurring the men to greater frenzy. Behind them she saw a rank of white-robed druids raising their hands and casting curses on the Romans.

Fear squeezed Cinnia's chest; her heart shuddered and her breath came in gasps. Surely her gods would protect the sacred isle. She squinted, trying desperately to spy her father, but the distance was too great. She looked at the lowering skies and prayed. "May Andrasta honor our sacrifices and give strength and victory to our people." She cut her thumb with the knife and allowed a few drops to fall to the roots of the sacred oak. "Keep Father safe, please?"

The Romans seemed to ignore the people on the island and concentrate on their tasks. When the tide ebbed, the infantry marched to the boats, filled them in an orderly fashion and cast off. A huge flotilla rowed toward the island. The cavalry mounted their horses and urged them into the surf to wade and swim the brief distance.

Cinnia stifled a cheer when a boat capsized and the heavily armored Romans sank like stones. Another, then another boat overturned in the currents. The treacherous water swept away some horses and their riders.

The Roman losses seemed to spur the warriors on the island. Several two-wheeled war chariots careened across the open field between the water and the massed tribes. Warriors ran along the poles between two ponies brandishing their spears at the approaching enemy, while others drove the wicker fighting platforms.

Cinnia rose to sprint down to the shore, as the last of the Romans shoved off and the first made landing on the Sacred Isle.

The shouting charioteers surged toward the first Roman boats. Cinnia heard a sharp twang and whistling sound as Roman archers loosed a cloud of arrows from the incoming boats. Immediately the cries of the chariot warriors turned into sounds of pain and fear. Several teams went down, entangling others. The Romans formed up and threw a flight of deadly spears at the surge of warriors following the chariots. The *pila* caught in the warriors' shields, bent and entangled them making the shields difficult to maneuver, if not useless.

The tribes milled in confusion, then charged again, but it was too late. The Romans locked their large shields together, pushing the struggling warriors back and stabbing with their short swords. They moved on, leaving the dead for the ravens that already began to flock to the killing field.

"Father," Cinnia whimpered, tears flowing down her face.

TWO DAYS LATER, Cinnia crept out of her hiding place and walked slowly to a fen north of the abandoned Roman camp. She had watched as the fires died down on the island and the Romans returned to the mainland with their booty. No captives. No slaves. Her heart and body chilled, Cinnia pulled a round leather coracle from a reed blind. Cold water seeped into her leather boots and soaked her wool trousers. Long before she reached the other shore, smoke from burning trees and the sickly sweet stench of roasting human flesh stung her nose. She beached her coracle and walked through the carnage.

Desolation and death.

Cinnia couldn't take in the enormity of it all.

Everyone dead. Men, women, children, animals. All dead.

She staggered through the sacred oak grove. Every tree lay toppled to the ground, killed by Roman axes. Burned bodies, with arms outstretched, as if to protect the trees, dotted the grove like grisly flowers.

Feeling like she walked in a dream, Cinnia approached the druid village. Smoking piles of naked bodies guarded the gate. Cinnia held her cloak over her nose and tried to breathe through her mouth, the smell of shit from voided bowels, vied with the stench of decay. She had seen people die of sickness and wounds, but never in such numbers. She doubled over and retched until her throat burned and her stomach ached with its emptiness. She sat, head in hands, not wanting to find her father among the dead, unable to erase the visions of butchery from her mind.

She heard others on the path and panicked. Had the Romans returned? She ducked behind a tumbled stone wall and peered out. A small group of men, with the same shocked look on their faces as on hers, stared gape-mouthed at the destruction. A tall man, with the sunburned look of a farmer led them. Cinnia dried her tears, wiped the snot from her face, and stepped onto the path.

The farmer looked her over. "We came over from the mainland. You have kin here?"

She nodded.

"So do I." He looked around at the devastation, jaw set; anger smoldering in his eyes. "May Taranis eat the bloody Romans' balls and crows peck out their eyes."

Cinnia barely heard the curses.

Tomorrow. Maybe tomorrow she would be angry. Today she just felt empty.

Chapter Three

Kush, south of Meroe

THE WEATHER WAS HOT AND DRY on the plain leading south, so the pre-dawn coolness felt good as Afra surveyed the Roman camp. The soldiers began to stir as the sky reddened in the east. A Roman trumpet sounded and they tumbled from their tents, grumbling and farting. After twenty days traveling, she admired their discipline. The Roman troops shouldered their heavy packs, marched at least fifteen miles a day and built a defensible camp at night. Over and over, they built to the same design, pitched their eight-man tents in the same order and ate the same food. She wondered if they ever tired of it.

Afra's own nightly assignment was near the temporary southern gate with a delegation of Roman traders. One, Lucius Marcius, emerged from his tent and fed dried mule dung to the cooling embers of his own fire. The meager flames flickered, casting his eyes in shadow.

"You would do better putting it out," she told him. "We move soon."

Marcius drew in a sharp breath. "Mercury's balls, Afra, you gave me a start!" He surveyed the dying fire, kicked dirt over the coals, and mumbled. "I *hate* breaking my fast with cold barley. You can bet that fancy-assed general is eating warm bread and cheese."

She smiled. Asina most likely breakfasted on cold roast meat from the gazelle she shot yesterday. Afra supplied the general's table for a bonus. She left the grumbling trader to prepare her own pack for the day.

Marcius caught up with her late in the day. Huffing a little at her pace, he scratched the salt from his three-day's growth of beard. "I've never been in a land that robs your very skin of moisture. In Rome and Alexandria, at least, the sweat rolls off. How do you live here?"

"I don't."

"Who does? I've seen tracks at the watering holes."

"Nomads. They travel from oasis to oasis with a few goats and cattle."

Marcius glanced at Afra from under a furrowed brow. "We've seen little on this trek but sand and scorpions. It almost seems as if you lead us through the worst land."

She shrugged. "You've traveled down Mother Nile. What did you see beyond the shores?"

"Desert."

"What makes you think anything would be different in Kush? We cannot travel by the river. It twists and turns and has many cataracts. This is a shorter trail."

Marcius gave her a sharp look. "We're upland. In my experience, when you gain height the weather cools. Besides, I've seen the gold, ivory, animals, and slaves flowing from your land."

"Through, not from. Kush is merely a place on the road from beyond to beyond." She waved along the horizon. "Ships from the East come to our shores. Caravans trek to Mother Nile beyond the cataracts."

Marcius blew dust from his nostrils and wiped his nose on this sleeve.

"What business do you have with Rome—this expedition?" she asked.

"I'm a hunter."

Afra snorted her disbelief.

"It's true! I work for an association in Alexandria scouting for wild animals for the games."

As she thought, a trader, not a true hunter. "Games?" She raised an eyebrow.

"Blood sport. The Roman people like to watch skilled hunters and fighters. We buy wild animals and send them to Rome to be hunted in the arenas."

"What sport in watching?" Killing animals for defense, sacrifice, food, or testing personal skills seemed reasonable. But killing for the entertainment of others?

"It depends on the *venatore*—the beast hunter—and how good a show he puts on." Marcius pulled a water skin from his belt and took a swallow. "How long will this trek take?"

Afra shrugged. "As long as the general wants. He says he's looking for the source of the Nile."

Marcius kept a placid face. His demeanor might not betray the true nature of this expedition, but his questions did—exploitation and possibly conquest. She pointed her spear toward the rugged terrain ahead. "Maybe another ten or fifteen days."

Marcius winced as he put a foot wrong on a stone and twisted his ankle. "Gods blasted shithole of a country..." He muttered to himself as he fell behind her long strides.

THE EXPEDITION CAME DOWN from the dry highlands to travel along a tributary of the Nile. The light sandy soil supported scrubby grassland and silted the river, giving it the name "White Nile."

Afra squatted next to Marcius at a campfire on the edge of the encampment. A lion coughed in the brush, a deep "hunh hunh" sound.

Marcius raised his head. "Anything other than lions around here?"

"Cheetahs, gazelles, giraffes." She ran her hand over her stubbled head. Like many, she shaved her head to avoid pests and lessen the heat. Her hair was starting to grow back. "Further on, elephants, birds, crocodiles."

"It's a long trek to bring them back." Marcius frowned. "Most would die."

"Egypt has crocodiles and hippos; Libya, many lions. Less work."

The lion coughed again. Afra stared into the blackness beyond the fire. "Don't leave the camp. Piss in the sand or take a torch."

"I've been in the wild before," Marcius muttered.

She rolled herself in her cloak and settled for sleep, back to the fire and spear in hand.

The next day they reached the Great Swamp. From horizon to horizon lay a drowned land, punctuated with grassy hammocks and tangled plants. The Romans pitched a soggy camp and Afra went out to procure the general's dinner. Flocks of ducks, geese, storks, and sacred ibis blackened the sky at any noise. She unslung her bow and pulled several small arrows from a leather quiver.

At the sound of mud sucking at feet, she turned around. Marcius stood, hands on hips, frowning at the horizon. "Any way around this?"

"I've walked for many days in both directions and never came to the end." She swatted a mosquito from her arm.

A leopard cried in the distance and a flock of saddlebill storks rose with a thunder of wings. Afra swung around, took aim and shot one arrow after another in rapid succession. For every arrow, a bird fell from the sky.

"Well done, Afra. I've seldom seen such skill with a bow." Marcius rubbed his hands and smacked his lips. "Fresh meat for dinner. A treat after days of journey bread and beans. I'll help you gather them."

"Stay back." She slung her bow and hefted her spear to test the ground on her way. Afra heard Marcius blundering after her and called out, "Walk in my steps!"

Too late.

"Afra, help!" The Roman sunk to his knees and struggled in a sink hole.

"Don't move!" She rushed back to the edge of the quicksand. Marcius stood, several feet away, white surrounding his dark eyes, sinking to his hips.

"Struggle makes it worse. Here." She tossed her spear toward Marcius.

He grabbed it, the fear on his face momentarily changing to puzzlement. He struggled and sank deeper. "Help me!"

"Idiot! Don't move. The sand will suck you down. Slowly…put the spear on the surface, lie back on to it. You will float."

Panting, Marcius did as she said. As his chest and arms floated to the top, his breathing eased.

"Relax. Now move the spear under your hips."

His hips and legs resurfaced.

"Slowly…use your arms to row towards me… Don't flail! Be calm. Go slow."

Inch by inch, Marcius made his way. When his head and shoulders touched solid ground, she grabbed him under the arms and slowly pulled him toward safety. Finally, his legs and feet came out of the sinkhole with a distinct, sucking sound. Marcius lay on the ground trembling.

"Always listen to your guide in a strange land." She retrieved her spear and wiped it off with a handful of grass. "Stay. I'll get the birds and come back for you."

Marcius stayed.

On the way back to Meroe, Afra listened to the grumbling and complaints among the soldiers and traders.

"Nothing but sand or mud…scorpions or mosquitoes."

"People have nothing but goats and even they're tough and stringy."

"No wine…just brackish water…if there's water at all."

She seemed to have accomplished her mission. She smiled to herself. *Soon, Asata, soon!*

The night before they entered Meroe, Marcius sought her out by her fire. "Afra, I have a proposition for you."

"What?"

"I've watched you on this trip. You're one of the best hunters I've come across. Even in that cursed desert you managed to find a hare or two."

"So?"

"I want you to come back with me to Rome. Skilled hunters are in great demand for the games. You could earn a good deal of money."

"What need have I for Roman money? My *Kandake* provides shelter, food, and money."

Marcius frowned. "For the experience, then. Don't you wonder what the world is like beyond Meroe? There are palaces, five times bigger than your queen's, and they belong to merchants not nobles. You can wear cloth from India softer than the fur of a cat. Taste food sweetened with honey from Spain. Hear music from Greece."

She raised her hand to ward off further words.

"Do you have family to care for? Aging parents, siblings, a child?"

"You do not ask about a husband."

"You don't act like a woman around men, flirting or shy. I assumed you were a *tribade*—a woman who loves other women." Marcius shrugged. "Some *tribades* marry, but no husband would allow his wife to travel among men as you do."

"These…*tribades*…are they common in Rome? Accepted?" The idea startled her. She knew no one who shared her feelings except Asata; but Afra lived her life among men. Maybe there were other—*tribades?*—among her countrywomen. She shook her head. She wanted Asata, no one else.

"Not common, but known. Accepted?" He scratched his beard. "I'd say tolerated. All have heard the stories of the rich and their orgies: men with men, women with women, both with beasts. Some consider that an abomination, but the rich do as they please. Common women? They have to provide for themselves as best they can. Generally what happens behind closed doors is no one else's business."

Afra sat silent, poking the fire. A place where she and Asata could live together; be…tolerated. Her step-mother accused her of corrupting her step-sister—leading her away from her natural path as wife and mother—but Afra believed Mesbat's anger had more to do with losing the prestige of a connection with the king's first minister.

Mother Isis, can this be true? Can Asata and I live together, love together in a far-off land?

"I have no family myself, just a…" Marcius paused, his eyes hooded.

"My mother died when I was born," Afra said. "My father married a widow with a daughter two years younger than I." Her lips curled into a sweet smile at the thought of Asata, then faded. Rome was a distant dream, possibly as ephemeral as a desert mirage. She couldn't drag Asata to a foreign land.

"Afra, you could earn a lot of gold for your family. If your father gave permission? I could talk to him."

"My father is dead. My step-mother banished me from her house, and I am forbidden to see my step-sister. She is married to the son of Kashta, the king's chief advisor."

"Afra, you're a free woman!" He clapped her on the shoulder. "Come to Rome with me. I'll make you rich."

"I will think on it, but my loyalty is to my *Kandake*." *And Asata.*

AFRA MET WITH THE QUEEN the evening after they reentered the city. The queen raised her from her abasement with a smile. "General Donkey seemed unimpressed by the country to the south. My agent confirms he plans to report to his emperor that Kush is too poor and too far away to be worth conquest." She placed a fat pouch of clinking coins in Afra's hand. "You did well, my daughter, and earned your reward."

Afra bowed low, blood running warm from the praise. "My only wish is to serve. Thank you, *Kandake*."

Leaving the queen's quarters, she counted the coins then tied the pouch onto her belt. Now she had enough money and could make amends.

"TELL YOUR MISTRESS, her sis—a friend bearing gifts has come to visit." Afra looked over the man's head into the interior of her step-sister's splendid house. Brilliant yellow, green, and blue frescos, showing leopards hunting river birds on the shores of the Nile, adorned the walls of the reception room. It put her poor room over the stables to shame.

The servant looked her over and sniffed. Afra's blood rose. She had bathed and dressed in her best red linen tunic with yellow embroidery for her audience with the queen, but it obviously wasn't good enough for this servant.

"My mistress is in bed and my master is at the Roman feast. Come back tomorrow."

"Why is Asata in bed? Is she ill?" Afra pushed the man aside. "Asata! Where are you?"

"Stop!" The servant grabbed her arm and looked closely into her face. "My master forbids you entrance. Be gone!"

She shook him off and spied a frightened-looking girl carrying a tray of food. "You! Where's your mistress?"

The girl squeaked, dropped her tray, spilling a tureen of lentils and a flagon of wine.

Afra rushed toward the girl, the male servant raising an alarm behind her.

"'Mani?'"

She turned at the sound of her childhood name. Asata stood swaying in the entrance to a sumptuous bedroom. Oil lamps flickered on white walls draped in gauzy blue-green fabric, giving the room a look of being underwater.

"I have your bride price, Asata." Afra fumbled at her belt for the bag of coins. "I can take you away from him. He'll never hit you again."

"You're too late." Asata said in a dull voice. She turned back into the room and the oil lamps momentarily outlined her figure, rounded in pregnancy, beneath her sheer linen shift.

Afra followed her to the low wooden bed carved with sacred ibis and papyrus fronds. She gathered Asata in her arms, feeling the warmth of her skin and smelling the sandalwood-scented oil she used to dress her hair. "It's never too late."

"Give me your knife."

"What?" Afra held her at arm's length. Her sister's face set in haggard lines; dark circles bruised eyes bright with fever or madness, her full lips thinned in pain.

Asata cupped her bulging stomach with both hands. "This is what keeps me tied to him. Give me your knife and I'll cut it out."

"No! You are unwell. Let me take you from here. We will deal with your husband tomorrow."

"He knows I hate him and it…excites him. The more I resist, the more he enjoys it. Now I carry his child. He will never let me leave," Asata mumbled, her eyes glittered with hate and despair.

Afra recognized the look of a cornered animal and her heart quaked.

"Give me your knife. He keeps all such from me. The servants watch me all hours." Asata pleaded, looking toward the open door. "'Mani, the knife. Please, I have no one else!"

Afra smoothed the straggling hair from her love's face, looked deeply into her mad eyes and clasped her tightly. "I'm so sorry. This should never have happened." She rocked Asata, seeing again the proud and satisfied face of her step-mother when she had announced the prestigious match between Piye and her daughter. The horror on that face, when Afra told her they were lovers and would not be separated. The hatred as she had the servants beat Afra from the house and into the street with only the clothes she wore.

I should have come back, stolen Asata away. Afra's grip tightened.

"What is this? Leave my house!" Afra turned to see Piye dressed in his finest saffron-colored linen and backed by two brawny men standing in the doorway. The male servant smirked over his shoulder.

Asata shivered and muttered, "Give me the knife."

Afra rose, sheltering her love with her body. "I'll not go without Asata."

"She's mine. If you don't leave now, I'll take great pleasure in letting my men beat you before throwing you out."

Afra eyed the men. She couldn't prevail, particularly in such a small space. Horror crossed Piye's face. "Asata, no!"

Afra whipped around to see the bed in flames from the oil lamp, the fire spreading toward Asata. She reached for her, but her love backed across the bed, behind the flames, laughing. The acrid stench of burning feathers stung Afra's nose.

Asata's laughter turned to shrieks of pain as her shift caught fire.

Afra grabbed the first thing to come to hand, a richly embroidered cloak, and tried to smother the blaze. Tears streamed down her face as she coughed and fought the blaze.

Ignoring the pain from the fire, she grabbed Asata's arm, dragged her out of the burning bed and rolled her in a woolen carpet. As Afra stopped to catch her breath, pain exploded in her head.

CHAPTER FOUR

Britannia, land of the Iceni

TENSION DRAINED FROM CINNIA'S SHOULDERS **as she entered her own** tribal lands. The people of the Cornovii and the Coritani tribes had offered her the obligatory hospitality in their forests and hidden valleys, but their leaders were uneasy. She was not the only one spreading the word of the massacre at Mona. Those druids not killed on the Sacred Isle sent messages throughout the land demanding retribution. The Cornovii and Coritani remained neutral…for now.

Most of the Iceni people were farmers living with their extended families on their land: cleared fields alternated with open woods on rolling hills. Cinnia spied the occasional large round house with thatched roof set in the barren grain fields. Shaggy cattle and brown sheep, tended by older children and herding dogs, dotted the open meadows.

Cinnia stopped at a spring at the bottom of the path leading up to her brother's village. Several women had gathered there to fill buckets with fresh water for their families and to gossip.

"Oriana!" Cinnia greeted her sister-in-law.

The plump blond woman dropped her bucket and grabbed Cinnia in a fierce hug. "We heard of Mona and feared you dead."

"Father is gone." Cinnia swallowed her tears. "At least I think so. We couldn't identify many."

"Oh, Cinnia, to see such a thing."

This time, Cinnia couldn't hold back the tears and she sobbed in Oriana's arms. "I know the druids teach that he will be reborn, but I miss him now." The other women murmured soothing words and patted her on the back.

"Come dear."

The flock of women struggled up the hill with their burdens of water and grief. A bored-looking older man, in patched leather and wielding a worn spear, guarded a packed earth path bisecting a flat-bottomed ditch and wooden wall that surrounded the tiny settlement village. His eyes crinkled in concern at the women's obvious distress.

"Cinnia, the bard's daughter, isn't it?" He leaned on his spear, peering closely at Cinnia.

"Yes."

"We thought you dead on Mona."

"So I've heard." Cinnia's lips turned up into a sour smile. "There are many uneasy spirits about in the land, but I'm not one of them."

"What news from the west?"

"Enough!" Oriana glared at the man. "Can't you see the girl's exhausted? You'll hear soon enough."

The warrior grumbled, but the women hustled Cinnia through the gate. The rest split off, heading to their homes and to spread the news of Cinnia's miraculous return. The villagers had adopted the Roman town plan of oblong houses, set around a square for meetings and markets. Their village was too small for a temple, but druids came to preside over the main festivals. Young children chased each other screaming between the houses. Women took advantage of the light to spin wool or repair clothing on the benches outside the houses, but there were no young men loitering, playing bones, or sharpening weapons.

"Where are the men? Where's Dumnor?"

"Your brother has gone to the king's *oppidum* with the other village men. The king is ill and the queen has called a gathering."

It was not unusual for a queen to co-rule a tribe or rule in her own right. Cartimandua had ruled the Brigantes in the north since before Cinnia was born. Prasutagus had two daughters, but no sons. His wife Boudica would rule—as long as her subjects wished to have her as queen.

Oriana ushered Cinnia into her brother's home, a well-tended house of wattle and thatch, painted white with lime. They entered a dim room lit by a central hearth. Straw stuffed pallets and sleeping furs were piled against a wall. A few sets of extra clothes hung on pegs by the door; smoked meat and dried herbs hung from the rafters. A cauldron, held by a chain hanging from an iron tripod, bubbled over the fire. Cinnia's stomach rumbled and mouth watered at the smell of rabbit seasoned with rosemary. For the first time in days she wanted to eat for the taste and not just to keep up her strength.

A slimmer version of Oriana—her younger sister Melva—sat next to the fire in the center of the hut spinning wool into yarn with a drop spindle. Cinnia, with practiced ease, plucked a swaddled baby from a basket set at Melva's feet. She nuzzled his belly with her nose, sending him into gales of giggles. She liked babies, how they smelled, how they smiled, their vulnerability. They touched a place in her heart that roused an intense need to nurture and protect. One day, when she found a man good enough…

"Cinnia! We thought you—"

"—dead on Mona." Cinnia chimed in. "I know, but my stomach tells me otherwise. Could you possibly give me some of that stew?"

Melva blushed to the roots of her blond hair. "Of course."

She filled a wooden bowl with stew—rabbit, barley, and turnips— and offered it to Cinnia with a chunk of brown bread. Cinnia put the baby back in the basket and grabbed the food. He started to cry. Oriana retrieved him, unpinned her brown wool tunic at the shoulder, bared a breast, and put him to suck. She smiled over the baby's head at Cinnia. "You're not the only hungry one."

In between bites Cinnia told her story. "Dumnor must know Father is dead. I must go to the king's hill fort."

"It's another day's journey." Oriana put the full baby on her shoulder and gently rubbed his back to make him burp. "Stay the night."

The thought of a warm bed and a hot breakfast appealed to Cinnia after her journey. "I will." She picked a burr out of her long braid. "And I could use a wash and combing."

Late the next day, Cinnia, passed through the gate into the Iceni king's *oppidum*. It differed little from other villages except in size. There were ten times as many mud-daubed huts, some white-washed with lime, inside the wooden palisade. Sturdy chariot ponies grazed in the adjoining fields with the cattle. Smoke rose from a blacksmith's foundry and beehive shaped ovens where women brought their bread to bake. Men and women crowded the streets. An open space before the kings large house, built of timber and decorated with carvings of horses and wheels sacred to the gods, served as a gathering spot and impromptu market. A temple to the triple goddesses sat across from the king's house. White-washed timber pillars flanked the carved double door and marked the sacred entrance. Cinnia looked for her brother in the crowd, but didn't see him.

A blast from a ram's horn sounded a gathering, sending a mournful sound to the ends of the village and beyond. Iceni warriors pushed the people back to make an open space in the plaza. An ancient druid exited the king's house. The old man looked wild—twigs sprouted in his long white hair; mud caked his feet and the hem of his robe. He pulled a green and brown checked cloak tighter about his shoulders.

That must be what I looked like traveling the forest. She smiled at the thought.

The druid leaned heavily on an oak staff. Their queen, Boudica, a tall woman with flaming red hair and the strong arms of a chariot driver, joined him. Two girls, her daughters, by the cast of their faces and color of their hair, followed her. Cinnia knew Brianna, the eldest to be three years her junior, fourteen; Maeve, at twelve, had the gawky look of a child becoming an adult and uncertain in her body.

The druid pounded his staff onto the ground three times and the murmuring crowd quieted. Boudica stepped forward, her face streaked with tears. "Prasutagus, your king and my husband is dead. We will send him to the afterlife with ceremonies befitting a king."

A low moan went up from the crowd. A few women screeched in ritual grief. Cinnia saw her own pain and loss reflected in this royal family's eyes and tear-stained faces. Royal, noble or peasant—everyone died sometime and their families grieved. Her heart found some space for these young girls, left fatherless, like herself.

"What of Mona?" a man cried.

Boudica's head swiveled and pinned the man with a glare. "We bury the king, and then take counsel."

The man shrank back into the crowd.

Boudica and her daughters returned to the house followed by the druid. The village people scattered to their homes and tasks. Cinnia spied her brother across the plaza.

"Dumnor!" Cinnia shouted.

Her brother looked up and a smile rearranged the sharp planes of his face, softening it. He wove through the crowd to pull her into a bear hug. "I thought you dead on Mona."

"For a while, I wanted to be. Father is gone. They all are—the young and the old, the hale and the halt. The Romans destroyed them all." She shuddered and her face twisted to match the ache in her heart. Her eyes glistened with tears. "The bodies…the trees…" She looked up at her brother "They cut down the sacred grove and the gods did nothing."

Her brother wiped tears from his own eyes and shook his head "It's not for us to question the gods. You are alive and that's all I care about… for now." He put a protective arm around her shoulder. "Come. Food will make you feel better. I'm staying with our cousins. There should be room for you by the fire." She nestled into his side. Food would be good, but his sheltering arms were better.

THE NEXT DAY, Cinnia and Dumnor joined their people in the king's funeral cortege to the burial mound. A cart carried the king's body, followed by their mourning queen and her daughters. Drums beat and pipers played a mournful dirge. The warriors clashed their swords on their shields as they walked. Cinnia let the tears flow, wailing with the other women for her father and her king. They arrived at a pit dug into the top of a low rise where the ancient druid waited for them. Beside him was a pile of carved and decorated wood, which, Cinnia realized, was the king's dismantled chariot.

The old man seemed to have bathed before the ceremony. He wore a clean white robe, plain brown mantle and leather boots. His beard was free of twigs and his flowing white hair lifted in the cold winter wind. The land seemed to mourn with the people, looking brown and drab, the trees stripped of their finery, and the sky leaden with clouds. Cinnia smelled rain in the air and shivered.

The druid raised his arms and face to the sky and the crowd quieted. "Our king is gone!" The crowd moaned and swayed. Cinnia caught up in her grief, scratched her face and pulled her hair. She vaguely felt her brother's restraining arms around her. "Cernunnos, the Horned One has claimed him to feast at his side, until such time as he is returned to us."

Four warriors hefted the king's body from the cart and lifted it on a wide wicker bier to their shoulders. Prasutagus' body was dressed in his finest yellow wool tunic and trousers, worked with red and green embroidery. A gold pin in the form of a horse clasped his blue cloak. The druid gestured to the royal family. Boudica stepped forward with the king's sword, shield, bow, and iron-tipped arrows which she laid on the body. Stooping, she kissed the dead man's lips. Briana placed a silver platter holding a joint of mutton, a flagon of wine, and a jeweled cup on the bier.

Maeve stepped forward and broke into an ancient song. Her voice was high and pure, but thin. Her sister and mother joined her, then the rest of the people. The music soothed Cinnia's nerves and calmed her heart. She joined the swelling chorus with a fluting descant. When the last notes echoed down the valley, Cinnia stood shuddering in her brother's arms.

Good-bye Father.

The druid next ordered several of the king's attendants to lower the body into the pit. They covered it with the wheels, chariot body, pole, and yoke; before shoveling in the fill dirt. As the last shovelful hit the mound, the clouds let loose with a thin sleety rain. The mourners trudged back to the hill fort. Cinnia, exhausted, skipped the feasting and went to bed by her cousin's fire. She didn't hear her brother stumble to the other side when he came in several hours later.

RAIN AND SORE HEADs kept most people inside the next day while the queen met with her advisors. Cinnia sat by the fire contemplating a disturbing dream when her brother entered.

"Cinnia," Dumnor said, "the queen requires your presence. She wants to hear your tale and your thoughts on the mood of the western tribes."

Cinnia pulled her wool cloak over her head, grateful for the natural sheep oil that kept her dry, and followed Dumnor to the royal house. As she entered her eyes widened and only a conscious effort kept her jaw from dropping. There were warm carpets on the floor and walls. A scribe sat at a richly carved table, making notes on parchment paper with a quill pen. The queen drank wine from a silver cup crusted with red and green gems. Oil lamps hung from the high ceiling, bronze braziers blazed to chase the chill away, and the queen's sleeping area was curtained off with shiny brocade fabric. Cinnia had only seen such luxury in the Roman towns where they settled the retired soldiers; usually at rich merchants' homes where her father occasionally sang or told tales.

The queen noticed her glance around the room and frowned.

Cinnia forced her attention back to where it belonged. The ancient druid sat on a stool at Boudica's side and a few of her closest counselors crowded around. Cinnia made a small bow. "How may I be of service, my Queen?"

"Sit." Boudica indicated a stool. "And tell me what you saw and heard."

Cinnia repeated her tale automatically dropping into the rhythms of a bard. When she finished, a servant discreetly offered her a cup of wine in fine redware. She took a gulp and nearly spit it out. The wine was strong; sweetened with honey and herbs. Not nearly as good as the beer brewed in the villages.

The druid turned to Boudica, his eyes blazing with hatred. "See, my daughter. The Romans intend to bow us all to their will. We must fight. The Romans build a temple to their dead emperor Claudius and worship him as if he were a god. I met Claudius when he came to our land. He was flesh like you and me. The Romans insult our gods, murder our people, and take our lands!" Spittle flew from the druid's mouth.

"And the rest of you?" Boudica turned to face her chosen counselors. "Do we fight?"

One of the younger men hissed, "Yes. We should push the Romans back into the sea. They take our land, goods, cattle; and treat us little better than slaves."

A grayer head shook his disapproval. "The Romans are far better armed. Remember they defeated us a generation ago, though we had more men. In this time of peace, our cattle have grown fat and our few swords rusty."

The discussion continued, growing more heated as they drank more wine. They seemed to have forgot Cinnia and she listened eagerly, but of two minds. She wanted the Romans punished for what they did to her father and the others on the Sacred Isle, but she knew war brought devastation to land and families. Dead warriors were honored, but dead men couldn't provide food for families, make love to their wives or tell their children stories.

"Enough!" Boudica clapped her hands. "I have heard you all. It is not time—and might never be time—to fight. The Iceni have few allies but the Romans. We've been at peace with them since I was a babe in my mother's arms. With his dying breath, my husband counseled peace. He left a will gifting half his lands to the emperor. I will honor his request."

The ancient druid stood. "You will rue this day, Boudica. You can never be friends with the Romans. They ravage these lands like wolves.

Like wolves they should be hunted and destroyed. Only by strength can we survive." He limped to the door, opened it and left, letting in a gust of cold damp air that chilled all.

Cinnia sat in shock. She had never seen such a breach between druid and ruler.

Boudica's face flooded with color and she clinched her hands. "Out! All of you!"

The advisors left, muttering under their breath. Cinnia caught up with her brother. "When do you go back to our village?"

"Tomorrow. We'll leave in the morning after first light." He rubbed his head and smiled. "That is, if I don't drink too much tonight. Our cousin brews a good beer."

"I'm not sure I should return with you." Cinnia tugged unconsciously at her tunic. "I had a curious dream last night. Clouds of crows darkened the sky, looking for carrion. I stood over two wounded fawns and kept them safe, with spear and shield, from a pack of wolves."

"You have more insight than I when it comes to omens." Dumnor scratched his chin under his bushy beard. "But, maybe you're supposed to return home and help Oriana care for my son."

"Dreams *are* tricky things and can have many meanings." Cinnia smiled. "But I think I'm supposed to stay. At least for a while. It feels right."

"We'll talk again, later." He put his arm around her shoulders. "The times are unsettled. I want you home, safe."

A FEW DAYS AFTER DUMNOR left the *oppidum* for home, Cinnia sat on a bench outside her cousin's hut, wondering why she still lingered. She felt restless and on edge, her dreams troubling, but something kept her here. She spotted an empty bucket and sighed. Her mother's sister's son and his wife were kind, but she felt the strain her continued presence brought. She helped out where she could, but spinning wool and telling stories to their children at night didn't make up for the food she ate. *Tomorrow I'll leave*, she decided. She grabbed the bucket *Might as well make myself useful until then.*

Cinnia crossed the muddy market square heading for a spring down the hill. The rain had stopped, and a thin watery sunshine pulsed through the scudding clouds. Women and children scurried on errands or chatted with neighbors. Everyone smelled of wet wool and wood smoke. Most of the merchants had left with the decamping mourners. Only one man, with a milky white eye, sold leather wares from his cart next to the shrine to the Triple Goddess. Most of the village men were hunting in the forest or tending the animals in the fields. They'd bring the herds in soon to butcher for the winter, then they'd have a great feast.

Cinnia lifted her head at the sound of tramping feet and shouts at the open gate leading to the Roman road. Heads poked out of huts. She ran for shelter between the temple and the granary, before she realized she was moving. Her heart beat with the uneven rhythm of fear and she didn't know why. She crept along the wall to look into the plaza.

A contingent of forty Roman *beneficiarii*—retired legionaries tasked with collecting taxes, tolls, and local policing—marched through the gate. Graying, hard-faced men; most sported scars and one wore a patch over a blind eye. They wore a livery of thick blue wool mantels over matching tunics and brown trousers; their chests covered in boiled leather cuirasses, they carried leaf-bladed thrusting spears that the Roman's called *hastii*. A couple also wore the short *gladius* sword favored by the Roman infantry. They flanked a litter carried by four slaves, marked, in the Roman way, with an iron ring around their necks. Three other men, with the pale faces of those who spent their lives inside, trailed after the litter, carrying official-looking leather pouches. Two large empty wagons stopped at the gate.

They marched into the center of the plaza where the slaves lowered their burden. An underdressed Roman stepped out of the litter and into a freezing puddle. He shivered in a white linen tunic and an elaborately embroidered, but inadequate, green cloak, clasped on the shoulder with a large gold *fibula* in the shape of a sacred Celtic spiral.

Cinnia snorted. Stupid Roman didn't have the sense to wear trousers or socks with his sandals. At least his body guard dressed for the season with socks laced up their calves. But where did he get the gold clasp? It was obviously of native manufacture.

He glowered at the slaves. "Start there." He pointed at the leather merchant. "Seize his goods and money." The old man blocked his small cart with his body, but one of the armed men shoved him aside, punching him in the back with the butt of his spear for good measure. The old man screamed and fell to the ground writhing. The sparse crowd milled in uncertainty till the armed Romans started shoving them to the ground. The women screamed and the old men cursed, as the Romans beat them about the shoulders and took liberties pinching and patting the younger women. Cinnia edged deeper into the shadows.

Boudica came out of her home, dressed in mourning clothes, a long dark blue cloak thrown over her shoulders. Her daughters stood in the open door. "Who disturbs the peace of the Queen of the Iceni?"

One of the pale clerks announced in a voice too deep for his narrow chest, "Procurator of Rome for the Province of Britannia, Catus Decianus, has come to claim the lands and goods of King Prasutagus in the name of Imperator Nero Claudius Caesar Augustus Germanicus."

Catus Decianus waved his hand casually at the houses. "You know what to do." Half of the body guard split off and started to ransack the huts, carrying off anything of value—coins, bronzeware, fabrics. "The young women and older children, too; for the slave market."

A grinning guard snatched a young woman by her hair, dragging her screaming to the square. Cinnia huddled in the shadows, glad her cousin's wife and children were in the forest herding the pigs.

"Stop this!" Boudica, face red with rage, shouted. The men hesitated and looked back at Decianus for instruction.

"What right do you have to come to my lands and take what isn't yours? I am Queen of the Iceni."

"Queen? Of what? This pig sty?" Decianus laughed and his guard joined in. "What right? By the right of Rome to collect what is owed to the Emperor."

"The Iceni are free people. My husband has a treaty with the Emperor. We are a client and ally of Rome. I have pledged to continue that support."

"Your support is no longer needed. When your husband died so did the treaty. Your husband left his lands and goods to the Emperor. The Emperor's Divine Father Claudius loaned great sums of money to your nobles. We have come to collect on both counts."

"The king left half his wealth to Emperor Nero and half to his daughters." She put her arms around the two girls. "I will provide you with an accounting after the mourning period. And those loans from Claudius have already been collected by agents from Seneca on behalf of your Emperor, leaving my nobles considerably impoverished."

"*You'll* provide *me* with an accounting?" The procurator twisted his lips into a sneer. "My clerks will make a full accounting of all land, coin, plate," he sniffed "people, animals, anything of value that belongs to the Emperor."

"But…" Boudica began to protest again.

The Procurator flicked his hand. "Stop that woman's mouth. She annoys me."

When the men approached, Boudica pushed her daughters behind her, crouched in a fighting stance, and leaped at the nearest one, knocking him down and grabbing his spear. She turned to do battle, hamstringing one guard and cracking another's head.

"Subdue her!" Decianus shouted. "Will you let a woman threaten Rome?"

The *beneficiarii* surrounded Boudica. A spear from behind, tangled her feet and sent her to her knees. She rolled, but her elaborate robes tangled her legs and two men grabbed her arms. She spit curses until one of the men stopped her mouth with a kerchief and leather belt.

"Show the *Queen* of the Iceni how Romans reward rebellion." Decianus ordered the men. "Lash her." The two men hauled Boudica to the temple, tied her arms and legs spread-eagled to the front columns, and ripped her clothes down to her waist. The *beneficiarii* kept the protesting crowd at bay.

Brianna and Maeve threw themselves at the Decianus, clawing and screaming, "Let our mother go!"

Two of the guard grabbed them before they could do any damage to the procurator's fine cloak.

Cinnia broke out of her horror. While all eyes were on Boudica and her daughters, Cinnia ran down the wall of the granary toward the fence. She knew of a hole where the children wriggled through to the escape their parents.

She crawled through the hole and crept into the meadow. There, she grabbed the halter of a dappled mare, larger than the short chariot ponies, and led it over a rise. When she felt safe, Cinnia threw herself on the horse and kicked it into a gallop. The farmers and hunters couldn't be too far away. She shouted her news to all she encountered. "Romans! At the *oppidum*!"

Chapter Five

Meroe, Kush

AFRA WOKE IN THE DARK, head throbbing from the blow, with no knowledge of how long she had been unconscious. The smell of smoke from her clothes almost masked the reek of dirt and urine from the cell. At least the dankness soothed the burns on her arms and hands.

She rose to her knees and stretched out her arms. A rough wall on the left and another on the right. *Mud brick?* There wasn't room to lie on the floor full length, even corner to corner. She stood and her head bumped the ceiling. Her hand followed the wall to a thick wooden door, barred on the outside. Afra pounded on it and shouted, but no one answered. She slumped, back to the wall, hoarse from the smoke and the shouting, dazed from the shock.

She sat there for what seemed a lifetime, till she dropped into real sleep, dreaming of Asata and flames.

The second time Afra awoke, the pallid light of an oil lamp crept beneath the door. She tried shouting again, but her throat was sore, mouth dry. The noises that came from her sounded more like squeals from iron on stone than speech.

The light strengthened and she heard stirrings beyond her prison—muffled voices, the wooden bar withdrawn. The door pulled open and blinding light streamed around a dark figure that poked her with a spear. "Back to the corner."

Afra scuttled on hands and knees and croaked. "Where am I? What's happening?"

"Here." A second figure put a bowl inside the door and disappeared.

The door shut and she surged forward, to pound on the wood. "Wait! Tell the *Kandake* where I am. Let her know! I can pay!"

Muted laughter trailed away on the other side.

Afra patted her tunic and found the pouch gone. Of course. If Piye hadn't taken her money, the guards had.

Her toe bumped the bowl and she reached down. She sniffed. Thin barley gruel. Her stomach clenched at the thought of food. How long since she had eaten? Afra gulped the slimy mixture and licked the bowl for the moisture as much as the nourishment. Thirst tortured her. She pissed in the bowl, but could not bring herself to drink it. Maybe later.

What seemed like hours, and might have been moments later, Afra heard voices approaching—a deep husky voice blended with a lilting female tone she recognized—Mesbat, her step-mother. The door swung open and she slouched unsteadily to her feet. "Mother?"

The woman advanced, raised her hand and struck her a ringing blow on the ear with her open palm. "You demon spawn!" She struck again with her other hand. "To be cursed with such a snake in my home!" Afra covered her head with her arms and ducked; letting her step-mother rain blows and curses on her burned skin.

Finally, Mesbat stopped, shaking with anger and fatigue. "Asata?"

"Dead…and the babe." Mesbat's face twisted in grief. "My only child!"

Tears filled Afra's eyes and closed her throat. She stifled a sob and reached for Mesbat's shoulder.

The woman hissed like a cat and slapped her hand away. "You cursed her. You drove her mad! *You* should be dead, not my beautiful girl."

"I loved her!"

"But not as a sister should!" Mesbat's eyes blazed with hatred. "May Ammit eat your bones and your *ba* be forever lost. But I hope you don't die too soon. I want you to suffer each and every day…cold, hunger, thirst, pain. I want your flesh scourged and your soul damned."

Afra sat, arms over her head barely listening to the stream of curses. *Asata, my light, my love, my sister. I would give my life for you.*

A sharp kick in the ribs brought her back.

"The *Kandake* is too merciful. You're condemned to slavery in the stone quarries. Your past service saved you from death."

Mesbat stalked past the guard who had witnessed everything. Afra thought she saw a glimmer of pity in his eyes.

"Please…" Afra reached toward the retreating back.

The door clanged shut in her face.

AFRA BEGAN TO DESPAIR of ever leaving her reeking cell. At least, they had given her a slop bucket and increased the water ration, although thirst continued to torment her. The darkness not only clouded her vision, but invaded her soul. She had always been better at living in the present than planning for the future or dwelling on the past; but the present was too horrific and the future too hopeless to contemplate. Her mind turned again and again to her girlhood.

Running in the hills. Bringing wounded animals back to the house. Once she had a pet lizard that lost its tail and miraculously grew it back. But her favorites were always the cats. Sacred to Bastet, they roamed the streets of Meroe and patrolled the granaries. One particular beauty, black as scribe's ink with five white hairs on her chest, frequented their garden. When Afra set out food, it stood on its hind legs, begging to be picked up before eating. Asata named her Sheba and carried her around the garden inspecting the plants; talking about her dreams.

One day Sheba didn't come. Afra hunted for her through the alleys and granaries, but found no trace. Asata cried for days until Afra brought her a yellow tabby kitten, a bedraggled little mite whose mother was killed by a dog. They fed it goat's milk and he grew into a fierce mouser, bringing his kills back to Asata and Afra for approval. Asata screamed the first time he brought her a dead mouse…

"Asata!" Afra sobbed.

She remembered the first time they lay in each other's arms, giggling, exploring their bodies. Touching their secret places. Mesbat thought Afra's body too tall, too thin, too flat, but Asata loved her the way she was. They fondled each other's breasts, kissed softly, and fell asleep clasped in each other's arms. Family and friends delighted in their closeness, remarking how well the two different girls got on.

If Mesbat hadn't arranged that horrible marriage…

If Piye hadn't been a brutal man…

If I could have raised the money earlier…

There was no comfort for her body, heart, or mind. She slept to forget.

ON WHAT SHE THOUGHT was the fourth day of her captivity; the guard pounded on the door, warning her away. Afra crawled to a corner and slumped against the wall.

"Afra?" A familiar gruff voice. "Jupiter's beard, girl. What have they done to you?"

She squinted up at the dim figure. "Marcius?" she croaked.

"Come out here." He offered a hand and Afra surged to her feet, joints stiff and muscles sore from the cramped position. Even stooped from her confinement, she topped the Roman by half a head.

He led her out of the cell. The lamp held by the guard blinded her and Afra blinked away tears. They walked down a narrow corridor of stout wooden doors to stairs that led up into light. When they reached the top, she knew where they were—the guards' barracks. She had been here many times and not suspected the cells underneath.

They continued to a large room fronting onto the palace grounds where a clerk looked up from his papyrus. "This the one?"

Marcius nodded and presented a folded paper. "Signed and sealed."

The clerk looked closely at the writing, then squinted at Afra. "You understand? By the queen's order you are condemned to slavery. This Roman…" his gaze strayed back to the document, "Lucius Marcius has bought you. Go with him and serve him well. He saved you from the quarries."

"This way, Afra." Marcius put his hand under her elbow. "First a bath, then food. I'll explain."

AFRA TUGGED AT THE IRON COLLAR that marked her a Roman slave as she ate boiled grains flavored with shreds of meat of dubious origin. She could swallow with ease, but *the fact* of the collar choked her. Her stomach tightened and the food lost what little taste it had. She looked across the table at Marcius, who watched closely. "Why?"

"You saved my life."

"Then free me. I did not keep you in bondage after dragging you from that sink hole."

"I wish I could, Afra." Marcius shrugged, "But—as you've pointed out to me—there is little in Kush to recommend to my backers. They will be unhappy, but your hunting skills will make me a rich man."

"I thought your association already had suppliers."

"I'm not talking about collecting animals for the arena. You'll make a first class *venatore* in the games."

Revulsion rippled across her face. "I won't kill for the entertainment of Romans."

His face hardened. "I saved your life. Don't make me regret it."

"I saved yours and already regret it."

"You'd rather rot in that cell or die working in a stone quarry?"

"Perhaps. Death is not to be feared."

The blood drained from Marcius' face at the prospect he might lose his investment. He must have paid a high price for her. His voice took on a tone of desperation. "Unless your soul is weighed with sin. Are you ready to meet your gods?"

Afra chewed her food in silence. Did she want to die? Maybe. Asata was beyond the cares of this world. Afra knew that such a gentle soul as Asata's would be welcomed in the golden halls of Osiris, but she missed her with a pain that stopped her breath. Maybe slavery was the price demanded by the gods for her actions. Mesbat certainly thought so. She tugged again at the iron ring.

"Afra, slavery doesn't have to be forever." Marcius ran a hand through his hair. "Many in the provinces sell *themselves* into slavery to get the opportunity to go to Rome and become affiliated with a powerful family. Many of the Emperor's most trusted advisors are freedmen."

"So?"

"Skilled hunters are in great demand for the games. You could earn a good deal of money—buy your freedom."

"For what purpose? I no longer have a family…" Her voice caught in a sob which she turned into a cough. "My *Kandake* has turned her back on me. Maybe death is preferable."

"Don't throw your life away before you've lived it."

"Will you permit me to seek advice from my gods?"

"Your gods have no influence with me. However," Marcius raised an eyebrow. "If they reconcile you to your fate, I'm willing. I've invested a lot of money in you, Afra. I want it back."

Marcius was as good as his word. He even bought incense in the market as a votive offering, before delivering Afra to the temple of Isis for prayers. The Mother's temple was smaller than others, but built solidly of stone, and decorated with rich frescos of Isis searching the reeds of the Nile for the scattered parts of her husband/brother. A prominent fresco showed Isis suckling a *Kandake*, giving her blessing to the female ruler. A gilded and painted stone effigy of the goddess sat on a marble throne in the farthest recesses of the temple. Worshipers could come as far as the outer courtyard and first two rows of columns.

Afra prayed, unrolled a reed mat, and fell into an uneasy sleep. She dreamed.

The god Horus stood on the top of Taharqa's pyramid tomb and shot an arrow north. It flew beyond sight into darkness that filled her with dread. The sky goddess Nut appeared and filled the darkness with stars and a full moon that reflected a bright path on the calm water of the upper Nile.

Afra stepped on the path and slid, like a child sliding on mud down a hill to the river, going faster and faster until the speed tore her breath away. She did not land in water, but sand soaked with blood. A wall surrounded her and the smell of death rose from the ground. Horns sounded faintly, a great distance away.

An opening appeared in the ground and Osiris, God of the Dead, came up flanked by a large dog-like creature, the Roman's called a wolf, and dog-headed Anubis with his scales. From another opening—this one in the wall—Isis, the Mother Goddess, appeared flanked by a great lioness and the dwarf god Bes in his feathers, playing a bright song on his pipes. A roar like rocks sliding down a mountain came from beyond the walls.

The lioness and wolf leaped at one another, biting and clawing, until both lay panting in the sand, bleeding from many wounds. The cat dragged itself to Isis and collapsed at her feet. Bes played a song and the cat was cured of its wounds. Anubis put the wolf on his scale which clashed to the ground. Osiris picked up the wounded wolf and carried it into the dark. Its frightened howling lasted until the door shut in the floor.

Afra came to Isis and bowed at her feet. The goddess lifted her up and put a hand on her head filling her with strength. The lioness stared with golden eyes, and then stood on its rear legs, its paws on Afra's shoulders. She felt no fear. Warmth flooded her body and her heart felt light. Isis smiled. Bes played a lively air while they walked away into the darkness.

Afra woke on her thin mat, turned to the north and stared as if she could see through the thick stone wall. When an ancient priest came to light the morning lamps, she dropped onto the floor in a deep obeisance. "Honored one who serves our Mother Isis, I need guidance."

"In what, daughter?" His black eyes sparkled with concern.

"My *dominus*—my master..." she stumbled over the term and continued, "wishes to take me from Kush to a far land. I am unsure."

He eyed the iron ring. "You are a slave?"

"Once free. Now a slave to a Roman merchant. He purchased me from the prison."

"Your life belongs to another now. You owe a debt of service."

"I don't believe so." Afra shook her head and tugged at the iron ring. "I saved this man's life. I believe the debt paid and my life my own. I have no family left here. Maybe death is the better path."

"There is honor in death for the right reasons, but you have given me none." The priest looked on her with compassion. "Why were you in prison?"

Afra hung her head. "I caused the death of a loved one."

"So a life debt *is* owed." He frowned. "The gods sometimes exact punishment in this life so you may enter the next free of burdens. Did you dream last night?"

"Yes."

The priest listened carefully as Afra described her dream, nodding at key moments. "It seems you are fated to go on this journey. There will be pain and many trials, possibly death; but if you persevere, Isis will smile on you and Bes give you joy. Your debt will be paid."

"I don't believe I can ever feel joy again." Her chest tightened with unshed tears.

"You are young, my daughter, and have much to learn from life." He smiled and patted her hand. "Trust the gods. Serve them well wherever you travel." He hesitated, then took a small amulet strung on a cord from around his neck. "Take this with you to know that the Great Mother, Queen of All Gods, Goddesses, and Women looks after her own."

Afra stared at the small wooden carving of the goddess, smooth and worn from much use.

"I can't…"

He curled her fingers around the talisman. "You can. I give it freely to a daughter in need."

She bowed her head. "Thank you."

Chapter Six

W HEN CINNIA RETURNED, the queen's *oppidum* was in turmoil. The gate stood open, broken. Ruined goods littered the ground. Old women wailed before their huts. Boudica sat on the steps of the shrine cradling her youngest daughter. Maeve whimpered like a beaten dog and covered her face with a once-fine cloak, now ripped and covered with blood. Brianna leaned on the wall of the temple for support. Her hair hung wild; her face white, blank. Dried blood stained her ripped gown and crusted her legs.

"What happened here?" Cinnia muttered.

The crowd hissed and moaned. The old women tore at their hair and scratched their faces. The men bellowed curses and shook their fists in the air. The noise escalated until Boudica stood, clasping her daughter to her breast. Her face set in a terrible cast, rigid with fury, she shouted, "The Iceni are no longer allies to Roman. The *procurator* took your wives and daughters as chattel, stole our goods, and claimed our lands for the greedy Roman Emperor. When I, as queen, protested, he had one of his lackeys do this." She turned so all could see her flayed back.

Cinnia gasped and the crowd moaned. Boudica's wounds were horrific but not fatal…unless infection set in. Bloody stripes crisscrossed her back where the skin had been peeled away with a whip exposing the muscle below. Blood soaked her ripped gown.

Boudica turned to face her people again, her eyes flashing. "The cursed Romans held my daughters down and raped them again and again, forcing me to watch."

Cinnia felt like throwing up. *The two fawns? I wasn't here to protect them. Was that the task the gods gave me in my dream? Could I have done anything against all those Romans?*

Maeve shivered in her mother's arms, whimpering. Low moans came from the crowd. The queen raised her daughter's body over her head as if offering a sacrifice to the sky gods. "On the heads of my ravished daughters; on the grave of my dead husband, I swear to you, the Romans will pay for this day's blood with rivers of their own. The Iceni are at war with Rome!"

Cinnia joined the crowd as it roared settling into a chant. "Boudica! Boudica! Boudica!"

BOUDICA SENT RIDERS TO ALL THE ICENI VILLAGES—round up the breeding stock, pack up preserved food, hide the grain stores, destroy the rest. Leave nothing for the Romans—not coin, grain, beasts, metal or leather. Boudica and her clan melted into the hills and forests. Men retrieved hidden arms. The smiths packed up their forges and ingots; merchants their wares. Distant valleys rang with the shouts of children and the clang of swords, battle axes, and spears being made.

Cinnia stayed with the queen. An old woman healer worked her magic with spells and poultices, but healing was slow. Boudica held her back stiffly. Maeve could barely walk, much less ride a horse. The old healer had a cart fitted with a pallet for the girl and Cinnia stayed close, heeding her dream.

A dozen other women, mostly young, but two older—with the ropy muscles of hard work and sword training—joined Boudica. They brought their weapons and formed an informal body guard for the queen and her daughters. One loaned Cinnia her second best sword until she could get one of own. When they camped in the deep woods, the more experienced male warriors trained the farmers—and any women who cared to learn—the arts of war. In a generation of peace, the tribe had lost some skills with sword and shield, but not their fierceness of spirit. Most nights Cinnia went to bed aching and bruised, but content.

One morning Boudica called her guards and advisors together. "I intend to unite the tribes to drive the Romans from our land. Tomorrow we ride southeast to treat with the Trinovantes."

CINNIA WALKED WITH HEAD HELD HIGH in Boudica's train as they entered the meeting house of the Trinovantes. The king stood among his advisors as Boudica and her women trooped into the open space. All waited as a young druid burned food and offered prayers to the gods at an altar in the far end. The familiar rites sent a prickle of tears to Cinnia's eyes and raised a lump in her throat. She coughed, pretending the wood smoke irritated her throat, while tamping down her feelings of loss.

"Boudica, Queen of the Iceni." The king of the Trinovantes approached her queen. "News of the Roman outrage has reached us. Do you seek sanctuary here among our tribe?"

"Sanctuary?" Boudica spat. "I seek vengeance!"

"Seek among the Romans who caused you harm." The king's voice reflected ice to Boudica's fire.

"I also seek alliance. You have suffered from the cursed Romans as much as we. The Roman *colonia* at Camulodunum have treated your people like slaves, taking their land and forcing them out of their homes to starve. The Romans not only set up a temple to a false god, but charged you ruinous taxes to build it. Join us in defeating them. Let us push the cursed Romans back to the sea…together."

"The Romans have also taken our arms and razed our villages as punishment for past rebellions. Why should we risk their wrath again?" This loosed a wave of mutters and frowns among the Trinovantes nobles.

"Because they are divided and vulnerable. Paulinus is mired in the West. Cerealis and the Ninth are in winter quarters in the North. More tribes join me every day. Combined we are a vast number. Far more than the Romans can muster. Now is the time." Backed by her female guard, Boudica leaned on a spear looking each Trinovantes noble in the eye, one by one. Some cast their eyes down, others grinned a wolfish smile, most mirrored their king's impassive face. "I have no doubt you have arms hidden in the woods and the hay stacks. We did. Tomorrow I return to my tribe. The day after, we go to Camulodunum to destroy the cursed temple of Claudius and revenge our people. Will you let the Iceni gain all the glory?"

Stung, the nobles mumbled. The king growled, "Leave us, Boudica. We will consider your offer."

Boudica stamped the butt of her spear on the floor and gave them a grim smile. "Camulodunum is a fat city. Join us there…" she looked around the assembled men and sniffed, "…or not."

Cinnia grinned at a young warrior as the women left. He didn't look happy.

"The city is defenseless, no walls or ditches; a handful of old soldiers with few arms." Cinnia overheard a scout report to Boudica where they camped outside Camulodunum. "It will be an easy victory."

"What of the neighboring garrisons?"

"Only two hundred soldiers in Londinium. The Ninth Legion will take three days march—once they hear—to reach us.

"Good." Boudica grinned. "Their road runs through a forest a day from here. We will prepare a surprise for Cerealis. We will not need our full force to take the city. I'll send the rest to stop the Ninth. With the gods' help we will prevail."

She turned to her women. "Tonight we go to the sacred spring. Bring your sacrifices."

Cinnia spent an hour sharpening the knife her father had given her. She ran her thumb over the symbol carved in the bone hilt; a wheel for the protective sky god. It was her dearest possession; not dear in coin, but in sentiment. She had nothing else of her father's but memories.

When dusk deepened the shadows under the trees where they sheltered, Cinnia picked up a torch and started her solitary journey to the sacred spring hidden in the deep forest. Although the tribe fought together, each warrior fought alone and must make the sacred journey on her own. She moved in silence, thoughts turned inward.

Andraste, Mother of War and Death grant me courage and strength!

At one point, Cinnia lost her bearings and stopped, panting, eyes wide. She caught sight of lights flickering among the trees. A bramble pulled at her trousers and scratched her hands. She fought her way through the thicket and came onto a path. She recognized a boulder that looked like a hunched dwarf and hurried past it, not wanting to miss the ceremony.

Cinnia came into the narrow clearing where a spring gushed from a broken rock face to fall into a deep pool. Boudica stood by the edge, red hair gleaming in the torchlight, face mottled by shadows. Several women had already made their sacrifices and stood at her side.

Cinnia approached the spring with her knife. Mist from the falls wet her face, masking her tears as she broke the knife with a stone and dropped it in the water. She watched the pieces fall into the dark, glittering with the light of the moon, as she muttered the ritual prayers. She had hoped to feel the goddess' touch, be flooded with power and confidence; but she felt nothing except foreboding and sorrow. Did the goddess sense her reluctance to part with the knife?

When the last of them dropped their sacrifices into the spring, Boudica retrieved a gold wine cup from a sack at her feet. She filled it with water from the falls, pricked her finger, let her blood drip into the cup, intoning, "We call on Andraste, goddess of war, patroness and sacred to the Iceni. Give us courage and justice in our fight with the Romans. Give us strength of arms and heart. Protect our warriors and give them victory or an honorable death."

Boudica drank from the cup and gave it to the next woman. When the cup reached Cinnia, she gulped the iron-tasting water. Although cold on her lips, it hit her stomach with fire. Warmth spread through her limbs and filled her with the certainty that her gift *had* pleased the goddess.

When the cup returned to Boudica, she held it high. "Accept our sacrifices, Andraste, Mother of War and Death. Strike terror in the hearts of our enemies." She dropped the cup into the spring and shouted, "Give us victory!" Their shouts echoed off the rocks, sending a covey of birds screeching from the nearest trees.

Boudica brandished her spear, "Today we take Camulodunum! Tomorrow Londinium!"

The warriors cried out, "Boudica! Boudica!" and clashed their swords on their shields. The Iceni streamed down a hill in chariots and on foot toward the city. Boudica and her guard sliced through the meager resistance of retired legionnaires and fat merchants to spill along the broad Roman streets killing everyone they encountered.

Cinnia ran screaming with the rest. Overtaken with rage, vengeance, and the goddess' fury; she fought as if in a shadow land. Cries of terror and triumph faded to a distant roar in her ears. The people she cut down, faceless and insubstantial flesh. She felt none of the cuts and blows that came her way. Her sword ran with blood slicking the hilt. Cinnia found herself in the center of the town, facing the cursed temple to the "god" Claudius. A small contingent of defenders had retreated to its stone walls and held the two heavy brass doors open for refugees.

She stood over a terrified boy, sword raised for the kill. Her senses returned. Every muscle in her body shook with fatigue. The back of her left calf throbbed. She grimaced to see blood seeping from a shallow wound. Smoke from burning buildings filled the air. She coughed; her eyes ran with tears. Cinnia stared at the boy just coming into his manhood, face spotted with pimples, tunic stained with urine, and the battle frenzy left her.

She kicked him and screamed, "Run!"

He scrambled to his feet and ran into the temple.

Boudica drove her chariot into the plaza.

Cinnia looked up and raised her sword in a tired salute.

"Leave the temple," The queen cried to her forces. "We'll deal with them later. Take what you want. The city is ours!" She descended from her chariot and prowled the open area, looking on the destruction and bodies with a grim smile.

Women from the baggage train joined the warriors combing through the wreckage of the city, plucking jewelry from bodies and pots from houses. Cinnia lifted a fat pouch of coins from the belt of one dead man, a broad brass buckle and a pair of stout boots from another. But her best find was a short Roman sword. She hefted the *gladius*, stabbing and slicing at an imaginary Roman. With this, she could fight with a shield or knife in her left hand. Its lighter weight was better suited to her strength than the longer Celtic sword, which required both hands.

As the sun started to set, Cinnia made her way back to the temple district, hungry and so tired she could barely heft her small bag of loot. She saw some warriors pushing two-wheeled carts piled high with silver plate, bolts of fabric, and armor. She hoped Dumnor and Oriana got a good share. Although she lodged with the queen's household, she made a point of finding Dumnor and his family whenever possible.

The Iceni women set up cooking fires. Men carried amphorae of wine from looted cellars into the square. Boudica sat in a throne-like chair salvaged from one of the houses. She stared at the temple, stony-faced, from the top steps of the town basilica, sipping a goblet of wine. Cinnia approached and bowed.

"My Queen, can I be of service?"

Boudica's gaze darted from the temple to Cinnia's face. "No. Go enjoy the feast."

The smell of roasted meat made Cinnia's mouth water and stomach rumble. She bowed again and made her way to the growing crowd milling around roasting spits.

"Cinnia!"

She turned to see Dumnor, smudged with soot, but otherwise unharmed, plowing through the people.

She grinned and rushed into his arms for a hug. He smelled of smoke, sweat, and dried blood.

He held her at arm's length, looked her over, frowning at the cut on her leg. "You need Oriana to see to that."

"It's just a cut."

"Cuts can go bad if not tended."

He hauled her into the basilica, where Oriana, and other village herb women, treated the wounded. Cinnia spied Melva, with the baby in a sling, tending a cauldron of boiling water and waved to her. She gave a weary smile and turned to push the bandages in the cauldron with a large wooden spoon. The inside of the huge brick building was whitewashed; ready for new frescos which would never be painted. Boudica would burn the building when they left. Remarkably few wounded lay on pallets or sat on the floor. The worst was a young man with a terrible gash across his stomach. An older woman packed his intestines back into the cavity, bound the wound, and shook her head. Cinnia knew no one recovered from such a wound. He would be dead of fever in days, if not hours. If he were conscious, he would have asked for a mercy stroke.

Oriana looked up to see both of them and a huge smile lit her weary face. "Thank the gods you're both all right." She clucked over Cinnia's wound, washed it with wine, spread honey on it, and bound it with a clean linen cloth. "That should do it. Keep it dry and stay away from ants." She eyed Cinnia's sack of loot. "That's all you got? You can put it over there with Dumnor's." She inclined her head toward an impressive pile of armor and household goods.

Oriana stretched, hands on back, looking around. "I'm done here. Let's eat."

They gathered Melva and the baby and wended their way to the food, piled bloody meat onto stolen plates, and sat on the steps chewing. Cinnia had never tasted anything as good as that half-roasted calf. She washed it down with a goblet of harsh red wine. The heat of it went to her head, making her muzzy. She'd get water next time.

The strident call of a *carnyx* echoed through the plaza. Everyone turned to Boudica standing on the steps, waiting for the chatter to cease.

"The gods gave us victory today!"

The crowd surged to its feet roaring, "Boudica! Boudica!"

"But they wait for one last act!" She pointed at the temple. "We must destroy this temple to a false god." She made a gesture. A group of warriors herded fifty or more wailing women and children into the square. They were covered in ashes, bruises, and blood. Many made no sounds, but stood dazed, blank-faced. Some begged for mercy for themselves or their children. A few spit curses at their conquerors.

Boudica strode to the temple steps, pointed her sword at the doors, and shouted in Roman, "We have your women and children. Do you want them? Open your doors."

Silence from the temple, but the doors opened a crack. Cinnia could make out eyes peering from the dark; light glinting off a sword.

Boudica gave another signal. The warriors beat the women with the flats of their swords herding them toward the temple. When they saw the open doors, they ran for the shelter. Cinnia could see hands reaching for the refugees, pulling them inside. With the last in, the doors shut with a clang.

Boudica punched the air with her fist. "Now!"

Warriors, with oil-soaked rags on their spears, launched their missiles at the temple roof. These were followed by arrows blazing with fire. Others built bonfires at the doors of the temple. Soon the roof of the temple blazed from one end to the other, throwing flickering red light and eerie shadows across the square. Warriors danced, shouted, and shook their spears at the cries of terror coming from the temple. Soon smoke flowed from the doors, followed by silence. The roof fell in with a crash and flying sparks.

Cinnia winced. She should have killed the boy and spared him the pain of a fiery death.

"Can't you keep your warriors under control?"

Cinnia watched as Boudica paced in front of the tribal nobles. The Trinovantes had joined the revolt. As word spread of Boudica's success, more warriors from outlying tribes flocked to her standard. "For days, all they've done is eat, drink, and squabble over booty!"

One of the Trinovantes nobles spoke up. "They deserve to reap the rewards of our success! We destroyed the Ninth in the forests and sent Cerialis running for his life back to his base. Londinium and Verulamium are no more than a heap of ashes."

"General Paulinus and his troops speed from the west and their conquest of the Sacred Isle. They move fast with no women, children or baggage." Boudica clenched her fist under the man's nose. "When we crush them and sweep our land free of the Romans, we can rest and revel. Now we need to move!"

The nobles grumbled, but when Boudica left the next day, they followed with their women, children, and wagons stuffed with loot.

CHAPTER SEVEN

Alexandria, Egypt

AFRA SAW WONDROUS SIGHTS as they sailed down the Nile: massive statues of long-forgotten pharaohs, towering obelisks, and sprawling temples. Even Marcius said that Rome had nothing to compare with the Pyramid of Khufu shining white in the desert. It certainly outshone the pyramid tombs clustered outside Meroe. Her heart swelled with pride tinged with sadness. Her people had once ruled this mighty nation many generations ago. Now Kush cowered in the south, reduced to deceiving embassies of stronger nations.

During the weeks they traveled, they fell into an easy camaraderie. Marcius rarely reminded her of her slave status. He rented her out to help on the boats occasionally, but always paid her a share of what she earned. He gifted her with a leather pouch—her *peculium* he called it—to keep her earnings. Afra suspected his attitude and generosity were signs he knew he did wrong by keeping her in bondage—or he coddled a valuable asset, knowing she could escape into the desert or into death, any time she wished. Maybe it was a little of both. Whatever the reason, she welcomed the trust and chose to stay for her own reasons.

Alexandria rose white and beckoning from the flat plain of the delta. Perched on a ridge between a huge freshwater lake and the salt sea, it was visible for many miles before their party reached the limestone walls. Afra stared as they walked through massive bronze gates into a city clad in marble. White, green, rose; each building polished to a shine. Painted statues stood in niches; covered columns paraded down each side of the broad boulevard, providing shelter from sun or rain. People in clothes from all corners of the world swarmed in the street like termites on a mound. The city was a riot of color. Afra heard a dozen different languages spoken.

"Did your people build this city?" Afra craned her neck looking left and right.

"The Greeks built it." Marcius smiled. "But Rome conquered it." He waved his hand down the avenue. "This is Canopus, the main street. We'll take this to the Rhakotis district. This is the Jewish quarter to the north, next comes the palace district…"

Marcius kept up a running commentary as they walked. Afra's head began to spin with all the names: streets, districts, temples, theaters. And monuments! Every block seemed to house a marble pillar, painted statue, or carved stone fountain dedicated to a long-dead ruler or city benefactor. They entered the *agora*—the heart of the city—a large plaza where two main streets met. The plaza was faced with temples, government basilicas, and a covered market; all overflowing with people of all types. Richly dressed city councilors followed by clerks or slaves in livery strolled up the steps of the government buildings. Soldiers stood guard at the market where merchants haggled with their customers. Beggars and cutpurses waited in the shadows of the temples where people of all classes gathered for daily sacrifices and rituals.

Marcius frowned at the lines of people spilling out of the eastern gate in a wall enclosing several blocks of the city. "Damned tourists! Everyone wants to see the tomb of Alexander the Great. See that?" Marcius pointed at a golden colored sandstone pyramid rising above the marble-faced, brick walls of the enclosure. "The great conqueror's tomb. Regular people can't see the body of course, but Caesar and Augustus both visited the burial chamber when they were here. Most just come to gawk at the gardens and statues and to be able to say 'I saw the tomb.' "

Afra's face screwed up into a puzzled frown. It was hard keeping track of the famous men Marcius chattered about; their times, deeds, and names were a jumble. It seemed that every emperor in Rome was named Caesar Augustus for the past hundred years. Which one was he talking about? She shook her head and put those thoughts away. No need to worry about anyone but her master at this point. She would never meet an emperor.

Marcius pulled on her sleeve pointing to a modest building down a side street. "No lines there and just what I need."

Afra sniffed as they approached. A public toilet. She had wondered how they kept the streets so clean. They entered the light stone building and Marcius paid the attendant two small bronze coins. The attendant handed him a sponge on a stick. From the smell the sponge was soaked in vinegar. Open windows high above their heads provided welcome ventilation. Stone benches, with oval holes cut out at regular intervals, lined the walls. A couple sat next to one another chatting. A woman with a child and three men occupied widely separate seats.

Marcius chose an open hole, hitched his tunic and dropped his breechclout before settling with a sigh. "You're paid for, Afra. Better here than a pot at the inn where you have to dump it yourself."

Afra chose a seat and relieved herself. She heard water rushing below the bench, flushing the waste away. *Much better than a pot or the bushes, indeed.*

After their brief stop, Marcius led them to a markedly poorer district. The multi-story buildings were made of mud brick and crowded around dusty squares. Dark-skinned women gossiped at the fountains, while children in meager ragged clothes squealed and chased one another.

"Rhakotis, the native Egyptian district." Marcius explained. They approached a building, distinguished from the rest by the faded sign of Tyche, the Greek goddess of good fortune, painted over the door. An old woman with a bloody bandage over one eye sat outside, begging.

Marcius nudged her with his toe. "Mother, do you know if Clio lives here?"

"The snake woman?" Spitting in the dust, the old woman held up her index and little fingers in the sign to ward off evil. "What business do you have with her?"

"That's none of *your* business, old woman." The tightening of Marcius's jaw deepened the creases around his mouth and eyes. "Is she in?"

"At this time of day?" The hag squinted at the lowering sun with her good eye. "You might find her in the next square outside the Inn of the Jackal dancing with her cursed snake." As Marcius walked away, Afra heard the old one mutter, "Or more likely inside the inn dancing on her back."

Afra followed Marcius. He typically babbled like a stream in spate, telling far more than she was ever curious about. Now, he remained silent, as he plowed through the crowds.

"Who is this Clio?"

"My wife."

"You never spoke of a wife."

"We didn't part on the best of terms. She might have divorced me."

Afra waited, but he said no more. They left the shadow of a narrow street for a small square with a public fountain. A few women clustered around the stone basin waiting their turn to fill jars with fresh water. The music of a flute drifted from a corner shaded by a twisted olive tree. A crowd—mostly men, but a few children—watched a woman dance with sinuous fluid movements.

As they moved closer, Afra gasped. The woman wore a sheer linen tunic over her full figure. Lustrous black hair cascaded down her back. Her hips gyrated to the erotic sounds of the flute. A large python coiled around her waist and drooped over her shoulders. The snake's head swayed with the music, its forked tongue flicked the air.

Marcius smiled. "A beauty, isn't she?"

Afra thought Clio's face a bit hard, with thin lips, a knife-blade nose, and too much makeup, but her lush body unexpectedly roused her.

The music took on a more urgent note and Clio pulled the snake between her legs, rubbing, riding the muscular body. Clio whirled, caressing the snake and being caressed in turn as it flowed between her legs and over her breasts. As the flute hit a high note, she cried out in seeming ecstasy, stiffened in a pose with her arms raised, and threw her head back to reveal the milky column of her throat.

Many of the men in the crowd reached for their genitals and rubbed vigorously. Marcius stood slack-jawed, blood draining from his face. Afra had to shake off the snake woman's spell, as well. She shrugged and took a deep breath, willing the blood throbbing through her veins to slow. The exquisite ache in her groin ebbed slowly.

One of the better dressed men approached Clio as the flute player passed a basket for money. Marcius muscled his way through the crowd, Afra in tow.

"…for your services?"

Marcius swung the man around with a rough hand. "She's my wife and not for sale."

"Are you sure, friend?" The man smiled, revealing small crooked teeth. "She seems most willing."

"Marcius, you son of a diseased whore." Clio advanced, both fists clenched at her side, the snake peering over her shoulder. "How dare you come back, after leaving me in this shithole without two denarii to rub together?" She drove a fist into his stomach, sending the air whooshing from his lungs.

Afra grabbed Clio's arm before she could scratch Marcius' face with her talon-like nails. Clio bellowed like a hippo and turned on her. Afra let go and stepped back when the python hissed and bared its fangs. Clio stood, panting with anger. Marcius stood, panting for breath. Clio's erstwhile customer looked back and forth, between the two.

"Leave us." Afra glowered at the man. He backed away as he took in her imposing form, disappointment warring with laughter on his face.

The rest of the crowd drifted a short distance, waiting to see if there would be more entertainment. Marcius turned to them, brandished a fist, and bellowed, "Show's over. Go."

Clio turned her rigid back on them and coaxed the snake into a basket.

Marcius approached. "Clio, my love. I told you I would make my fortune and I have." He pulled a jingling pouch from his belt. "Now we can go to Rome. I can buy you all those pretty things you want."

Clio turned, pursed her lips, and eyed the pouch. "That doesn't look like enough to get us passage, much less set us up in comfort."

"The money isn't all. I also have her." Marcius gestured at Afra.

" *'Her?'* " Clio's mouth tightened as she surveyed Afra's muscled arms and flat chest. "You went to Kush to get gold and come back with a female slave? And not even a pretty one. If you had to get a female, at least you could have got one we might rent to the brothels."

"Afra is one of the best hunters I've seen. She'll earn us her price many times over. I promise."

Afra stiffened. "What of my fr--"

Marcius pulled Clio into a hug, shaking his head at his slave. "Later," he mouthed.

Clio broke loose from the embrace and grabbed the basket from the flute player. She carefully counted the coins. "Not what that crowd should have brought in." She frowned. "You're bad for business, Marcius."

"You won't have to do any business from now on, my love." Marcius stroked her hair. "I'll take care of you."

Clio batted his hand away, pointedly pouring the coins into her own money pouch. She tossed a couple of the smaller ones to the boy flute player, who deftly snatched them from the air, grinned, and scampered off. She pointed her chin toward an open air food stall. "I'll let you buy me a meal and consider your offer."

They approached a small shop with a large opening onto the walkway. Four clay pots with lids set into the wide counter, from which the proprietor ladled food for the crowd of ill-dressed patrons who flocked to his window. He seemed to do a brisk business, so his food must be good, cheap, or both. Afra's mouth watered at the savory smell of cooked onions, garlic, and cardamom. Clio pored over the pots, finally settling on a dish with a few shreds of lamb in lentils and onions, served in a hollowed loaf of brown bread. Marcius bought portions for them all, and escorted Clio to a small table behind the counter, out of earshot.

Afra eased her pack from her shoulders, squatted in the dusty street, and broke off a piece of bread for dipping. Fatigue, heat, and a full stomach had her nodding within seconds of finishing her meal.

I hope Marcius won't be long.

*****

"Afra."

Someone shook her shoulder. She started out of a comforting dream. The humid heat was wrong; the smells of unfamiliar spices confused her. *Asata?* Memories of Asata came flooding back, but the pain was more distant, less insistent than in weeks past. She regretted that. Her love was slipping away. She looked up at a rugged male face and a frowning female one. She remembered where she was.

"Is she simple?" Setting her hands on her ample hips, Clio regarded Marcius with suspicion.

"No." Afra rose and stretched, muscles cracking.

" 'No, *Domina.*' That's the proper address." Clio gave her an appraising look and shoved a covered basket into her arms. "Here. You carry Astarte."

"Astarte?" Afra hefted the basket.

"My snake."

She nearly dropped the basket, as the snake shifted its weight. Clio gave her a vicious smile. Afra was beginning to dislike this woman.

"Clio, don't be a harpy." Marcius draped an arm around his wife. "Afra's no ordinary slave. She saved my life."

"As any slave should."

"*Before* she became my slave. She's a skilled *venatore*, not a house servant."

"What's the use of having a slave, if she won't carry my things?" Clio sniffed and removed Marcius' arm. "Let's go home. I'm tired."

By the time they reached the crumbling mud-brick tenement, Afra shouldered a jar of wine, olives wrapped in grape leaves, and a small round of hard yellow cheese; as well as her pack and the basket. The building, a hollow square of four floors, stood hunched and dark on the side street. Small balconies overlooked a narrow shaft in the middle, which provided light and air to the rooms on each level. The lowest levels suffered a perpetual twilight except at noon. Afra eyed the rickety stairs wearily.

"My room's at the top." Clio smiled. Marcius leered at his wife and patted her on the bottom.

They trudged upwards. Women sat nursing babies on the landings outside their rooms. Children shouted as they chased each other up and down the stairs. The fetid stench of human waste wafted from the center shaft; it was obviously used as a communal midden. When they finally reached Clio's room, Afra heartily longed for the rough camps and fresh air of their journey.

Clio pushed aside a flimsy mat covering a doorway to reveal a small room filled with a pallet and a stout locked chest. Soot from an illegal brazier streaked the once-white walls. Afra deposited her burdens in the empty corner.

"I'll take that from you." Marcius grabbed the jar of wine and his wife. He motioned with his chin to the balcony.

Afra left to make a rude bed of her cloak outside the door. She fell asleep to a chorus of squeals, grunts, and giggles from within.

Afra stood on a dock, waiting for Marcius, as the treasures of Africa flowed into ships bound for Rome. Slaves hauled amphorae of oil, olives, and wine. Others bowed under loads of ivory, bales of animal skins, and boxes of ceramic goods. Most numerous of all were wagons groaning with grain. A constant stream of slaves hauled bags of wheat and barley harvested from the banks of the Nile to the waiting grain fleet—huge boats, twice the size of most of the ships moored in the double harbor. Marcius claimed the grain more precious than gold, as it fed the ever-hungry hordes of Rome. Nearly as tall as the Pyramid of Khufu, the famous Pharos lighthouse brooded over the scene, watching the wealth of Egypt pass out of its sight.

An elephant's fearful cry preceded a general uproar further down the wharves. Curiosity piqued, Afra walked toward the shouts. A boat specially built to hold large animals—deep keeled with built in cages and thick iron rings for chains—floated at a dock. A stout wooden ramp leading from the dock to the boat bobbed from the gentle waves. A young female elephant, her legs shackled in massive iron chains, balked at the ramp. A burly man hauled a chain to guide her onto the boat, while a red-haired man poked her from behind with a barbed spear. The elephant was obviously terrified of the swaying ramp and refused to move, trumpeting her distress.

Afra approached the man on shore. "Turn her around."

"What?" he snarled, prodding harder with the spear.

"Back her up the ramp. She won't see the swaying."

The red-haired man stopped poking, looked her up and down, while wiping his sweating face with a dirty rag. "What do you know about elephants?"

"Enough." She shrugged. "They are intelligent creatures. If you saw danger ahead, would you walk into it?"

He grinned, showing yellowed teeth. "I suppose not." He turned to his partner and yelled instructions. They soon had the elephant on the boat, where she stood shifting from side to side straining against her chains. The burly one locked the chain to a stout beam.

"Do you have any food for her?" Afra asked.

"Over there." Red pointed to a basket of partially rotting fruit.

She picked up several dates and approached the animal, fruit on open hand. "Great one, take this humble offering from your sister."

The elephant stopped swaying and turned her massive head toward the sound of a kind human voice. Afra drew closer. The animal tentatively picked a date from her hand with its sensitive trunk and popped it into her mouth. The elephant ate another and another, until they were gone, then used her trunk to explore Afra's face, snorting sticky date juice into her hair.

Afra laughed and caught the animal's trunk, patting it. "You are a playful one."

"Are you as good with other animals as with this one?" Red asked. "I have an ailing cat."

He motioned toward a covered cage on the dock. Afra clambered down the ramp to the cage and whipped off the heavy cloth. A cheetah panted on the floor, her fur patchy and eyes glazed. Three small spotted cubs shared her cage. One didn't move. Flies gathered at its mouth and crusted eyes. The other two butted their mother's belly looking to suckle, but getting nothing.

"Special request, worth a great deal of money to me. The cubs were born on the trip down the Nile."

Afra stroked her chin. "She's in a bad way. In this heat she needs fresh air and lots of water. Cats eat meat. Mothers eat more."

"If I get rid of the cubs will she recover faster?"

Afra reluctantly nodded.

He looked Afra over, noting the iron slave collar. "Who do you belong to? I could use a good animal handler."

"She's mine, you pirate."

" 'She'?" The man turned.

"Afra." Marcius nodded at her, then the other man. "Rufus." Marcius grinned and punched the other man on the shoulder. "Trying to take my *venatore*?"

Rufus scowled, "Who're you to call me a pirate, you thief."

"Fatherless son of a cheap whore."

Afra stood puzzled while the two men continued to call each other names, until they roared with laughter and pounded each other on the back.

"Afra," Marcius gasped. "Rufus works for my former association. We've had many a good night together drinking and whoring."

" 'Former association'?" Rufus laughed. "Did they get smart and kick your sorry ass onto the street?"

"No. I'm starting my own business. With what I can earn from Afra, I'll build a troop. The Emperor's agent for the games is looking for acts—*venatorii, beastiarii,* comedy—you know—everything except the gladiators."

"That's quite an undertaking." Rufus whistled. "If you need a partner…"

"Why would I want a lazy pile of shit like you working for me?" Marcius put his arm around the man's shoulders. "Come, I'll buy you a drink."

"Let me take care of this cat first." Rufus called over the burly man. "Put her cage in the bow, with one side uncovered, so she'll get a breeze. Make sure she has plenty of food and water and get rid of the cubs."

The burly man, reached in to take the live cubs. It was a sign of how far gone the mother was, that she didn't take his hand off. He dropped the mewling cubs into an empty grain sack.

"What will he do with them?" Afra pointed at the sack.

Rufus shrugged, "Feed them to one of the other animals, probably. They always appreciate fresh meat."

"Such a small meal for a large animal." She shook her head. "Marcius will buy them. His wife keeps a snake which likes live prey."

"What?" Marcius stood gaping.

She pulled him aside. "Buy the cubs. I'll train them for you."

Marcius frowned. "No."

"Two fully trained hunting cats. How much will they be worth?"

His eyes gleamed. "How long?"

"Less than two years till they are fully grown."

The frown returned.

"They will cost little as snake food. I worked with the royal animal trainer. They will more than pay for themselves." Afra couldn't explain her sudden need to rescue the cubs, the emptiness in her chest when she thought of the helpless creatures, alone, ripped from their mother.

Marcius studied her face. "Fine."

He strolled over to Rufus. "What will you give me to take those cubs off your hands?"

They haggled briefly. Marcius turned over several small coins. He handed the wriggling sack to Afra.

"I'll need money to buy a goat."

"What?" Marcius' face turned red.

"The cubs will need milk for a while. A goat is best."

"Here." He gave her a large brass piece. "They better be worth it. Buy milk in the market. We'll talk later about the goat." Marcius turned back to his friend. "Come on, Rufus, before Afra costs me more money." They sauntered off the docks toward a wine shop.

Afra grinned, put the brass in her pouch, and left with the cubs.

Afra woke to Clio's high-pitched complaints. "Keep it down, woman!" Marcius growled and clutched his head.

"Where have you been?" Clio hissed through clenched teeth, "I send you out in the morning to book us passage and you come home after dark, stinking of wine. Did you gamble away our money as well?"

"Got our passage. Day af'er 'morrow. An' I got somethin' for you… here somewhere…"

"And wild cats! That crazy slave of yours said you bought them." She screwed her thin lips into a moue of distaste. "I can't abide cats. The cursed Egyptians worship the flea-bitten things or I would drown every single one I could catch." Clio's eyes blazed. "How much did you pay for them?"

"Almost nothin'." Marcius vaguely patted at his body. "Here!" He pulled a blue faience necklace from a pouch. "Jus' for my lovely wife."

Clio grabbed the necklace and frowned. "Cheap tourist stuff."

"I paid good money for that!"

"You were robbed."

Afra rose and checked on the cubs sleeping in a small box lined with straw. Marcius and Clio would either argue, make love, or both. Either way she wouldn't get much sleep that night.

Chapter Eight

Cinnia spiked her hair with lime. Another woman blackened the area around Cinnia's eyes with soot, drew protective spirals on her arms in blue woad, and decorated her cheeks with parallel blue lines. The fierce face Cinnia saw reflected in her sword thrilled and disturbed her. So much had changed since she started on that journey to the Sacred Isle, months ago. Her life, her dreams swept away. She couldn't see beyond the next day.

Today they would meet the Romans in battle—maybe the final one. General Paulinus had failed to defend Londinium and Verulamium. Both lay in smoldering ashes. The Iceni had chased Paulinus, the XIV *Gemina*, and the XX *Valeria* to this hill. Not only did Cinnia's people have the advantage of greater numbers, but they held the high ground, ranging their baggage wagons across the crest of the hill. The Romans had their backs to deep forest. There would be no escape. Cinnia sighed. Maybe they could all go home after today.

"Andraste, sacred to my people, Mother of War and Death, give me strength." She prayed, as she sharpened her blade. "May the Morrigan take the Romans and eat their balls."

Cinnia looked up as a *carnyx* sounded the assembly of the warriors. She put on her heavy leather belt, graced with the looted bronze buckle, over a short summer wool tunic. The sun climbed above the tree line, glaring down on the bustling people. Sweat dampened her tunic under her arms and breasts; trickled down her bare legs. She picked up her small round shield, sheathed her Roman *gladius,* and moved with the other women toward Boudica in her chariot.

A vast sea of warriors watched the Iceni queen. There were men from many tribes, dressed in their looted armor, decorated with their sacred symbols. For every Roman soldier there were ten Britons. The crowd thrummed with a taut, nervous energy. Cinnia's mouth dried and her muscles twitched in anticipation.

Boudica stood in her chariot, sun glinting off her armor and red hair. She faced her army and shouted, "This is not the first time the Britons have followed a woman into battle! But I did not come to boast of ancestry, or to recover my kingdom or the plundered wealth of my people. I take the field, like the meanest among you, to assert the cause of liberty and to seek revenge!"

A roar rolled across the mass, as Boudica's words were sped on.

"To the pride and arrogance of the Romans, nothing is sacred; all are subject to violation; the old endure the scourge and virgins are deflowered. But the vindictive gods are now at hand. A Roman legion dared to face us. They paid with their lives. Those who survived the carnage of that day think of nothing but how to save themselves by an ignominious flight."

The vision of frightened fleeing Romans elicited laughter and many rude gestures, as the Britons banged on their shields.

Boudica pointed down the valley toward the distant Romans. "From the din of our preparation, the Romans even now shrink back with terror. What will be their case when the assault begins? Look round. View your numbers. Behold the proud display of warlike spirits. Consider the motives for which we draw the avenging sword. On this spot we must either conquer or die with glory. There is no alternative. Though a woman, my resolution is fixed. The men, if they please, may survive with infamy, and live in bondage."

Cinnia lifted her sword with the rest as they chanted, "Boudica! Boudica!"

Her heart lifted. Resolve strengthened as her queen rode toward her female companions. Boudica pointed to the five oldest and most experienced women. "You with me. The rest will guard my daughters."

"No!" Cinnia joined in the chorus of dismay at being left behind.

Boudica's face softened. "You have been my most loyal warriors. I ask this of my best. If the gods are against us this day, take my daughters to safety. Two valleys to the north on the left rock face is the cave of a druid. You will know it by a black boulder with a flat top. Hide them there."

Cinnia looked up at her queen and recalled her dream of so many months ago: *she guarded two wounded fawns from attacking wolves. Had the gods sent her a message of doom?* She shook her head. That couldn't be the import.

Boudica saw the look on Cinnia's face. "Do not fear, faithful ones. We will be victorious. I take a mother's precautions."

Cinnia ducked her head so Boudica couldn't see her tears.

Cinnia shaded her eyes as sunlight glinted off the swords of the Romans, rank after rank of them. She stood atop a wagon, piled high with loot from the Roman cities they had destroyed. The baggage train formed a half moon across a ridge. Women, children, the wounded, and the old watched with eagerness as the huge mass of British warriors streamed down a narrow valley toward the waiting Romans.

"There's Mother!" Maeve pointed. A blue streamer sporting a white horse and a spoked wheel—sacred to the Iceni gods—floated from her charioteer's spear, marking the queen's chariot.

"I see!" Cinnia's heart lifted as Boudica led the chariot charge. The light wicker chariots pulled by short-legged ponies bounced over the rough ground, but not a driver or warrior fell. The chariot rush slowed and packed more tightly, as the valley narrowed. The women and old men of the baggage train shook their weapons, ready to join the battle if needed. A wild ululation seared Cinnia's throat as she joined with the others urging the warriors on. The chariots were followed by a huge mass of screaming, fearsome warriors—most in mail and helmets with their long Celtic swords flashing in the sun. A few fought naked dedicating their lives to the warrior's gods. The sounds of the *carnyx* wafted over the din of the men and women surging forward toward the ranked Romans.

Cinnia could only imagine the terror of the Romans cowering behind their wall of shields as the frenzied Britons descended on them with swords flashing and the fury of the gods in their shouts. The earth shook under their feet. She wondered they did not break and run into the forest. The Romans *couldn't* survive against such a large force, but her dream nagged her. Cinnia looked behind. One of the other guards had horses saddled, and a pack animal ready, in case of flight. She made the spiral sign to ward off evil. The roar of battle cries brought her attention back to the charge.

When the chariots spilled out of the valley, the Romans sent a deadly wave of spears toward the Britons. Ponies screamed, chariots overturned, forcing the warriors to fight on foot. A second wave of spears rained down on the Britons. The deadly *pila* shattered the warriors' shields or stuck in them, making them useless. The stream of warriors continued surging toward the waiting Romans.

Brianna screamed, "Where's Mother?"

"There!" Cinnia pointed at the blue banner in a knot of warriors on foot.

"Thank the gods." Brianna sobbed. "Why didn't she let me go with her?"

Cinnia patted the younger girl on the back. "Look! Our people swarm the field." She watched, exultant, as the never-ending stream of warriors descended toward the Roman soldiers, shouting their war cries.

The Romans shifted their positions, forming into a blunt triangle, pointed toward their attackers. They started marching toward the Britons, pushing them back with their large red shields, stabbing them with their short swords, and stepping over the dead bodies to take on the next wave of warriors. The tenor of the battlefield noise changed. A note of frustration entered the cacophony, occasionally punctuated with fear— but not from the Romans—from her own people.

The Romans pushed the Britons into the narrow valley where the following warriors piled up behind their fellows pressing them forward to their deaths. There was no room for the warriors to swing their long swords or throw their spears. When one rank of Romans wavered with fatigue, they stepped back, a fresh rank took their places, hacking and killing; their short swords gleamed with the blood of hundreds.

Cinnia watched with growing shock as the mighty British force broke against the solid Roman army and came crashing back toward the baggage train. Caught between the encircling wagons and the onward press of the Romans, they threw down their weapons and ran. Once though the defile, the Roman infantry opened up to allow the cavalry through. They set upon the fleeing warriors, cutting them down by the hundreds.

Cinnia grabbed the girls and pushed them off the back of the wagon. "We must leave. Now!"

"But, Mother…" Maeve's mouth hung open in a silent scream.

"Has provided for your escape. Brianna, help your sister onto her horse."

They both boosted the girl into her saddle then Cinnia helped Brianna. Her own mount bucked and pulled at the reins in the chaos.

One of the other guards grabbed Cinnia by the shoulder and screamed into her face, "Ride! We'll cover your retreat." She held the horse steady as Cinnia leapt into her saddle. "Go!" She turned back to fight the advance of Romans, giving Cinnia a few more precious seconds.

Cinnia wheeled her horse around, grabbed the lead rope of the pack animal, and shouted. "Follow me!"

She thundered down the opposite side of the hill, followed by Brianna and Maeve. Cinnia looked left and right for flanking cavalry. She wasn't a natural rider and crouched over the horse's mane holding tight as it stretched its neck and ran flat out over the rough ground. Cinnia feared falling off more than confronting the Romans. The horse seemed to sense her uncertainty and slowed. The girls passed her, speeding for the forest. Her horse, not wanting to be left behind, sped up again.

By the time they reached the forest, both the horse and Cinnia were blowing and lathered. She slowed to a trot and was nearly scraped off by the low-hinging bough of a fir tree. She came to a stop, trembling. She heard a noise ahead and unsheathed her sword.

Brianna came into view with a sobbing Maeve. "Are you all right?" They seemed to sit their horses with a lot more confidence than Cinnia.

She wiped the sweat from her brow, smudging her soot and woad. "I am now." She looked around the forest; spotted a faint path. "Come. Your mother left instructions."

She led the girls down the valley beside a stream that cut through a meadow filled with summer flowers. Birdsong stilled as they approached, starting again as they passed. Everything seemed so serene and normal, that Cinnia wondered if she dreamed the horrors they left behind. She turned to see the forlorn huddled figures of the girls. A sob rose to her throat.

What of Dumnor and Oriana? Melva and the baby? Did anyone survive?

In the second valley to the north, Cinnia spied the black boulder up a ridge of loose rock. If there was a path, it was well hidden.

"I think we should leave the horses here and go up on foot."

"Why?" Maeve cried.

"Because I don't think the horses could make it up that slope."

"I mean, why should we hide?" Maeve's voice trembled. "Mother is dead. We have no home, no people. We should take our own lives before the Romans catch up with us."

Cinnia had no answer.

Brianna moved her mount closer to her sister and pushed the hair from the younger girl's face. "Because Mother wanted us to live."

"Like this?" Maeve gestured around her. "Hunted, alone?"

"We're not alone. Mother provided a guardian. Let us choose to live one more day. We don't know what tomorrow will bring."

Maeve hung her head. "One more day."

They hobbled the horses in a small glade where they could graze, hid the saddles and tack under a stack of evergreen boughs, and shared out the supplies from the pack. Cinnia took the largest share; mostly food, but a couple of blankets and cook pots, as well. She discovered a heavy bag of coins in the middle of the pack and gave that to Brianna.

The girls hiked up the ridge of loose rock, past the black boulder, around a bend. Under a twisted fir clinging to the side of the rock, Cinnia spied a narrow opening. She slipped off the pack so she could slide in sideways. The opening broadened into a smallish outer cave but the passage turned at the back. She spied light flicking on the other side of the turn. Cinnia approached, knife out, crouching. A quick look around the wall confirmed a small fire; the smoke drifting toward the back of the cave toward a crack to the surface. A dark figure sat by the fire, his back to Cinnia.

"Come in."

Cinnia started. "How did you know?"

"I may be old, but my nose works. I could smell the fear on you."

Cinnia sheathed her knife as her eyes adjusted. She recognized the ancient druid from Boudica's court. "I have the queen's daughters. The Romans…" Cinnia choked back a sob.

"I know. I warned Boudica. My dreams were filled with crows and ill-omens. I told her to send the princesses here if there was need." He looked past her shoulder. "Come in, my daughters."

Maeve and Brianna crept past Cinnia and sat at the old man's feet. He laid his hands on their heads. "The triple goddesses have you under their protection. Tomorrow we will go north to the wild tribes where no Roman dares to go. They will honor Boudica's children."

"What of Mother?" Tears glistened on Brianna's cheek.

The old man shook his head. "I foresee her death. She did not want to be captured by the Romans and dragged through their streets in chains. I gave her a potent draught. If needed, it will bring a quick death." The girls sobbed, hugging each other. He looked at Cinnia. "And you, my child? Will you journey with us?"

"Boudica left her daughters in my care. I'll go where they go. No Roman followed that I know of. They were busy slaughtering those they could catch on foot. Distributing the loot from the baggage train will slow them down, but soon they will scour the land looking for the last of us."

The old man nodded. "You are all tired. You should sleep before we journey. I've laid protections on this cave. We are safe."

Cinnia doubted her gods' ability to save them from the Romans. They had failed so far in spite of the bloody sacrifices made of captives from the towns they took. She shuddered away from the gruesome memories, but the druids had insisted. In war, the gods needed blood and better that be the blood of the enemy. She felt she should scout the area looking for survivors or Romans, but at the old man's suggestion, exhaustion crept through her limbs. She barely dragged in her pack and unrolled a blanket, before falling into a deep and dreamless sleep.

NEXT MORNING, Cinnia left their shelter to relieve herself and spotted a small Roman cavalry detail coming over the pass into the valley. She bolted back into the cave.

"Romans! Not more than an hour away. We must move." She started to pack their small store of provisions.

"We can't go." Brianna hunched over her sister. "Maeve has a fever."

Cinnia looked at the druid.

"I have medicines, but she can't be moved."

The girl groaned and cried out.

"Hush, sister." Brianna wet a strip of cloth from the water bag and washed the younger girl's face. "I'm here. You're safe."

"They don't know we're here." The ancient druid put a hand on Cinnia's shoulder. "They will not see us."

"These Romans have the look of hunters. A traitorous Briton rides with them."

The old man tugged at his beard. "If they know what they are looking for, they might see."

"They will find the horses and come looking for us. If they have a scout trained in woodcraft they will find us. There is a path." She tuned to Brianna. "Douse the fire. The smoke will give us away. Stay with the druid. I'll take the horses, lead the Romans away from the cave, and double back when I'm sure they've given up the chase."

Brianna's lips trembled. "Come back to us, please?"

She touched the younger girl on the shoulder. "I'll try. Your mother charged me with your lives." Cinnia looked at the druid. "Can you get them to the north if I don't come back?"

His eyes crinkled with concern. "I've lived in these woods all my life. I know the secret ways and can keep them safe."

"I'll be back as soon as I can, but don't wait for me. When Maeve can travel, go." Cinnia hugged Brianna and knelt for the druid's blessing.

"May the sky gods protect you and keep you safe, my daughter."

Cinnia grabbed a blanket, but left the food and water. She wouldn't need it.

CINNIA STIFLED A GROAN as she slid off the horse at the stream. Not used to riding, her back ached after hours in the saddle. Her inner thighs felt raw. She eyed the stream, wondering if she had time to sit in the cool rushing water for relief. She decided against it. The stream was exposed in a broad meadow, which had been grazed by sheep or cattle the year before. She needed to move on before someone spied her from the woods edging the meadow, but she couldn't resist an extra moment out of the cursed saddle.

Did I miss anything? Cinnia mentally sorted through her actions, looking for mistakes, thinking ahead. She had obscured the path to the cave and rode the horses through soft ground leaving a clear trail. After a couple of hours, she sent two of the horses down a side path, hoping to split the Roman forces following her. The third horse went lame shortly after, leaving her one mount. How long would they bother to follow her? Were they looking for Boudica's daughters or mopping up escaped Iceni? She lowered herself to drink beside her horse, who noisily snuffled the water, before seeking a few blades of grass.

Then it raised its head in alarm, looking toward the woods.

Wolves? Cinnia saw the glint of sun on helmets. *Yes, the Roman kind.*

She pulled herself into the saddle. A Roman road lay on the other side of the hill. If she made it there, her pursuers would have to divide again to follow. She would send the horse in one direction and disappear into the woods on foot. If the Romans caught up with her, she had her sword and knife.

As the shadows deepened under the trees, Cinnia limped south beside the Roman road, hoping never to have to ride a horse again. The hour before, she had hid in a thicket, while a small squad of five Roman cavalry passed her. For the first time that day, she felt confident that her ruses worked. She took the time to harvest a few handfuls of late berries to satisfy her complaining stomach. When the last light leached from the forest, she fell into an exhausted sleep, covered by last year's leaves.

She woke with a spear at her throat.

"Found him!" A grinning soldier shouted in Roman.

Cinnia heard bodies crashing through the woods and Roman curses as brambles scratched at exposed legs and arms.

"Thought you'd be clever, eh? Sending the horses off?" The soldier spoke in a heavily accented dialect. "Horses are herd animals. They don't go far without a man riding them or a wolf chasing them. When we find the horses, we know to go opposite."

Cinnia ground her teeth. *How could I have been so stupid?*

Two more soldiers entered the clearing, grabbed her arms; took her knife and sword. One brushed his hand against her breast as he searched her and started.

"This's a girl!"

"Fun tonight, boys!" The spear-wielding soldier's grin grew broader. "Tie her up."

Cold settled in Cinnia's stomach; horror paralyzed her limbs. She stumbled through the woods toward the road wishing the druid had given her a vial of the deadly poison he had provided Boudica.

Chapter Nine

Afra watched the Pharos grow smaller in the distance, its fiery eye visible long after the white walls of Alexandria had disappeared. Her eyes unexpectedly prickled with tears. Would she ever return to Africa? Did she want to? She clutched her amulet. The priest in Meroe had told her to honor the gods wherever she went, but the small figure of Isis gave Afra no comfort as the coast slipped away. Maybe she should have asked for the Roman sea god's favor, as the crew and other passengers did before leaving the harbor.

She surveyed their meager possessions piled on the deck: Clio's snake basket, her own pack, three bed rolls, a small cage for the cubs, and a basket of fresh fruit and herbs to supplement the ship's fare. Clio's wooden box, Marcius' much more substantial pack, and the other passengers' kits were stowed below deck with the cargo—amphorae of oil, wine, and fish sauce—along with fourteen days' supplies of food and water. Afra hoped the voyage wouldn't take more than the usual seven days. She had a limited supply of dried meat and cheese for the cubs. They were a little young to wean, but she had little choice. If necessary she would chew their food for them.

Three other passengers voyaged with them. She spotted Marcius chatting with a well-dressed man in a peaked cap, who looked annoyed at being cornered. Clio clung to the rail, retching, along with two others who were poor sailors.

Afra picked among the basket of herbs, found a sprig of mint and crushed a few leaves into a cup of water.

"Try this." Afra held the aromatic cup out to Clio.

"You insolent slut!" Clio turned her green-tinged face toward her. "Call me '*Domina*' and don't talk to me unless I ask."

"Yes, *Domina*." Afra sketched a bow and retreated to sip the water herself. She felt mildly unsettled, but the mint-flavored water helped. She surveyed the ship. A medium-sized merchant vessel, with a crew of four, its deck accommodated ten people in a space Afra could cover in twenty strides from bow to stern and five from side to side. No way to get away from Clio and her tempers. It was going to be a long voyage.

A school of large sleek fish leaped out of the water on either side of the ship, slipping gracefully in and out of the water. One stood on its tail and chittered at Afra; its eyes gleamed with intelligence, and mouth curved in a smile.

She heard Marcius come up behind her. "You should see your face, Afra. You look like a small child who has seen her first shooting star."

Entranced, she reached over the rail as if to touch one. "What are these creatures?"

"Dolphins. The Greeks say that a ship of sailors tried to seize the god Dionysus who traveled in disguise and sell him as a slave. He turned the oars and ropes to snakes and the men jumped over the side to escape. Poseidon turned them into dolphins, forever fated to lead ships to safe harbor."

Afra raised an eyebrow. "Not a bad fate for such evil doers."

"Sailors who go beyond the Pillars of Hercules talk of dolphins bigger than a ship, all colors and markings." Marcius shaded his eyes. "They're moving off."

"What other strange creatures do you know of?"

"Bears, wolves, great horned elk." He put his hand up to forestall her questions. "You'll see them all and more in Rome."

She grinned for the first time in weeks. "Maybe I'll like this city after all."

*****

"PORTUS, HO!"

The sailor's shout roused Afra from a nap. They had been skirting the coast of Italia for a couple of days, heading for Rome's main sea port. A hint of green earth smell tainted the briny sea breeze. She rose, shaded her eyes, and looked off the bow. A massive lighthouse rose from the horizon, thrusting its slender tower into the sky.

"Quite a sight, isn't it?" Marcius came up behind her, holding hard to one of the ropes running to the mast. "Claudius built it taller than the one at Alexandria. Similar plan, but bigger. See the figure on top?"

Afra nodded.

"On the Pharos it's the sea god Poseidon. Here, it's the Divine Claudius. He built the Portus harbor too. Ostia—you'll see it on the right as we pass—is a river port. As Rome grew, it needed more goods. Ostia can only take shallow bottom boats." He looked around at the sailors taking their positions. "We should get our gear together."

Afra helped tie up their few bundles with plenty of time to spare to watch the crew. Two sailors manned the lines which ran through an ingenious series of horn rings sewed in vertical rows on the front of the great square sail. Two men could easily pull the sail up or lower it as the captain and a fourth sailor managed the tillers on both sides of the stern of the ship.

As they got closer, she saw a white gleaming *stoa* running the length of a mole reaching into the sea. It terminated in a temple, so the ship broaching the gap between the sea wall and the lighthouse island sailed between gods. The other passengers made small sacrifices at the portable alter in the stern as they sailed through, furled the sail, and came to a stop, gently rocking in the artificial harbor. Within minutes, a small boat, powered by a row of oars and carrying an officious-looking little man, pulled up to the side. The captain lowered a rope ladder and hauled the man aboard.

Marcius sighed, grumbling. "Damn, tax men. Can't a citizen go anywhere without paying?"

After the captain showed his papers, the tax official inspected the cargo, made notes on a wax tablet, and took a turn around the deck, poking at the various bundles. When he came to the cheetah's cage, he pushed the cover off and stepped back. "Who owns these?"

Afra heard the cubs' chirping cries and started to step forward. Marcius, put his arm in front of her. "They're mine."

"And you are?" The tax man looked up at Marcius.

"Lucius Marcius, citizen of Rome. These are my cats."

"Do you have a license? The Emperor carefully regulates animal importers."

Afra clenched her fists in frustration. She could do nothing if Marcius gave up the cubs. They were hers only in her heart. He glanced at her pleading face. Over the tax man's shoulder she saw Clio pick up her snake basket and disappear down the hatch. Afra wasn't the only one who might lose her pet.

"These aren't for the games. Special order for Senator Cotta"

The tax man snorted in derision. "Papers?"

Marcius handed over his papers. Afra saw a glint of silver drop into the tax man's hand. He quickly glanced through the papers. "Everything seems to be in order."

Afra released a long slow breath she hadn't realized she was holding.

Eventually the tax man left. Clio emerged from the hold with an empty basket, wearing a voluminous mantle. Sweat speckled her brow. She swayed up to Marcius, gave Afra a venomous glare, and hissed, "How much did that cost us?"

"Nothing compared to what I'll get when they're grown and trained, my love."

She sniffed. "If I hear that excuse one more time, I'll feed them to Astarte myself." At the sound of the snake's name, her robe shifted and undulated. Clio put a gentling hand on her waist and murmured a few soothing sounds.

When they finally tottered down the swaying ramp of the ship to a stone quay, each carried a substantial burden. A clutch of men stood along the quayside shouting their services. Marcius chose a likely looking fellow and handed him Clio's wooden box and a couple of their packs. Afra carried the cage, her own kit, and a precious leather cylinder enclosing a Kushite bow and arrows Marcius had bought for her in Alexandria. They followed the man under the marble stoa, past the lines of slaves off-loading the dozens of merchant ships, toward a large building on a canal.

After the magnificence of Alexandria, the Portus harbor seemed new and raw. Construction crews worked on several buildings close to the harbor. Piles of timber, brick and marble facing hulked nearby. Warehouses? More men carrying wax tablets or leather pouches stuffed with papers came and went from a central administration building. Travelers—coming and going—made offerings at another temple shrine. Afra murmured as they passed, "Praise to Mother Isis for delivering us safely from the sea. I'll make an offering when I can."

To Afra's relief, they stopped under a stoa by the side of a busy road. Marcius and the porter went in search of a hired wagon to haul their possessions to Rome. Clio sat on her wooden chest, back against the cool stone, and fanned herself. Afra took advantage of the break to take the cubs out of their cage for little air. At two months, they fit in her lap, but would soon outgrow it. The cage was already cramped. Afra smoothed the fuzzy spotted fur while the cubs purred and butted her leg. They would lose their baby coats soon and look more like adult cheetahs. They already had their spots and the distinctive black stripe from the inside of their eyes to the outside of their mouths.

"Have you named them?"

Afra looked up, startled. Clio had paid no attention to the cats on the voyage. With little to do, Afra had spent most of her time feeding and working with the cubs, training them to the leash and to respond to simple commands.

"This one's Mari. That's Cari."

"How do you tell them apart?"

"Mari has the bold spirit of the hunter. Cari is shy, but cunning."

Clio raised an eyebrow. "I thought it had more to do with their spots."

Afra graced her with one of her rare smiles. White even teeth flashed, rearranging the planes and angles of her face into a mask of exotic beauty.

"Mari has two rows of three small spots here." Afra pointed at the cat's left cheek. "Cari has a white spot on the tip of her tail."

"When will they be fully trained and ready to sell?"

Afra clutched Mari a little too hard, and the cub gave a soft chirping sound of distress. She loosened her grip. "A year at the earliest. Best if I train them until they are fully grown. About two."

"That's a long time." Clio frowned. "How will you feed them? We can't afford meat for ourselves, much less wild animals."

Afra had worried over that question herself, until she knifed a rat trying to steal their food on the boat. She pointed to a bold rodent scurrying across the road heading for the grain warehouses. "Wherever there are people, there are mice and rats. I will trap them until the cubs can hunt on their own."

"Good." Clio nodded. "Get an extra one or two for Astarte, next time you trap. Live hares are expensive."

CLIO SNIFFED AND LOOKED down her long nose at the dingy room they shared with several other travelers at the Rearing Horse Inn.

"It's just until I get my contract, love. Then we'll move. I'll find you a fine home." Marcius' voice trailed off under Clio's withering stare. "Afra, you and the cats will stay in the stable. This way."

Her heart lightened. The prospect of sharing space with horses and mules seemed much more pleasant than Clio's company.

"YOU'LL DO." The next day, Marcius looked Afra over with a critical eye. She wore his spare tunic—a pale yellow with embroidered roundels at the shoulders. Because of her height, it came to just above her knees. She was used to wearing men's clothes, but for some reason, this time she felt exposed. Maybe it wasn't the clothes but the new place. She knew nothing of Rome except some fantastical stories Marcius shared with her.

"Here's your bow. We're going to meet with the *procurator munerum*, the emperor's agent. He may want a demonstration of your abilities."

Afra carefully unwrapped her bow which stood nearly as tall as she. She ran her hand along the polished wood and inspected the sinew string for weaknesses. She had been more than pleased when Marcius bought it for her in Alexandria. He had been reluctant to part with the coin until she pointed out that her skill was with the Kushite bow not the inferior Roman ones. It took months to layer the wood, sinew, and horn that made the bow supple and strong and gave her better accuracy. If he wanted her to show her skills, she needed good tools, and Kushite bows were considerably cheaper in Alexandria than they were in Rome.

Their inn was inside the city boundary off a side street intersecting with the Appian Way. Rome was a much different city than Alexandria—bigger in every way—dirtier, noisier, more people. Whereas Alexandria was laid out on a grid system, Rome seemed to sprawl in all directions. Lavish villas crowned the hills, while the lower lying areas were crowded with *insulae*, apartment buildings that towered as much as five stories. The narrow streets twisted and turned, stinking of human waste and dead animals.

"Are the Romans as crooked as their streets?"

"Pretty much." Marcius laughed. "See that gang of toughs heading into the wine shop? They're probably the *collegia* paid by the local merchants to maintain the local shrine to the *lares*."

She raised an eyebrow.

"The *lares*—the minor spirits that protect crossroads and springs," he hastily explained.

"You mean that?" She pointed to a *fascinum*, a fired clay representation of a winged penis that seemed to be over every doorway.

Marcius laughed until tears came from his eyes. "No. Those are for good luck."

"Those men don't look like priests."

"They're not." Marcius wiped the tears from his cheeks. "The merchants pay the *collegia*, not only to maintain the shrines, but to protect their businesses."

"Protect from whom?"

"The *collegia*."

"Ahhh." She nodded.

"It's the Roman way. Everyone gets his cut."

They exited the twisted streets onto a broad boulevard which ended in a wide space packed with people smelling of sweat and strange spices. Basilicas and temples clustered around the various *fora* at odd angles and levels. Marcius traveled the twisted streets with practiced ease.

He pointed. "That's the *Forum Romanum* and the *rostra* where Senators speak to the people. They rarely have anything to say, but it's free entertainment." On a platform, a man in a purple-bordered white toga harangued the people. Some listened; some shouted back, others drifted away.

"Why have Senators if you have an Emperor?"

"I'm not sure myself. They used to be important during the Republic." Marcius lowered his voice and looked around to see if anyone seemed unduly interested in their conversation. "Every so often, the Emperor kills a bunch and takes their property. The next thing you know, there's a bunch of rich lack wits trying to take their places. It doesn't pay to be too rich in Rome, especially when the Emperor has a war to finance or a building project.

"Enough of politics. It makes my head hurt." He pointed to the right, "The procurator's office is over there, next to the amphitheater where the gladiators fight."

They approached an immense wall that curved away to the right. It looked like stone, but Afra soon realized it was wood, painted to look like stone with arches, pillars, and statues in niches. *Clever to trick the eye.* They approached a smaller wooden structure, with an equally ornate door guarded by a hulking man. He was taller than Afra and twice as wide, muscles rippling in his arms and legs, but going to fat around his middle.

"Ex-gladiator," Marcius mumbled and tried to pass.

The mountainous man stepped in their way. "Your business?"

"Is with the procurator."

"Do you have a letter of recommendation?"

"No." Marcius' jaw jutted forward. "I have a *venatore* from Ethiopia." He waved a hand at Afra.

The ex-gladiator slowly swept her with his gaze. "End of the line," he grunted, and let them pass.

They entered a dim, cavernous room lined with benches, most of which were filled with a motley crew of tough-looking men. Marcius stopped inside to let his eyes adjust. "Over there." He pointed to a rabbity man, sitting at a table outside a door and scribbling on a wax tablet.

"Lucius Marcius to see the procurator," he announced to the clerk.

"You and all these others." The clerk indicated the filled benches.

"Ah, but the procurator is a particular friend of mine and will be most interested in seeing me." Silver flashed as Marcius passed a coin to the clerk under the table. It disappeared so fast, Afra wondered if she really saw anything. She was beginning to wonder where Marcius got enough money for all his bribes. He always seemed to have an extra coin or two.

"Take a seat." The clerk nodded his head. "You're next."

"The Roman way?" Afra settled on a hard bench.

"Everyone gets his cut." Marcius sat and patted the pouch tucked in the fold of his belted tunic. "I hope there aren't too many cuts between me and the procurator, or I'll have to make another trip to the money lender and Clio wouldn't like me pawning the pretty new jewels I got her."

Uneasiness prickled Afra's skin. "What does the moneylender hold for that?" She nodded toward his pouch.

Blood crept up his neck to suffuse his face. Marcius looked away.

"Me?" She gritted between her teeth.

"Only if I can't pay by the end of each month."

"I owe *you* a life debt of service, not those others!"

"This is Rome, Afra." Marcius' low voice took a harder edge. "I own you. It's legal. I can do with you as I wish."

"Truly?" She crossed her arms and stared down her nose at the shorter Roman. "I can always choose escape or death."

His face went pale. "Escaped slaves are crucified. You don't want that death." He ran his hand through his dark hair. "I promised you a chance to buy your freedom. I stand by that. I need money to see the procurator. No procurator, no contract. No contract, no money. No money, no freedom. It's an investment."

"It's my life."

"Your life is mine. Trust me and you'll get it back. Fuck me over and you'll die in chains or nailed to a cross."

She sat, back rigid, one hand clasped tight on her bow, the other on her amulet, so as not to throttle him. She took several deep breaths to calm herself. The wood warmed under her hand. *Mother Isis, give me strength for the trials ahead. I am a stranger in this land. Give me wisdom and guide my actions.*

"Lucius Marcius!" the clerk cried.

She tamped down her emotions as they entered a smaller room lit by oil lamps. A man of medium build, with the dark complexion and hooked nose of the eastern provinces, sat at a table piled with scrolls. Animal skins covered the floor. Afra recognized the distinctive pattern of a zebra hide, but not the dark brown furry pelt with a dog-like head and a mouth full of sharp teeth. Horns of many types, including rhino and elephant tusks, adorned the walls.

"Procurator." Marcius made a deep bow.

"Sub-procurator in charge of *venatorii* and *beastiarii*."

Marcius made the slightest of hesitations before resuming his upright posture. "Just the man I wanted to see!" He smiled. The sub-procurator did not smile back.

"Your business?"

"I have a superb *venatore*." Marcius indicated Afra. "She's a dead shot with a bow. Can hit anything moving within arrow range."

"She?"

"I understand our August Emperor is interested in seeing females in the games." A thin line of perspiration formed on Marcius' upper lip.

The sub-procurator raised an eyebrow. "What kind of bow? What distance?"

Afra presented her bow and held it out for the sub-procurator's inspection. Her stomach clenched as he ran a finger over the fine finish.

"I've seen such bows among the Scythians north of the Black Sea—long range weapons, accurate, but they take a lot of strength to master." He eyed her well-muscled arms. "Show me."

She bent the bow almost double to string it, pulled the string back to her ear and let it go with a twang.

The sub-procurator grunted.

"Let Afra demonstrate her skill on a target, Excellency."

"Tomorrow, second hour, at the stadium on the *Campus Martius.*"

"Thank you, Excellency." Marcius bowed low, backing toward the door. "I guarantee you will be pleased."

"Tell the clerk what you require." The man flicked his fingers as if shooing a fly and turned back to his scroll to make a note.

THEY ARRIVED EARLY to the appointment the next day and found Afra was not the only one to perform. The rabbity clerk who had taken Marcius' silver the day before gave them a pottery scrap with a number written on it. "You're number five." The clerk made a note and nodded toward the entrance. "Through there. Wait with the others until you're called."

They walked through a tunnel lit with torches in sconces. A boy waved them into a room next to the exit on the sands of the amphitheater. A dozen men in various stages of agitation lounged on benches or paced around the room.

Marcius drew her to a corner. "Ready?"

Afra wiped a sweating hand on his yellow tunic. "Yes."

"Do as we discussed. The fancier the better. Remember, these are not only demonstrations of skill, but entertainment for the people of Rome and glorification of our gods and the Emperor."

She nodded and swallowed. Afra wasn't nervous about her skills, but the "fancy" part bothered her. She had never performed for an audience and her fate rested on her ability to entertain the sub-procurator and win the contract for Marcius.

Afra sat on a bench, eyes closed, breathing deeply, picturing the arrows flying to their targets, feeling her muscles stretch, pull, and relax. Four times the boy came to the door and called out a number. Four times a man or group of men rose and followed him out the door. When the boy called "five," Marcius touched her shoulder. "It's time."

They exited onto the oval stadium floor. Tiers of wooden seats rose around them separated from the sand by a decorated wall. The sub-procurator and a small crowd of spectators sat in the prime seats opposite the Imperial box. A stationary leather target with a crude drawing of a deer on it stood at the far end. A small circle behind the shoulder marked the best kill spot.

Marcius approached the spectators, bowed, and announced in a booming voice, "I present to you, Afra—from the land of Kush— what the Egyptians of yore called 'The Land of the Bow.' She will first demonstrate her strength and accuracy from a distance."

A driver with a two-horse chariot drove Afra to the opposite end of the stadium. She stepped down from the chariot and studied the target. The sun's heat already radiated off the sand making the image waver and dance, but there was no breeze. She drew out three arrows, took aim, and shot one after the other. They all clustered inside the small circle for good "kills." A slave ran onto the sand to take the target to the sub-procurator. There were a few smiles at her prowess.

"Now Afra will demonstrate her celebrated skills as a huntress!"

She took out lighter arrows and jumped into the cab of the chariot. The driver zigzagged across the stadium as a slave opened a cage of doves. A flock of five burst into flight over head, but plummeted to the ground one-by-one, as her arrows found their marks. Again the watchers smiled and nodded, but the sub-procurator's face remained impassive. Her skills were not enough. Afra's heart thudded—one more chance.

"For her final feat…"

A scream cut across Marcius' voice. A massive black bull raced from the shadows of the far gates dragging a young man tangled in a rope attached to the bull's halter. A bull? She was supposed to hunt a gazelle!

The animal stopped, swaying its head, blinking from the bright sun. The tangled man took advantage of the bull's temporary halt to saw at the rope knotted round his arm with a knife.

The chariot jolted as the horses reared and plunged, providing a new target for the enraged animal. The man screamed again as the bull bolted towards them, dragging him through the sand.

"Control your horses!" Afra shouted as the chariot lurched again. She reached into her quiver—only a handful of the light arrows left— nothing that would bring down a bull.

"To the left!" As the chariot passed the charging bull, she sent her remaining arrows into its neck and flanks. This annoyed the animal and blood started to drip from its muzzle.

Something glittered in the sand. "Leave me!" She shouted, jumped from the chariot, rolled in the dirt and came up with the tangled man's knife. He had stopped screaming; hanging limply from the rope, bouncing behind the bull. The animal seemed to notice the weight for the first time and turned toward the body.

With a cry, Afra raced toward the bull's side, slashed its flank, and vaulted over its back. The bull turned to where she had been.

Afra cut at the rope, nearly parting it before the animal turned her way. With a final swipe the rope dropped free.

She ran in front of the bull, luring it away from the injured man. At a distance, she turned and stood as the bull charged. Her breath came in ragged gasps as sweat poured down her flanks. Her vision narrowed to the charging animal.

Within seconds of being spitted on a shiny black horn, Afra leaped aside and scored a deep cut on the bull's neck.

The bull, deprived of its target, shook its head, blood flying. It turned and charged again and again.

At each pass, Afra scored another cut before leaping away. But her leaps became shorter and her legs felt more leaden. She needed to end this while she had the strength. She faced the animal again.

Foamy sweat mixed with the blood on bull's black hide. It stood on unsteady splayed legs, tongue lolling. They both gasped for air.

Afra's nerves tingled as she bounced on the balls of her feet. She heard nothing but her heart beating and breath panting. The dust from the sand coated her mouth and throat. She spit, took the knife between clenched teeth, and settled with hands free, ready for the next charge.

The bull seemed to regain its energy and charged with all its weight behind a furious assault.

Afra leaped to the side and grabbed the bull's horns as it passed. She dug in her heels throwing all her weight to the side, bringing the bull to a standstill, neck twisted. The bull went to its knees.

She sliced the animal's throat and ululated a feral scream. Blood gushed as the bull fell to its side, legs twitching.

Afra stood, panting. Sticky blood drenched Marcius' tunic and matted her short hair.

It was only then she heard the roar of the sparse, watching crowd. She walked to the sub-procurator's box and bowed low to the chants of "Afra! Afra!" Marcius stood aside beaming.

"Well done!" The sub-procurator smiled, at last. "Marcius, you have a contract for the Emperor's upcoming games in the spring. See my clerk as you leave."

Afra bowed again and retrieved her bow from the chariot driver. The horses snorted and stamped at the smell of blood. The bull handler lay still in the sand at the far end of the amphitheater.

"YOU DID *WHAT?*" Clio screamed and aimed a blow at Marcius' head. He ducked, catching her wrist.

For once Afra shared Clio's sentiments. She could easily gut Marcius and damn the consequences.

He shook the bulging money pouch. "Afra is the foot in the door.

So I promised additional acts and got a larger contract. Using the guaranteed contract as collateral gives me cash to find the others. We have six months."

Afra clenched her fists and prayed for patience. She didn't understand the complicated arrangements with the moneylender, but knew the consequences if Marcius couldn't pay.

Clio seemed skeptical as well. "Where will you find these other acts? You're not the only agent in Rome."

"We'll move to Pompeii. The Emperor closed the amphitheater there a couple of years ago as punishment after a riot that killed several people. They have cheap housing and training facilities. We'll be ready by spring for the Emperor's games." Marcius pulled Clio into an embrace. "Care to dance for the Emperor, my love?"

Clio snorted, but a calculating look came over her face.

Afra tried, but couldn't dismiss the cold gripping her stomach or the bile in her mouth.

CHAPTER TEN

THE NEXT BUILDING ON THE LEFT," Marcius said.

Afra nodded. They stopped in front of a well-built brick building, taking up half the block just inside the walls of Pompeii. Marcius had heard there might be a bargain or two to be had. Besides, it was an excuse to get away from Clio's carping. After a month, she wasn't happy in Pompeii, thinking it a poor backwater compared to Alexandria or Rome. Afra much preferred the slower pace of the smaller city. Today was overcast and the sea breezes held the nip of winter. She pulled her cloak tighter against a chill wind.

Over the door hung a sign which Afra could not read, but recognized the picture of a sword and trident as one of the many slave markets catering to the gladiator trade. Although the arena was closed, there were many gladiator schools in the area and slave merchants flocked to sell their wares in the public auctions.

They passed into the dim atrium.

"Welcome to our humble establishment!" A rumpled man with a balding head and the quick dark eyes of a bird greeted them. His glance quickly passed over Afra. He focused his attention on Marcius, taking him by the elbow, escorting him to a room to the left of the atrium, prattling of the weather, and complaining of his heavy tax burden. Afra noted the crude murals of gladiator battles and the occasional graffito scratched into the walls. Not one of the more prosperous establishments.

"Please, noble sir, have some wine." A boy of about ten, dressed in a thread-bare red tunic much too big for him, brought a pitcher and two goblets on a wooden tray.

"What are you in the market for today, my good man?"

Marcius took a gulp and wiped his mouth on the sleeve of his tunic. "I train novelty acts for the games. Do you have any dwarves or hunchbacks?"

The slaver's face fell. "Not at this time."

"Singers, dancers, acrobats?"

"I'm expecting several Greek performers next month."

Marcius pulled at his lower lip, frowning. "Any bowmen or charioteers?"

"I recently received a boatload of slaves from Britannia. They are renowned for their charioteers. Take a seat and I will show them to you." He ushered them onto a wooden bench, polished and hollowed from the many rumps it had accommodated.

The boy refilled Marcius' goblet and stood in the corner with the pitcher.

"What do you think, Afra?"

She shrugged. "He seems as honest as any other."

Marcius spluttered his wine and laughed. "Meaning he would cheat me blind at the first opportunity?" He rubbed his close-shaven jaw. "I agree. He will have little to show us."

"He talked of Britannia. Is the land far?"

"I know little about it. Caesar invaded the island north of Gaul and the Divine Emperor Claudius claimed to pacify it a generation or so ago. The legions have been fighting with the native tribes ever since."

The slaver returned with a bull-like man pulling a line of eight men shackled hand and foot. They were tall and naked, with the light coloring of the northern tribes. They might once have been strong warriors, but now their muscles were slack and bellies hollow. All had scars and scabby wounds. Afra shuddered. Their eyes were dulled with hunger, but one or two mustered a sneer of defiance. They had little energy for anything else. But for Marcius, that could have been her fate.

"These are fit only for the mines." Marcius frowned. "You've wasted my time." He rose to go.

"Please wait. I have one other you should see. A girl. Emperor Nero is fascinated with female gladiators."

Afra's interest piqued. Marcius had mentioned that northern women often fought alongside their men. He settled onto the bench, mumbling, "Fine. I will see this girl."

The bull-man herded the starving Britons out the door followed by the slave merchant.

He returned shortly with a girl in her late teens. She was naked and shackled as the men, but better fed. The cold raised goose flesh on her limbs. The irons seemed unnecessary. Her eyes were blank, face slack. Afra noted the well-muscled arms, the right larger than the left, and a scar on her temple leading up into curly hair dark with dirt and sweat. When the girl flinched from the hands of the slave merchant, a similar revulsion rippled across Afra's skin. Something about the Briton called out to her, touched her secret self.

Marcius spat on the floor. "Her mind is gone. She's not even fit for the brothels."

"Buy her." Afra said in a low tone.

"What?" He turned to her.

"Buy her and I will cure her mind."

"Afra, this girl is beyond even you."

"Buy her. She can't be worth much." Afra's stomach clenched. She looked again at the girl and something broken inside her soul shifted. Is this what Asata would have become? Could she have cured her? Can she cure this one? She looked back at Marcius. "Trust me."

He looked skeptical.

"Will you not make a fortune with the cubs? I'll do the same with her."

"You've certainly done well with the cheetahs." Marcius searched Afra's face, his eyes calculating. "I don't know why I let you talk me into these things."

He turned to bargain with the slave merchant.

Afra approached the girl and looked deep into her eyes—an unusual shade of light brown flecked with gold and green. A shadow crossed the girl's face before she looked vaguely off into the distance.

"Yes," Afra said in her own musical language. "You are there, somewhere beyond the pain." She put a hand to the woman's cheek and brushed back a lock of hair. "Are you a gift from my Lady Isis, sent to lighten my heart?"

AFRA SETTLED THE BRITON on a pallet of straw in the stables where she lodged. The clean smell of hay mixed with the comforting smell of horse sweat. "You will be safe here."

She raised a wooden beaker of wine, sweetened with honey and mixed with sleeping herbs, to the girl's lips. "Drink this. Sleep. Dream. Find yourself." The Briton drank the brew as long as Afra held it to her lips. After half the cup, her eyelids drooped and she leaned onto Afra's shoulder.

Afra laid her on the pallet, covering her with a light cloak. She crushed mint to sweeten the air. Afra sat by the sleeping girl, singing a soothing song from her homeland until a wave of pain choked off her tune. The empty place in her soul, previously filled with Asata, had grown smaller with time; the pain dulled, but occasionally something brought it back sharp and poignant—the scent of sandalwood, a particular song, a fading dream of soft skin caressing hers.

She heard growling in the next stall and rose to check on her other charges. The pair of cheetah cubs hissed and rolled with each other, squabbling over a fresh scrap of pigskin. She leaned over the half wall and picked up each by the scruff of its neck, grunting at their increased weight. "Mari, Cari, sisters should not fight. They should cooperate; help each other in the hunt."

She put them in the straw by her heels. "Come." She walked out of the stall. The cubs followed, knowing this behavior always resulted in food. Afra scooped cooked grain from a small crock and mixed it with sheep's blood and marrow from the local butcher. The rats were harder to find after a month in one place. She'd have to lay traps farther out.

Marcius entered as she groomed the cubs with a comb and a scrap of soft leather. "How's the other one?" He poked his chin towards the back of the stables.

"She's asleep."

"Good enough. I hope she's worth it. Clio nearly ripped my balls off when she found out." He rubbed his jaw. "I came out here to give her time to settle."

"Your wife might like to have another woman's hand to help."

"Clio sees every female as a rival. She's even jealous of you!" He roared with laughter. "She hasn't figured out yet that *I* should be the jealous one."

Afra blushed under her dark skin. "Your wife does not appeal to me."

"There's no need to be celibate, Afra." He patted her arm. "I've seen how you watch other women. You're a slave. No one cares what slaves do in their beds. Maybe your Briton will be of a similar persuasion."

Marcius rolled a wooden ball across the dirt floor and laughed when both animals chased it. One cub caught the ball and the other leaped on her sister. They tumbled, hissing and scratching.

"No, Cari!" Afra grabbed the cub that had jumped on her sister, tapping her sharply on the nose. The cub blinked twice, settled on her haunches, and started grooming herself.

Afra gave a soft chirping cry. Both cubs ran to her. She ruffled them behind the ears and looked up at Marcius. "I hope they are not destined for the games."

Marcius snorted, looked closely at the cubs, and shook his head. "I'll try to find a private buyer. A rich Roman noble. A pair of hunting cheetahs will be a novelty." Marcius shook his head and walked out. He stopped in the door. "No guarantees."

"I understand." Afra stroked the cubs. They curled up for sleep next to her. Her thoughts turned to the sleeping girl in the stall. Was her spirit broken or licking its wounds in a dark place?

The Briton thrashed and groaned in her sleep:

*****

SHE FOUGHT IN A BLOOD-RED MIST, *mud sucking at her feet. Dark shadows flickered at the edges of her sight. She turned and turned again. The shadows kept teasing her, leading her on in the ruddy fog. Pain flared in her head. She dropped to her knees from the blow, her head throbbing to the beat of her heart. She crawled a few feet in the muck, planted a spear in the ground and levered herself up.*

She shouted, "Let me see your face!"

Mocking laughter came from her left.

She put the pain aside and lunged after the shadow, uphill, out of the mire. She drew closer. The shadow wore a ragged cloak that flapped in a non-existent breeze. The laughter turned into a raucous caw.

She burst through the mist into bright light at the top of a rocky hill. She shaded her eyes, letting them adjust. The light seemed to be coming from a tree, half on fire; half green, untouched by flame.

Joy flooded through her, washing away the pain and fatigue. "I died the good death. I will be reborn!"

The ragged shadow laughed again as it flew overhead and landed in the green branches. It preened its feathers and turned a cold eye on her.

"Let me pass, hag. It is my due."

"Hawwwww!" the crow cawed. "Your queen is dead, your tribe broken. The gods turn their heads away in shame."

The flame in the tree went out. The green leaves fell to the ground leaving the crow sitting on a dead twisted limb. A sharp keening rose around the hilltop. Out of the mist crawled people from all the tribes—men with horrible wounds, holding their own guts or severed heads in their hands; women carrying mutilated children, their own limbs showing bone and dripping blood. Old people, young: they all moaned or screamed in horror as the black crow grew bigger, rose from the tree, and covered them with the shadow of its wings. In the darkness, her soul shriveled in despair.

*****

"If you don't make her stop, I will." Marcius raised a hand to slap the keening Briton as she rocked, eyes wide and unblinking.

Afra caught his wrist. "No."

"Let go, Afra." Marcius grimaced, rubbing his bruised wrist. "You've had three days. We can't keep a mad girl. If you can't bring her to her senses, I'll have to sell her as beast fodder in the games." He left, mumbling about the waste of money.

Afra studied the moaning rocking girl, gave her another sleeping draught, and left.

Chapter Eleven

As with most large cities, Pompeii forbade gigs and chariots on the streets, so the stables were outside the walls. Afra followed the wall to the southern gate, the entrance onto Via Stabia which bisected the city from north to south. She joined the throngs of merchants, travelers, and the occasional noble, in from his country villa, entering the city. A guard stopped her. She showed the papyrus with Marcius' mark. That precious scrap gave her permission to walk through the city on her master's business without him.

It being a little after the noon hour, the crowds began to thin. The business day was nearly over. People sought the baths or their own homes. Afra crossed Via Stabia on the stepping stones that allowed wagons to pass to the market and rain water to drain to the sewers while keeping citizens' feet dry. Those wagons—coming from the country laden with produce, leaving with finished goods—wore deep grooves in the stone street. At the third intersection, she turned left and approached the Temple of Isis.

The building was but a tenth the size of the Temple of Venus, off the forum, but to Afra, it was a piece of home set down in the middle of a foreign land. The Great Goddess was the same whether in Kush, Egypt, or Italia. Egyptian priests cared for this temple. Afra had been surprised to find that most Roman temples had no full-time priests, although they did have full-time staff to care for the buildings and tend the shrines. Roman nobles themselves conducted the ceremonies and sacrifices.

She looked through the gate in the high wall. The daily public ceremony had yet to start. Good. Ibises, sacred to the Egyptians, wandered the small courtyard. A priest prepared a sacrificial fire on an altar in the middle of the space where ordinary people could watch. Great stone sphinxes flanked the colonnaded entry to the temple. Afra could see the shadowy figure of the Great Goddess within, holding her *sistrum* in her right hand, and an *ankh*, the Egyptian symbol of life, in her left.

Afra walked up the stairs, head bowed. When she reached the top, she abased herself before the marble statue. The Great Goddess stood tall, a kind smile on her face. Afra could feel the warmth of her love through the chill of the stones.

"Oh, Great Mother, source of all wisdom. A woman, like me, came from the ends of the Roman Empire. Like me, she searches for herself. Help me, Isis, Mother of Gods, Giver of Life. Help me do Your work and give this woman's life back to her."

"My daughter." A priest touched her shoulder. When she looked up, the man gave her a kind look. "The ceremony will soon begin."

"Thank you, Blessed One."

Afra retreated down the steps and joined the small crowd that gathered for the regular afternoon ceremony. Acolytes lined the stairs, shaven and dressed in traditional Egyptian garb; a white pleated linen gown that hung from under their armpits to their bare feet. At a signal from the priest presiding over the fire, a piper began an ethereal melody as the acolytes shook *sistra* and chanted.

The high priest came out of the temple and held up a vial of water. "Behold the holy water of the Nile, giver of life by the grace of Isis, Queen of the Heavens; Wife of the Great Osiris, Ruler of the Underworld; Mother of Blessed Horus, King of the Living. The holy river Nile feeds and nourishes our land. Let us praise the Holy Trinity, Isis, Osiris, and Horus. May they protect us in this foreign land."

The altar priest added the cones of the stone pine to the sacrificial fire and fanned the flames. Afra breathed deep of the aromatic smoke, swaying in time to the chants of the acolytes. The ritual usually gave her a feeling of renewal and peace, but, by the end of the ceremony today, she was still troubled.

She dropped a small coin in the collection jar, left the temple, and turned into a web of narrow allies abutting the city wall. A few moments brought her to the shop of an old woman with white hair, black eyes, and quick bird-like movements. Afra eyed the clumps of dried herbs, bottles, and charms lining the shelves.

"Grandmother, I have a special need."

"Most do when they come here."

"Of course." Afra blushed under her dark skin. "I'm caring for a girl who is lost in her mind. She comes from a far-off land. I fear she has been beaten and abused."

"Raped?"

"Most likely."

"Pregnant?"

"She shows none of the signs."

"A blessing, that. What have you done for her?"

"A sleeping draught of poppy juice and wine."

"Good. Sometimes sleep, rest, and time is all they need."

"I have no more time. "

"Hmmm." The old woman raised a quizzical eyebrow then turned to peruse her store of goods.

She used a staff with a hook to loosen three clusters of herbs from the ceiling and picked a dusty brown bottle off a shelf. She proceeded to grind sprigs of two of the herbs in a bowl with a pestle, releasing the cooling scent of mint. The old woman mixed the powder with the contents of the bottle. The overpowering scent made Afra's eyes water.

"What is this concoction?"

"Powder of peppermint and marigold, mixed with camphor oil. Put it on her chest. It will ease her spirit." She handed Afra the third bunch of herbs. "Take this rosemary. Make a strong tea. Dose her as often as you can. It helps with memory."

"Thank you, Grandmother." Afra put the items in a string bag and paid the woman. She turned to go.

"For an extra coin, I can give you a charm for good health." The crone held out a tiny sheet of lead, rolled into a scroll. "Put it under her bed for best effect."

Afra fingered her slim *peculium* and sighed. It was no time for half measures. She handed over the coin and put the charm in her money pouch.

Afra rubbed the pungent oil on the girl's chest. She had fine rounded breasts, marred by fading bruises. Afra smothered a sneeze caused by the camphor smell. She said a prayer to Isis and put the charm under the girl's pallet.

The Briton slowed her rocking and blinked her eyes. Tears flowed down her cheeks. Her keening wail subsided to a moan.

"Drink this." Afra put a cup of the rosemary tea to the girl's lips. She gulped it as if dying of thirst. She took another cup.

Afra sat knee to knee with her and turned the girl's face to hers. "Your spirit is deeply wounded, my sister, but fight the darkness."

The Briton's eyes rolled up in her head showing the whites:

She heard her own voice join the wails of all her people turned away from the glorious afterlife. No feasting in the sunny halls with gods and heroes. She was not worthy. She crawled down the rocky slope toward the slime. A sharp rock cut her knee. The pain streaked through her. She cried out. Tears welled in her eyes, but she dashed them away, streaking mud on her face. She looked at her muddy hands and shook her head. "I am not a worm to crawl on the ground."

She stood and looked back up the hill. The red mist thinned. "If I am to roam the earth as a shade, I will know why!"

She rose and strode toward the blasted tree. The crow looked smaller.

"Why do you return? Go away," it cried.

"Why did the gods abandon our cause? Was defending our land and Queen not just? Did we not honor them with sacrifices and praise? Why turn away those who died in honorable battle?"

"Go away!"

She felt strength return to her limbs. She approached the crow. It ruffled its feathers but now it looked no bigger than a normal bird. She grabbed it by the neck. "Tell me, you ill-figured hag. Why?"

The crow pecked viciously at her hand, tearing away a piece of flesh.

"You can eat my hand to the bone, but I won't let you go."

The crow rolled its eyes. "There are no answers here. You must seek elsewhere."

"Where?"

"In the world."

"But I'm dead."

"Not yet." The crow turned to ashes in her hand.

Darkness smothered her senses.

Afra wrapped her arms around the Briton. She felt shivers run through the young woman's body. Afra murmured a few British words she learned from a trader, "Follow me," over and over, in a sing-song chant.

The girl cried out, Afra stroked her back. "Let go your fear. You are strong. Come back." She gave her another cup of tea.

She felt as if she floated in nothingness—no light, no sensation of weight or touch. "The gods have abandoned me." For a moment she felt their loss, a hollow in the pit of her stomach, a chill in her heart, despair in her soul. She almost gave in to the despair, when a small spark of outrage flared.

"What faithless gods are these?" Her feet touched solid ground.

"Why should I fight and die for strengthless gods that cannot win against the Romans?" The air moved, chilling her flesh. She shook her fist at the black heavens.

"I will seek my answers elsewhere."

A light appeared in the distance. She saw a tall figure holding a lantern high. The figure was black as night, but it was not a crow. "Come," it cried in a soft voice with a musical accent. "Follow me."

Afra felt the Briton slump, as if her bones melted. She laid her on the straw and noted the deep even breathing of natural sleep. She smiled, stroking the girl's hair. "Sleep well, my sister. You are strong and will overcome."

Chapter Twelve

THE BRITON WOKE IN THE DARKNESS with an insistent urge to urinate. *I'm alive, but where am I?* Her nose told her she was in a stable, or barn, near horses or mules. There was a sharper scent—musky. *Cats? Probably to keep the mice out of the grain.*

She rose to her knees and nearly toppled from dizziness. She clutched her temples and cursed.

A soft voice came out of the dark. The girl didn't understand any of the words but she recognized the voice from her dreams. *Her dreams?*

The voice came again, but this time accompanied by a flair of lamp light. She blinked, covering her eyes.

"Come. Follow me."

"What? Who are you? Where am I?" The insistent urge grew stronger. She looked around the stall for a place to piss, shifting from foot to foot.

The dark figure approached, beckoning. From its height, the girl thought the figure male, but as she got closer, she smelled that peculiar scent women have when their moon time is upon them. The strange woman tugged at her arm and said again, "Come."

She let the woman guide her to a large pot outside the stable, the use of which was apparent from its odor. She pulled up her rough tunic, squatted, and let loose a long blissful stream. It gave her time to study the strange woman. The lamp light glistened on skin as black as charcoal and eyes like two holes in the night. Her people became deeply brown during the summer, but no one she knew had skin this dark.

My people? How do I know this? Who are they?

She searched her mind for faces, names, memories. She found vague grayness, shifting like fog. Frightened, she stood and raised her hand to touch the strange face to make sure it was real. The woman stood completely still, letting her fingers roam over the planes of her face, the full lips, flaring nose, the skin as soft as a baby bird's down. She dropped her hand.

The woman beckoned again, leading the way with the lamp to a tiny room—barely enough space for a narrow bed and stool. She gestured for the girl to sit on the pallet, put the lamp on the stool, and disappeared out the open door. A well-worn cloak hung from a peg on the wall; a pack hung from another. The girl rose, looked quickly out the door, and pawed through the pack—a patched spare tunic, worn sandals, a new pair of knitted socks, a sharp knife with a beautifully carved ivory handle, and a clay votive figure of a seated woman with a baby on her lap.

At the faint sound of rustling straw, the girl resumed her seat, secreting the knife under the pallet. The woman came in with a tray of bread, oil, cheese, olives, and wine. Not her usual meal of stew— cooked grain, chunks of lamb or deer, flavored with onions—and frothy beer. How did she know that? Why could she remember the food, but not the one who cooked it? Her stomach rumbled. She set aside her worries—momentarily.

She nearly spilled the lot, grabbing the tray from the woman's hands. For the first time a frown furrowed the dark face. She stuffed the bread in her mouth. The stale stuff nearly loosened a tooth. She dipped the rest in the oil to soften it. The cheese was better, sharp, pungent with a nutty taste. The olives, small, black, and bitter, puckered her mouth, but she doggedly chewed, spitting out the pits.

The woman watched her closely as she wolfed down her food. When she spat out the last olive pit and wiped her mouth on the back of her arm, she got a good whiff of her own strong odor. She wrinkled her nose. Her body smelled of stale sweat, urine, and a hint of shit. She wanted to take a bath or, at least, dump a bucket of water over her head.

The woman smiled—a white flash of teeth that seemed to light up her dark face. "How much Roman you know?"

"A little." She indicated a small amount with her thumb and forefinger. "Trade talk. You?"

"More."

"Where?" She threw her arms wide and looked around.

"Pompeii."

She frowned and shrugged.

"Italia." The woman pointed over her shoulder. "Rome."

"Rome?" Her jaw dropped and eyes went round. A trickle of anger and fear crawled up her spine.

Cold water…burned bodies…toppled trees…desolation…death.

She stiffened, shivering.

The strange woman pointed to herself. "Afra."

She opened her mouth, but nothing came out. White ringed her irises. Her eyes started to roll up in her head.

"No!" Afra clasped her body close and rocked till the girl's rigid body relaxed. "Drink."

She gulped another cup of tea through chattering teeth. She lay in Afra's arms twitching. Her eyes grew heavy—*something in the drink?*—and lapsed into sleep.

She woke the next morning to find the strange woman sitting on the stool watching her. The woman pointed to her pack. "Knife?"

She blushed. She hadn't meant to steal the knife. She wanted protection in this strange place. She reached under the thin pallet, retrieved the item, and handed it over hilt first.

With a set mouth and raised eyebrow, the woman put the blade back in the pack, evidently trusting her not to take it again. A name floated from the darkness.

"Afra?"

The woman smiled. "Yes,"

"I am…" She shook her head, trying to loosen the memory of her name.

"No…" Afra pointed to her own head…"memory?"

"I'm…" she shook her head, straining for the name that would not come.

"Leave be. Memories return when you're strong enough to bear them." Afra beckoned. "Come."

They left the stable and went around the corner. Afra pointed to a trough of water and handed her a sea sponge. "Wash."

She shrugged off the rough slave garment. Afra picked up a wooden bucket, dipped it in the water, and poured it over her head. She gladly scrubbed herself from face to toes, removing some of the fetid sweat and dirt. Another bucket and she felt almost human. She picked up the soiled tunic with finger and thumb, frowned, shrugged, and put it on. It was that or nakedness; and there was a chill in the air.

She ran her fingers through her hair in a vain effort to sort out the tangles. Afra handed her a wooden comb. Between them, they managed to unsnarl the worst of the knots. Afra looked her over, smiling. She smiled back, amazed to realize that the woman's approval meant something to her.

AFRA SMILED AND NODDED. She was a far cry from the mad girl Marcius had left her with. He would be pleased at the transformation. She handed the Briton a pair of worn, much-patched sandals.

With the girl in tow, Afra entered the city gate and strode down the pedestrian side of the Via Stabia. Wagons lumbered by, piled high with amphorae; baskets of produce; and cages of live fowl destined for the busy markets in the central part of the city. Shops opened for business on the first floor of the buildings, mingling the enticing scent of baking bread with the acrid stench of human piss used by the fullers to whiten cloth. She was used to the Roman architecture now, but suppressed a smile as the girl craned her neck and stared at the several-storied brick buildings.

They approached the inn where Marcius and Clio lodged. Although once painted a striking red with yellow trim, the colors had faded to the shades of thin wine and pallid fish bellies. Marcius stood in the courtyard arguing with a rat-like man with a sharp nose and several rings on his fingers. Marcius shrugged then stuck out his hand. "Done."

The man grasped Marcius' arm briefly, forearm to forearm. He handed over a small bag of clinking coins which Marcius put into a belt pouch without counting.

Afra's jaw clenched as she approached. "Another moneylender?"

"An investor." Marcius' eyes went wide at the sight of the Briton. "You are a wonder worker, Afra. I never would have known this was the same girl. How much does she understand?"

"She knows trade talk, but there are holes in her memory."

"Her name?"

"She doesn't remember."

"Probably for the best to have a new name in a new life." He made a twirling motion with his hand and finger. "Turn around. Let me see you."

The Briton hesitated. When he repeated "turn" and his hand motion, she turned in a circle.

"Very good! With a little training we can pair you two up as faux gladiators—the ones who entertain the crowds during breaks in the action. We'll call her Britannia." He spread his hands apart from in front of his face. "I can see the signs now: 'Britannia, Barbarian Princess versus Afra, Ethiopian Queen. A Battle of the Provinces.' "

"Kush." Afra stiffened. "And I am not a *Kandake*."

"To Romans, all black-skinned people come from Ethiopia." Marcius smiled. "A few months ago, you didn't want to be a *venatore*. Now you don't want to be a queen?"

"I won't caper for the amusement of Romans." Afra snorted. "Why train her to fight? Better a dancer."

"She's a Celt. They all fight. Look at her arms and those scars. She's seen battle. What do you think, Britannia? Would you like to fight?" He chucked her under the chin.

The girl slapped his hand away, snarling like a spitting cat.

"See? I told you." Marcius laughed.

Afra pushed the girl behind her and frowned at Marcius. "She's not ready."

"Afra." His eyes grew tired. "She is my property. I'll train her as I see fit to get my money back. Besides, the fights aren't real, there's no danger."

Afra folded her arms across her chest. "And me?"

"I'll try to buy someone else to pair her with." Marcius frowned. "You're worth more to me as a *venatore*, anyway. But Afra, don't test me. I allow you far too many liberties, as is."

Afra knew he was right, but it didn't settle her sour thoughts.

He reached into his pouch and pulled out two brass coins. "Take these. Buy her clothes. Have a good meal tonight." He wrinkled his nose. "And take Britannia to the baths."

BRITANNIA STAYED CLOSE TO AFRA as they threaded their way through the crowds. Afra was her anchor in this strange sea. Until she knew herself, she needed the woman for knowledge, safety, and comfort.

They stopped at a shop selling second-hand clothing. Afra pawed through a pile of women's garments, pulled out a tunic of sensible brown wool and began haggling with the shop keeper. They reached an impasse until Afra pointed to a red cord belt. The woman nodded. Afra handed over one of the brass coins.

So clothing was as dear as in her land. Raising and shearing sheep; days spent carding, spinning, weaving, dying; her mother's best gown her most prized possession.

She shook her head in frustration. How did she know this and not her own name?

A picture floated in her mind. *A young woman at a loom with a baby crawling at her feet. Her mother? Sister?*

Her hands clenched as she tried to see the face. The harder she tried, the hazier the picture became. She realized she was holding her breath and let it out with a sigh.

*****

Afra, noting the girl's agitation, put a gentling hand on her shoulder. "It will come." She folded the garment, securing it with the belt. They continued, crossed several smaller streets, and approached a large building faced with pink marble. Tall columns graced the entrance providing shade to three loiterers, playing dice until the men's hours started.

They crossed an outer chamber where women played games on painted boards or gossiped while hairdressers arranged their tresses in intricate braids and curls. Frescos, advertising the kind of sexual services that could be had in the brothel attached to the bath, adorned the walls. Britannia's eyes widened as she studied the pictures.

Afra hid a grin. She had had a similar reaction the first time she came to the bath. The women must be quite limber to achieve some of those positions. In the next chamber, they stripped, stored their clothes in a niche, and Afra gave the attendant—a wizened old woman—a small coin. They exited to a room filled with steam, one of Afra's favorites.

After a few minutes, the Briton started gasping and turned as red as a pomegranate. Afra tapped her on the shoulder, "Follow." At the other end of the room a large fountain coursed with water. Afra dipped a cool cup of water.

"Thanks." Britannia gulped the water, dipped a second cup, and fanned herself with her hands. "Hot."

The next room provided a cold plunge, which the Briton seemed to enjoy more. Finally, they entered a room with a large warm pool where women swam or talked in corners, occasionally laughing. In each room, Afra named things as Britannia openly gawked.

"Pool. Warm." Afra sighed as she slipped into the warm water. She had gotten little sleep these last few days. The water soothed her. Shaking her head to relieve the sleepiness, she pushed away from the side of the pool, using an efficient stroke to reach the other side.

When she looked back, the girl followed using a more awkward stroke, trying to keep her head above water. She likes the cold water and she can swim, but doesn't do it often. Another clue.

They left the pool for an open air courtyard surrounded by a colonnade. Vendors hawked food and drinks to the women lounging on padded stone benches and folding camp chairs. The sun shone brightly and warmed the still air, but most women wore a wrap of some kind against the slight chill. Afra found it refreshing after the warm pool. She walked to a fountain and cupped her hands under the stream of water issuing from a stone imp's mouth. Britannia did the same. Afra turned at the sound of giggles and girlish shouts. Girls, in soft leather breast bands and loin cloths, exercised and played ball in the open area.

Britannia snorted, obviously not impressed with the girls' performance. "Why ball? Why not..." She mimed clenching a sword and thrusting.

"Not warriors." Afra pointed at Britannia's well-muscled arms. "You?"

"No, I..." She screwed up her face in concentration. "...maybe...?" She shook her head in defeat.

Afra nodded at the giggling girls. "Roman women work beside their husbands in fields, shops, or crafts. The noble Roman women move through the city in closed litters. I've never seen either kind with knife or spear." Afra rose and stretched. "Men rule in Rome. In my land, the *Kandake* rules equally with the *Qore* and the Great Mother Isis commands the heavens and the gods."

The girl frowned and shook her head

Too many words, Afra thought.

"My queen..." Tears welled in her eyes.

Afra grabbed the girl's arms and shook her, before she could go inside herself. "That is past. This is now."

The girl drew a sharp breath. "My queen...Boudica." She turned a tragic face to Afra. "Sadness. Fear..."

Afra put her arms around the shuddering girl and held her tight, while she cried on her shoulder. "Crying eases the heart. Time heals it. I know."

Her heart ached for the girl's sorrow, but gradually she became aware of another feeling—an insistent, joyful, forbidden feeling. She looked around, to see if any noticed them. All seemed occupied except an aging matron who frowned at them from the next bench. She called over an attendant and whispered in her ear.

Afra held the girl at arm's length. "Time to leave."

Chapter Thirteen

Britannia let her sewing fall to her lap. The meager fire in Clio's brazier chased the winter chill from her room, but her fingers felt cold and clumsy. Afra, Marcius, and the cubs were gone again, this time to a local villa for the Saturnalia. They earned extra coins, which they always seemed to need. Marcius liked to play dice, the game the Romans called *tali*. Each time he returned with an empty purse, Afra became more silent and Clio more vocal.

Today, Clio did sums on a small wooden counting frame. Sharp creases furrowed the older woman's brow as she moved the little beads in the grooves with lightning speed, and wrote the results on a waxed tablet with a stylus.

With a final, "Ha!" Clio closed the wax tablet and looked at the younger woman. "Are you ill-wishing me?"

"No, Domina! I wouldn't curse you."

"You've been watching me all morning like an angry harpy ready to pounce."

"Harpy?"

"Never mind," Clio stood and put her hands on rounded hips. "Have you finished the mending?"

Britannia lifted the tunic she was trying to patch. "I'm not good with a needle."

But she was good with languages and after four weeks could speak as well as Afra, although with a distinct accent. The thought of the tall African brought a smile to her face. They had little time together during the day, but at night…Afra liked to comb out her long blond hair and braid it for the night. The soothing strokes brought peace to her troubled mind. During the day she served Clio, cleaning, mending, carrying packages, running to the food and wine shops. Sometimes she sang for Clio when she danced with her snake. But that only happened on market days and when Marcius was away. The music stirred memories, but none that she wanted.

Clio inspected the sloppy stitches and sighed. "What girl doesn't learn to sew? Were you raised by wolves in that wild forest of yours?"

Britannia clenched her jaw, but stayed seated. For all she knew she *was* raised by wolves. Why did the memories dance in and out of dreams, teasing her, just out of reach?

"You'd like to slap me, wouldn't you?" Clio smiled.

Britannia's face flushed red and she snapped, "Yes!" before she could curb her tongue. She wasn't really angry with Clio, but frustrated at the hole in her memories.

"At last, a little spirit." Clio poked her in the chest with a sharp fingernail. "Marcius has plans for you, now that you've regained your strength. The gods know you make a lousy servant. It's time you earned your keep." She unlocked her chest and shook out a short, sleeveless, red tunic. "Try this on."

Britannia caught the garment suppressing a shudder. "What's this?" The tunic was the color of fresh blood, the material much better than her brown wool—thinner, softer to the touch, with a shiny finish.

"Your gladiator costume. At least part of it. The laws forbid slaves running around the city with a sword or spear, but this will give the crowd a thrill." Clio gave a satisfied cluck when she pulled out a stunning black leather belt, studded with brass. "Here, use these." Clio held out matching wrist guards. The belt and wrist guards flashed in the sun. Britannia reached up to finger the iron slave ring on her neck.

She donned the tunic and brass-studded leather. She smoothed the rich red fabric over her hips and tugged at the hem that barely reached her knees. "Too short. I'll be cold."

"You're a northerner. You're used to the cold."

"We wear furs, trousers, and socks during the winter." An image of an underdressed Roman on a litter floated to the top of her mind. She frowned. *Two winters ago?*

"Here." Clio tossed her a wool cape. From a distance, it looked fancy, dyed a deep blue and edged with red embroidery, but Cinnia could see the worn spots and frayed thread up close.

"You'll accompany me on my errands. Men will look, women will be scandalized, but all will talk. When Marcius puts up his placards you'll be a bigger draw. Try frowning a little—look fierce."

"This is a costume? I'm not really expected to fight in this?" The idea of performing felt right, but the clothes were too fancy for battle.

"Of course. We're entertainers." Clio pulled a slender bag of coins from the chest. "Come with me."

Clio made a show of traveling the crooked streets of the old quarter to the Forum where the local people congregated. They did, indeed, gape and talk behind their hands. At first Britannia blushed to the roots of her hair to be displayed in such a manner, but she soon fell into playing the role with natural fervor. She growled at a band of children following them and grinned as they ran away squealing in pleasurable terror.

They wended their way to the Samnite *Palaestra,* an enclosed athletic area used by the gladiators housed in a nearby complex for training. Three ranks of wooden benches allowed spectators to observe the gladiators' practice. Clio led her up the steps to sit near the top. A crowd of rowdy young men passed a wine skin around further down the benches.

"Pigs." Clio sniffed. "They have nothing to do but drink and goggle at the gladiators."

"What are we doing?" Britannia raised one corner of her mouth.

"This is different." She sat and patted the bench next to her. "We're here so you can learn. Watch close."

Two men slick with oil and sweat, lunged at wooden stakes with heavy wooden swords. A third twirled a net over his head then tossed it at another stake.

"Those are Thracian and *myrmillo*." Clio pointed at the swordsmen. "See the blades? The Thracian's is curved. It's a *sica*. The *myrmillo* uses the *gladius*."

The *gladius*, sword of the Roman army. Short, deadly, stabbing, drenched in blood.

Sunlight glinted off the swords, rank after rank.

"What's the matter, girl?"

Britannia heard teeth clacking and realized they were hers. Her body was racked by shudders, she seemed unable to stop.

Roman soldiers…searing pain, blood, the blessed relief of blackness.

"You, there, bring me that wine skin if you have any left," Clio shouted at the rowdy men.

"You want a little taste of this?" A swarthy man with stained teeth, pursed his lips making kissing noises. "Or maybe this?" He grabbed his crotch, while his colleagues laughed. "Much better than the meat in the ring."

"Only the wine, you clot head, for the girl. Can't you see she's ill?"

One of the younger men cuffed the swarthy man on the head and grabbed the wine skin. "Can't you be a gentleman occasionally?"

Britannia watched the young man ascend the steps, trying to still her shivers. She could see the look of calculation in his eyes as he looked her over from head to toe, her legs and arms bare. She pulled the cloak around her shoulders and closed her eyes, but the stench of sweat, sour wine, and garlic gagged her as the man drew closer.

She straightened. "I'm all right, *Domina*. I need no wine."

"Are you sure?" Clio fanned her with a kerchief. "You look ill."

"Here, girl, try this."

Britannia started when she felt his hand on arm. Her skin crawled.

Hands held her down; breath foul with wine and garlic panting in her face; pain beyond bearing as man after man….

She leaned over and vomited on his feet.

"Filthy bitch!" He scampered back as she heaved again.

"Fine impression you make on women!" His colleagues laughed and made gagging sounds.

His face reddened and he left the two women, shaking vomit off his feet, muttering curses under his breath. Cinnia couldn't tell if he cursed her or his friends, but didn't much care as long as he went away.

She had remembered her name and what happened to her.

She immediately wanted to forget.

CINNIA WATCHED FOR AFRA in the courtyard. She needed to see her, needed her comforting presence. Clio's eyes were cold when they looked at her, like her snakes'. Afra's were warm, welcoming, but would they still be when she told her? She spied Afra and Marcius as they passed the gate.

"Afra!" Cinnia leaped up and fairly flew across the courtyard. She grabbed Afra in a hug that belied her feelings of weakness. "Thank the gods, you're back!"

Afra held her at arms' length. "Are you ill?"

Cinnia pushed a strand of hair behind her ear, faltering. "My stomach. Clio took me…"

Afra frowned. "Bad food? You shouldn't eat at the Persian's stall. He leaves his fish in the sun too long."

"I remember my name." Tears pooled in Cinnia's eyes. "And all the horrible things…"

"Hush." Afra pulled her close and stroked her back. "You're safe now."

Cinnia mumbled into her chest. "No. You don't understand…"

She shuddered until Afra tipped up her face and asked in a soft voice, "What are you called?"

"Cinnia."

"Does it have meaning?"

" 'Beauty,' but…"

Her bloody sword…Row after row of stakes…Roman women impaled, their own breasts stuffed in their dead mouths…Chanting Iceni as the druids led the rituals.

Afra put a finger over her lips. "You are well named." She turned to Marcius. "She's ill. I'm taking her back to the stable."

Cinnia clung to Afra's hand as they walked through the back alleys of Pompeii in silence.

They exited the Stabian Gate and made their way past the tombs of the dead. Rich family graves were marked with miniature temples, marble statues, beautiful vases; poorer ones with a simple stele giving a name, an occupation.

"Afra?" Cinnia pulled her to a stop among the dead. "Have you ever killed? A person, I mean, not a beast."

"I've caused death," Afra's face stilled, "That's why I serve Marcius."

"I've killed many."

"In battle?"

"I was raised to be a wife, though I wanted to be a storyteller," Cinnia whispered. "But the Romans took our lands and goods. They killed my father, desecrated our holy places, and beat our queen. I became a warrior. When we took their cities, we killed everyone."

"Women and children?" Afra looked out into the distance.

"I did what I had to, but…" she faltered, "I fear you might judge me."

"Your tribe fought for your land." Afra shrugged. "That is the way of war. I would do the same."

"The Roman gods proved stronger in the end. My family is likely dead."

"As is mine." Afra's voice cracked. She turned Cinnia's hand over and ran a thumb over the calluses, sending a sweet thrill through her body. "We could make new families in this strange land."

"Take husbands? Have children?"

"No. We could be…sisters to one another." A tear tracked down Afra's cheek and she turned it away from Cinnia. "Or more…?"

The other woman's pain touched something in Cinnia. She reached up to wipe away the tear. A jolt run up her arm, like when she rubbed a fur then touched someone, but a hundred times more. She longed to run her hands over Afra's beautiful face and taut muscles, but she pulled back. Sex among her people was natural and frequent, but also a sacred act insuring the fertility of the land. Women chose their own mates and could divorce them if they failed to provide her with children. Some women took lovers rather than divorce, if their husbands were good providers but couldn't satisfy them in bed.

She knew a woman could feel that need for another woman. There were two among Boudica's female guard who shared more than their blankets, given the moans that issued from underneath. Did sex between women affront the gods by denying fertility? Her gut clenched and blood warmed. Her gods had forsaken her and her people. Why should she look to them for guidance? Besides she had no wish to make the Roman lands more fertile. If she could, she would blight their fields with black rot, insects, and hail.

"You are more than a sister to me, Afra." Cinnia clutched the other woman's hand tighter and ducked her head, cheeks burning. "Let us leave the dead to the dead."

Afra sensed the change in Cinnia. For weeks the Briton had been uncertain, searching but afraid of what she'd find. Occasional flashes of memory gave her hope. Now there was sadness in her eyes; but anger, as well, in the set of her shoulders, clench of her jaw; an insistence— no, confidence—in leading them through the cemetery. Afra feared that, knowing the past brought Cinnia more sorrow than joy. Would she grieve excessively? Brood over the horrors done to her and by her? Would she turn her gaze outward, scorn Afra's affections as unnatural?

It was the last question that caused Afra to shake her head. She should be happy that Cinnia found the memories she sought, but a tendril of dread threatened to choke her joy.

Everything changes.

Cinnia turned her head, smiling.

Afra's heart leapt.

They returned to the stable shortly before dusk. Most of the work animals rested in their stalls, eating hay. Afra peered through the bars of the stall where the cubs napped. Britannia—*no, Cinnia; she had to get used to her new name*—joined her, shoulders touching. Afra's muscles twitched and she drew in a quick breath.

"They're funny cats." Cinnia pushed a strand of hair behind her ear. "Their legs are too long and feet are too big. They sound like birds and act like dogs."

"Some Romans believe they are dogs, but dogs don't purr. Their legs are long and feet big, because cheetahs are swift. Over short distances, I've never seen anything outrun one. They are also friendly and easy to train, unlike many big cats. My *Kandake* kept a hunting pair. She let them roam the palace, unchained."

"Will you be sad to give them up when they're grown?"

"Yes. They have been my only friends in this strange land," Afra's voice softened, "until...."

"Until?" Cinnia put her arm around Afra's waist and dropped her head to Afra's shoulder.

"Until I found you." Afra reached up to stroke the shining blonde hair. "I believe the gods sent you to me."

"Mine or yours? As punishment or reward?"

"You say such strange things, sometimes. But it doesn't matter." Afra cupped Cinnia's chin in her hand. The shadows deepened and she couldn't see her eyes. "Come to bed."

Afra led Cinnia this time. They lay their straw-stuffed pallets on the dirt floor, side by side, and faced each other on their knees.

"Is this what you want?" Afra put a warm hand on Cinnia's cheek. "You have only today come back to yourself."

"I don't know." Cinnia trapped the hand with own and kissed Afra's palm. "I know only that I am new born today. I thrill to it. You have been my savior, my friend. Afra, you give me joy."

They fumbled in the dark; pulling off their tunics, finding each other breast to breast, thighs entangled on the pallets.

Afra stroked Cinnia's back and kissed her eyes. She tasted salt tears and pulled back.

"Why do you weep?"

"I'm happy." Cinnia pulled her face down into a deep kiss. "I am happy your gods sent me to you."

Afra laughed deep in her throat, almost a growl. She nuzzled Cinnia's breasts, alternately sucking and biting on her nipples. They sprang up hard under her urging tongue.

Cinnia groaned.

An insistent ache spread from Afra's groin.

Afra dropped lower, tongue flicking across Cinnia's taut belly. She buried her face in the thatch of curly hair between Cinnia's legs taking in the alluring scent of a sea creature, salty, ripe, reaching for the wet cave she knew was waiting.

"No!" Cinnia stiffened and curled her hands in Afra's short hair. "Not there!"

Afra rose on her arms. "I'll do nothing you do not wish." She crawled back up to hold Cinnia in her arms as the younger woman sobbed.

"I'm sorry…the soldiers…"

"Hush." Afra crooned, her need subsiding. "I know. When it is time, I'll replace those memories with good ones."

Cinnia shuddered in her arms. "I'm so ashamed."

"Don't be."

They fell asleep clasped in each other's arms.

Chapter Fourteen

AFRA UNTANGLED HERSELF at first light the next morning. Her arm tingled where it had rested under Cinnia's shoulder. She lightly kissed the sleeping girl and rose.

Shrugging into her tunic, she went to check the traps by the grain bin. Two contained rats. Four sat empty. She frowned. Pickings were getting slim or the rats were getting smarter.

Maybe I should trap close to the sewers. There are always rats scurrying about there.

She snapped their leashes on and took the cubs out to a fallow pasture beyond the cemetery.

First she let them run. The cubs chased each other, tumbling, racing. She smiled. Hardly cubs anymore. They were more than half grown. The only part of their baby pelt left was a ruff of fuzzy fur on the back of their necks.

She called the cubs back, "Mari! Cari! To me!" They raced to her feet and sat, panting slightly. Afra loosed a rat from a cage. It ran a few feet and froze. The cheetahs stayed, but she could see their muscles tighten, their tails twitch with excitement.

"Mari." Afra gave the hand signal for "go" and the cat leaped forward. The rat fled at the sight of sharp teeth and spotted fur, but it was no match for the speed and flexibility of the cheetah. Mari twisted with each turn and reached out with her front claw to trip up the rat. She stood, her foot on the struggling rodent, but didn't kill it. Mari looked back at Afra for another signal. Afra had her release the rat and catch it three more times before giving the signal that Mari could eat it. A small meal for a big cat.

She repeated the ritual with Cari. Once fed, the cubs wanted to sleep, so she took them back to the stable. She would need bigger prey soon. A single rat or two wasn't enough to sustain the cubs for much longer. Plus, they needed to learn how to bring down hares, deer, and pigs.

As she put the cubs away and called to Cinnia, Marcius entered the stable talking with another man. Cinnia, hair sleek from a dunking, grinned when she saw Afra.

"Afra, Cinnia, come meet Paetus." Afra reluctantly left the cubs; she usually groomed them after a hunt.

Marcius clapped her on the shoulder. "Paetus will teach you the gladiator moves you'll need for the act."

The stranger looked the part of an ex-gladiator—stocky, well-muscled, with a scar the length of his left calf. He limped up to the women. "Let me look at you."

Afra stood still as he circled her, but didn't care for his tone. She was used to Marcius affording her some respect, in spite of her slave status.

Paetus looked at them with the eye of a shepherd about to cull the herd. He returned to his place beside Marcius. "I might be able to do something with them. Half now and the rest at the end of the month."

"Done." Marcius smiled, turning over a small bag of coins.

"What's this?" Afra took Marcius aside. "I thought you sought another to pair with Cinnia?"

"I have to go back to the original plan." He ran a hand through his hair in a familiar gesture. "I haven't been as…uh…successful in my other ventures. I can't afford another slave right now."

" 'Ventures' as in *tali* and chariot races?"

"You sound like Clio." Marcius' face went red. "I don't need another nagging female in my life. Trust me."

"That is getting harder, my friend."

"I paid off the Roman moneylender!"

Afra knew he owed money to men in Pompeii, but decided not to push. Marcius had managed to juggle all the balls…so far.

"Fine. Cinnia and I will train as play gladiators. Will she get a cut of the contract?"

"Not as much as you, but something."

"Good."

PAETUS TOOK THEM to a dusty courtyard just inside the walls, furnished with a stake and a pile of battered armor. "You're entertainers, not real gladiators. The crowd wants to see skill, but they also want to see drama. First one is winning, then the other. A falter, a slip, a comeback, these are all planned. The real blood comes in the afternoon."

He handed each a heavy wooden sword. "Now for the stake. Five hundred thrusts." Afra hacked at the stake until her arms burned with the strain and the sword shook in her grasp. Cinnia proved more adept at this exercise, having practiced with a *gladius* and used it in war. Afra's muscles were tuned to the bow, not the sword. Next, they practiced shield blocks as Paetus thrust and hacked at them. Here, Afra's longer reach had an advantage.

Finally he had Afra lifting heavy rocks, while he practiced sword and shield with Cinnia.

"Lift with your legs, not your back!" he barked, looking over Cinnia's shoulder at Afra.

She threw her stone to the ground. "Why do this? It has nothing to do with fighting."

Paetus stalked over to stare up at Afra. "Marcius told me you hunt."

Afra nodded.

"Do I tell you how to track? Which shot to take?"

Afra shook her head.

"I am the *doctore*, the instructor. You do as I say."

"I want to know why I do what I do."

"To what purpose? To challenge me?" Paetus sputtered, face turning a deep red.

Afra stood, arms across her chest, staring down at the man. He was right. She wanted the knowledge to argue against his commands. That was not her place. She picked up the rock.

By the mid-afternoon break, Afra felt bruised, battered, barely able to stand. To her consternation, Cinnia seemed less fatigued. She chatted easily with Paetus about technique as they shared a jar of water.

"She didn't spend hours lifting rocks," Afra muttered to herself, rising from a crouch, stretching her back.

Paetus took a drink of water from the jar, swished it around his mouth, and spit it out. He glanced at the sun. "No more today."

He eyed Afra's tired and dusty frame. "Go to the baths. Get a massage. Back here tomorrow, second hour."

Afra groaned. Cinnia shot her a sympathetic glance as she helped Paetus gather the wooden swords and shields. They left the rocks in the dirt.

"It gets easier," Cinnia promised as they walked toward the baths. "You'll feel better after a steam and massage."

"But why the rocks?"

"Paetus knows." Cinnia grinned. "He's a good *doctore*. Listen more. Complain less."

"I don't complain!"

"If you say so." Cinnia raised an eyebrow. "Learning a new skill is hard. I've spent months practicing the sword. Today was your first day."

A thought struck her dumb. *Am I envious of Cinnia's skills?* Of the two of them, Afra was always the leader, the one with experience and knowledge. Cinnia depended on her. Until today. Afra ducked her head. Tomorrow she'd do better.

AFTER A WEEK of sword and shield drill—and a few more hours lifting rocks—Paetus moved on to the most challenging part of the training— the fight as a dance. He taught them to thrust and parry, retreat, circle, feint, and lunge. By the end of the month they had mastered several combinations and were developing their own routines.

"A bit rough, but with practice you'll do." Paetus slid the coin pouch into a fold of his tunic on the last day. He departed without a glance.

Marcius watched his retreating back. "Did he smile once during the training?"

"No." Afra shook her head. "He barked orders, thumped us with the flat of his sword, and grunted."

"He's an odd one, but he got the job done. You two will put on a good show. Tomorrow's a feast day. You'll perform in the Forum." He flipped Afra a coin. "Go to the baths. See Clio afterwards. She'll have your costumes."

AFRA WATCHED AS CINNIA brushed imaginary dirt off her red tunic and admired her wrist bands. She looked beautiful, her long golden hair shining and braided. Afra's heart skipped a beat when Cinnia's white teeth flashed in a smile.

"Cinnia, you'll do, but Afra…" Clio frowned, walking, observing her from all angles. "The yellow coloring suits you, but I wish you looked more like a woman."

Afra's normally relaxed stance stiffened. She clenched her jaw, sorry echoes of her step-mother's criticism ringing in her head.

"Maybe a wig?" Clio bent over her open wooden chest, rummaging. She straightened, holding a shoulder-length wig of tiny black braids decorated with blue faience beads. "I picked this up in Alexandria."

"I won't wear that."

Clio's mouth pinched to a thin line. "Marcius! Tell her!"

Afra hid a smile behind her hand. Clio had given up threatening her with beatings when Marcius pointed out how valuable she was.

"Put it on, Afra." Marcius took a drink from a goblet while he lounged in bed. The room reeked of sex and sour wine. "You're supposed to be an Ethiopian queen."

"How can I fight with that thing sliding into my eyes and clacking around my ears?"

"A diadem will hold it in place." Clio turned again to the chest. This time she retrieved a thin white ribbon embroidered with gold thread. "Sit."

Afra sat on the room's one stool while Clio tugged the wig over her short cropped hair, tied the ribbon across her forehead, leaving the ends dangling from a knot at the back.

"Much better." Clio handed Afra a polished bronze mirror.

"You're a different woman!" Marcius agreed.

She hardly recognized the exotic face looking back at her. It had been so long since she had worn long hair, she had forgotten what she looked like.

"It itches." Afra grumbled.

"You'll only have to wear it for a short time." Clio shot back. "Trust me. This is what you need to make an impression."

Afra sneaked a glance at Cinnia in the mirror. The girl grinned and winked. Afra was grateful for the dark skin that hid the flush of blood rushing to warm her face. She had never been vain, but it meant something that Cinnia found her attractive.

"You'll do." Clio looked them both over. "Now strip. Back here tomorrow by third hour."

They donned their old tunics and left.

Outside, Afra put her hand to her eyes, gazing at the angle of the sun. "We have a couple of hours before dusk. Would you like to go to the Forum? See who's entertaining today?"

"No." Cinnia smiled. "I thought we could entertain ourselves."

Afra's gut tightened. Since that first night, they had had little energy for more than kisses and sleep. Afra quickened her step.

At the stables, Cinnia pulled her into their shared cell whispering. "It's time. I'm so much stronger now. The memories are fading."

Afra started to shed her tunic.

"No. Let me." Cinnia pulled the rough garment over her head, dropped her own, and pulled Afra to the pallet. A puff of dust tickled Afra's nose. She sneezed.

Cinnia laughed, almost a moan of excitement, and ran her hands down Afra's sides to rest on her hips. "Roll onto your stomach."

Afra complied, head on crossed arms, eyes closed. She felt the cool air where Cinnia's warm body had been but a moment ago, heard a rattling of bottles. The scent of musk and olive oil wafted on the air. She felt Cinnia's hands rubbing the oil into her skin, kneading the taut muscles in her back and buttocks. Afra relaxed with a deep groan. Her breathing deepened and slowed.

A sharp slap on the butt brought her out of that place between wakefulness and sleep.

"Roll over."

Afra half-opened her eyes. Cinnia's breasts glistened with the musky oil. She rubbed more onto her hands and gently stroked Afra from throat to belly, lightly circling her breasts. Heat built in Afra's womb. A feeling of pleasure, bordering on pain, spread along her nerves as Cinnia teased her nipples. She arched her back and moaned. She hadn't known such pleasure since Asata. A tear leaked from the corner of her eye to escape into her hair.

No, I can't think of her. She is gone. Cinnia is here.

Cinnia seemed to sense her distraction and stopped stroking.

"No!" Afra took Cinnia's hand and guided it to that small button hidden in the folds of her woman's flesh.

"What do you want me to do?" Cinnia whispered nibbling on her ear.

"Touch there. Rub it. Lick it. That's the secret to a woman's pleasure."

Cinnia lowered her head to lick and suck at the hard nub.

The pressure built until Afra writhed, crying out as wave after wave flowed from the spot to leave a pleasurable ache throbbing in her groin.

She pulled Cinnia's head to hers, kissed her deeply and rolled her onto her back.

"Your turn, my love."

Cinnia smiled, her eyes wide with anticipated pleasure.

The next morning, Afra woke to find Cinnia gone. Fear clenched her stomach and quickened her breathing before she heard her with the cats in the next box.

Mari and Cari alternately hissed and chirped in distress as they paced in the straw. Cinnia sat in a corner humming a calming tune. She looked up when she heard Afra at the bars and smiled. The light flooding Afra's soul rivaled the sun's.

"They've been like this for some time." Cinnia watched the disturbed cheetahs. "They didn't eat the mash I made for them. What's wrong?"

"I don't know." Afra frowned. The few horses and mules not out to work were restless as well—stamping, snorting, jerking irritably at their halter ropes. "But I don't like it. Animals are canny. Maybe a bad storm from the sea?"

Cinnia's eyes darted to the sun streaming in the open door and shrugged. "We should go."

They joined the noisy crowd of celebrants entering the city gates and made their way to the inn, Afra brooding over the cats.

Clio watched them dress with a critical eye while she caressed Astarte. The snake tried to slip off Clio's lap time and again. "What's the matter with you?" Clio held the snake's face close to her own. It flicked its tongue tasting the air, shaking its head side to side.

"Put that thing away. I don't like the way it looks at me." Marcius grumbled from a messy bed. He sat up looking much the worse for wine and in need of a shave. "It's probably hungry. Didn't you say it hadn't eaten in two weeks?"

"*She* doesn't need to stuff her belly every day." Clio sniffed as she put the snake in its basket. "You better get up or you'll miss the sacrifice."

"The magistrates don't care if a man doesn't attend the sacrifice, as long as he puts a coin in the jar." Marcius rose, scratched his belly, and farted. "Do I have time for the baths?"

"No. But don't come back to my bed without going sometime today." Clio wrinkled her nose, waving at the air in front of her face. "I don't sleep with dirty pigs."

"I don't sleep with poxy whores." Marcius pulled Clio into a hug and growled as he buried his face in her ample breasts.

She pushed and squirmed like her snake till she broke free of his embrace, cursing all the time in Greek.

"Do we go now?" Afra tugged at the diadem Cinnia tied around her wigged head.

Marcius laughed and pulled Clio back to the bed. "Meet me in the Forum in front of Jupiter's temple at the fifth hour. I'll have your swords and shields."

They escaped the room.

CINNIA'S SPIRITS ROSE as she observed the crowds: smiling women dressed in bright colors, men chatting in clusters, children running free from chores or study, merchants hawking votives and other wares. The sun warmed her skin and the hopeful mood of the merrymakers, lightened her heart.

They entered the Forum by the Via dell'Abbondanza , opposite the town basilica whose busy law courts were closed for the day. The two of them garnered some speculative looks. Cinnia had to admit they made a striking pair and preened a bit. Few people had their height or physique.

The Forum was a lively, impressive place, dominated by temples and civic buildings, each faced with marble, decorated with columns and carved capitals; bronze and painted stone statues of important people populated plinths and niches. Someday, Cinnia promised herself, she'd find out who all those people were. She looked toward the imposing temple of Jupiter, Juno, and Mercury at the far end of the Forum, where they were to meet Marcius. "What do the Romans celebrate today?"

"A feast for Juno *Sospita Mater Regina*."

Cinnia raised a quizzical eyebrow. "Juno Savior, Mother, and Queen?"

"Juno is the wife of their main sky god, Jupiter. That's why they share the temple." Afra shrugged. "Women who want to conceive, shepherds who want to increase their flocks, will seek the goddess' blessing. All can ask for her protection in the coming year."

They threaded their way through the crowds to approach the massive temple. Stairs led up both sides past a central altar with a huge bronze bowl on top. Flames flickered from the bowl. The smell of roasting meat vied with nose-tickling incense from the sacrifices. Two bronze statues of men on horseback flanked the stairs. *Roman gods? Emperors?* There had been an equestrian statue of Claudius at Camulodunum, which the Britons had pulled down and hacked apart.

Cinnia's mood darkened at the memory. "We have a similar feast at this time of year, *Imbolc*, sacred to the goddess Brigid." *Lambing time. Dumnor helping a ewe in distress. Oriana making the traditional stew from the docked tails.* She dashed tears from her eyes. "But nothing so grand."

Afra squeezed her hand. "All peoples herald the return of spring. Mother Isis is protector and goddess of increase for my land. We also have a spring festival."

"Juno, Brigid, and Isis seem little different from each other. Are they the same goddess by different names?"

"Isis lives in Kush, far south, and in Egypt. Even the Romans welcome her. Maybe she's the same as your Brigid."

"My father studied to be a druid, a holy man. He believed the gods inhabited places: mountains, rivers, trees. If you traveled beyond one god's territory there was another different god. I have traveled much farther than I ever believed, and the gods here are not so different."

"In Alexandria, there are people called Jews who believe there is one god and all others are false. They don't give him a name."

"If there is one god, how could there be others to be false?"

"The gods just *are*. It is not for ordinary people to question them." Afra shook her head. The beads of her wig clacked. She frowned. "Religion makes my head hurt. Leave it to the priests to argue the details. Let's eat."

Cinnia looked to the sun. They had an hour or so before they had to meet Marcius. Just to the right of the temple, the *marcellum*—a covered market—bustled with people going in empty-handed and returning with free food provided by the city fathers for the feast day. The smells of roasted meat and fish, redolent of rosemary and sage, made her stomach rumble. "Let's go before they run out."

They joined a stream of people entering through the right-hand arch to spill out into a courtyard surrounded by an interior colonnade. The fish stalls on the south and meat stalls on the north were closed, but tables heaped with their cooked wares occupied the middle section under a circular roof. The city fathers also provided bread for trenchers, several kinds of cooked beans, early greens dressed in vinegar and oil, olives, cheeses, and the last of the winter apples and pears.

"I haven't seen so much food in months," Cinnia cried. "I do get tired of pulse and porridge."

"Don't gorge. We have to entertain soon. You don't want to be sluggish or get overheated and throw up. Marcius would be most unhappy."

Cinnia laughed and pointed at a woman in a red *stola* and the traditional matronly *palla* pulled over her hair followed by a slave with two trenchers towering with meat and salad. "Don't worry about me. I'll eat like a dainty Roman lady."

They elbowed their way to the tables. Cinnia picked amid the abundance and came away with a quarter of roast fowl, salad, and an apple. They left the brightly painted market and found a shady spot at the base of the temple to enjoy their feast. Cinnia raised her chicken leg to the temple and intoned, "Thank you Mother, by whatever name you choose, for this bounty and any blessings you bestow on us in the coming year. I promise to sacrifice a white dove to you when I receive those blessings."

Afra clutched her wooden amulet and bowed her head for a moment. When she looked up, she smiled in that way that made Cinnia feel soft and melted inside.

"There he is!" Afra pointed to Marcius squatting with three other men under the peristyle next to the temple; the gaudy gladiator equipment piled neatly to the side. As they got closer, she could see he played *tali*. From the frown on his face, he wasn't winning. Her stomach clenched. "Fortuna, I beseech thee," she mumbled under her breath. "Favor Lucius Marcius."

Marcius put the four dice in a small box, shook them while whispering his own supplication, and tossed them to the ground. Each showed a different number I, III, IV and VI.

"Fourteen! Venus throw!" He whooped, reaching for a pile of coins.

One of the men grabbed his wrist. "Let's play again, friend. This time we'll use my dice."

Afra slipped to Marcius' side. "*Dominus?*"

The man let go Marcius' wrist.

"My bodyguards." Marcius indicated Afra and Cinnia as he poured the coins into his pouch. "Grab your gear, we have business elsewhere."

He stalked away, weaving between the crowds under the peristyle, Afra and Cinnia trailing with their blunted swords and flashy shields slung over their backs.

"Good fortune you arrived when you did, Afra."

"Yes, I…"

All the dogs in the city began to howl. The birds took flight, briefly blackening the sky.

"Mother Isis protect us…"

The stone under her feet trembled like a herd of elephants stampeded close. Soon it pitched and rolled like a ship tossing in a storm.

All around her people fell, but she couldn't hear their screams over the thunder of the earth.

Cinnia stumbled toward her. Afra grabbed her, yelled in her face, "Run!" and pushed her from under the collapsing peristyle.

Statues danced on their plinths and toppled in the Forum. Columns jerked and collapsed in the temples. The roar of the underworld ripping the earth apart smothered the wails of the dying.

Afra tried to follow Cinnia, but the floor cracked and rose at her feet, tripping her. She fell full length, arms outstretched, as a shower of dust and rubble blocked her sight.

A pain exploded in her head.

Darkness took her.

Chapter Fifteen

"A FRA!" CINNIA SCREAMED in the sudden silence as the earth settled. She scuttled forward on hands and knees to scrabble at the pile of rubble. "Don't leave me," she sobbed.

Moans, prayers, and curses rose from the people scattered in heaps in the Forum and on the streets. Bells clanged in the distance, signaling a fire. Broken water pipes from toppled fountains gushed into the gutters.

"Please Brigid-Juno-Isis let her be alive." Cinnia clawed at the rubble with bleeding hands, paying no attention to others crying for their loved ones. Tears cleared tracks down her dusty cheeks. She uncovered a hand, ebony skin pale with dust. "Please, please, please, Lady Fortuna, gods of all names and none, spare her. Spare her."

The prayer became a chant as she shoveled debris away with her shield. An arm. A shoulder. At last the back of her head. "Afra! Speak to me!"

Silence.

Cinnia renewed her efforts. A column lay next to Afra providing protection from larger blocks. The hated wig seemed to have cushioned her head from the worst of the rubble and the crumpled shield protected her from the large chunks.

"Love, please wake up." Cinnia stroked Afra's exposed face. She could feel her irregular breaths on her fingers.

The earth started to tremble again. "Take me! Take me!" Cinnia beseeched the gods as she pitched forward to protect Afra. This tremor was but an echo of the first. It lasted moments.

"Cinnia?" Afra coughed.

Cinnia's tears dripped on Afra's turned cheek, making dark puddles in the dust. "Yes, my love. I'm here. You're trapped under the rubble, but I'll soon have you free."

"Water," she croaked.

Cinnia looked around. A trickle ran down the gutter, but she had no cup. Using a sharp rock, she ripped a piece of her tunic from the hem. "I'll be back."

She ran to the gutter, soaked the wool strip, and brought it back. "Here, suck on this. Can you move?"

Afra wriggled her shoulders. "My legs…" Her eyes grew round with fear.

Cinnia stroked her face. "Stay still." She shifted more rubble, freeing Afra past her waist.

"Let me try." Afra rose to her hands and knees; shook the dust off, like a dog after a dunking. She pulled one leg free, then the other, and staggered upright.

Cinnia shoved her shoulder under the taller woman's arm. "Don't try to walk yet." They settled on a cracked pedestal. "Do you hurt anywhere?"

Afra flexed her joints from neck to toes. She flinched when she swiveled her left ankle. "My ribs hurt and my ankle is sprained."

Sitting in each other's arms, Cinnia took a moment to look around her. Juno's altar lay toppled down the temple steps, the fire dying, sacrifices scattered. Dust hovered over collapsed buildings.

A portly man walked up to them. Blood streamed down his dazed face to soak into his fine white tunic. "Fabia? Have you seen my Fabia?"

Cinnia shook her head. He moved off, mumbling.

On the temple steps, a small girl sat under a leaning marble statue, eyes round, sucking her thumb. A woman lay next to her, unmoving, half obscured by a large chunk of roof tile. Dust fell from the statue as it settled uneasily on its cracked plinth. Heart pounding, Cinnia rose to rescue the girl, but a dark-haired man stumbled up to the child. He pulled her into his arms, just before the statue smashed to the ground. He sat, sobbing, the girl clasped tight in his arms.

All around her, people dug in the rubble—some to free their loved ones, others to rob the dead and dying.

"Marcius?" Afra croaked.

Cinnia drew in a sharp breath and nodded toward the downed column. "It fell on him."

Afra's tears streaked her dusty face.

AFRA AND CINNIA SHOULDERED THE BIER carrying Marcius' body. They followed Clio through the Nucerian Gate to the cemetery. Clio saved a few coins by providing her own slaves for the funeral procession. The widow, dressed in dark robes, carried a covered basket. Afra tried not to hiss when the pain in her ankle flared. In one way the throbbing was a blessing, taking her mind off her fate now that Marcius was gone.

But today was given to the dead—dozens of them—so many that the funeral directors had difficulty accommodating them all. Today the poorer folk were to be cremated and buried. The rich were able to afford separate ceremonies at a later date.

Outside the gate, Afra saw the smoky fires concentrated in the southeast portion of the cemetery. They joined a string of bereaved families heading in that direction. The smoke thickened, as did the smell of roasting meat.

"This way." Clio pointed to the left as they drew closer. "The standard with the mark of Mercury."

Afra looked up to see a crudely drawn winged sandal on a wooden sign.

Mercury, god of commerce, thieves, and travelers; a fitting choice for Marcius after Fortuna deserted him.

Clio approached a bald round Roman with twinkling eyes, which seemed inappropriate for his profession. They talked in low tones. Afra shifted the weight off her aching ankle, wishing she could put her burden down during negotiations. Finally, after much arm waving, coins and a paper passed hands. Clio and the round Roman approached.

"My condolences, dear madam, on your loss." The funeral director lightly supported Clio's elbow. "Have your slaves place the body on that pile," he indicated a prepared stack of wood, chest high, cut from the ubiquitous poplar groves surrounding the city. A dozen identical pyres, awaiting their burdens, trooped in an orderly line. "Are you sure you want no singers or dancers to send your husband on his last journey?"

"No. Just the burning and the burial."

"An oration? A container? A marker?"

"I told you, my husband failed to join a funeral club, so this is all paid by me." Clio frowned at the man. "Should I take my custom elsewhere?"

"As you wish." The funeral director sighed. "My assistant will see to your…uh…needs." He called over an undernourished young man, dressed in a well-made dark blue tunic, and turned to deal with the next client.

They lowered the bier onto the pyre. Marcius' face looked peaceful, but Afra knew the rough grain sacks wrapping the body covered fearsome bruises; the flatness of the chest indicating where the column crushed his ribs. The assistant poured a jar of oil over the body and applied a torch to the kindling in the middle of the pyre. The oil-soaked body and wood blazed hot enough to send them back a few steps, coughing.

"He will take a while to burn." The assistant provided Clio with a folding camp stool. "May I bring you some wine?"

"Yes, thank you." Clio settled onto the stool. The thin man brought her a plain clay goblet. From the face she made, Afra concluded it was sour stuff, well-watered, or both.

Cinnia touched her shoulder. "Over there."

She pointed to a patch of grass under a poplar tree away from the fires. There was still a touch of winter in the air, but the fires heated the surroundings. The smoke settled in Afra's throat.

"Yes."

She limped to the tree, settled onto the grass, and took a drink of water from a leather flask. "Want some?" Afra offered the flask.

"Thanks." Cinnia took a drink and sat staring into the flames. "This seems a rather poor beginning for Marcius' journey."

"Marcius became a friend to me, as well as master, but he had many faults. I doubt Clio has the money for anything better."

"She keeps a plump sack of coins hidden in a false bottom in her chest."

"I doubt Marcius knew, or it would have disappeared." Afra frowned. "Where did she get the money?"

"When you two go away, she dances in the marketplace with her snake. I sing." Cinnia grinned. "She also lightened Marcius' purse by a couple of coins each time he got drunk. I suspect she has a good deal put aside."

"Did she give you any of the take when you sang?"

"No."

"Wretched woman!" Afra hunched her shoulders. "Marcius always gave me a few coins. How else can a slave buy back her freedom?"

"How much do you have?"

"Not enough."

"What happens to us now?"

"I don't know." Afra rested her chin on her knees. "I'm supposed to hunt in the Emperor's games celebrating *Cerealia* in April. That's two months. Marcius seemed to think I could earn my freedom quickly, once I hunted in the Roman arena."

"Will Clio honor the contracts?"

Afra shrugged. "She has no reason not to. My life debt was to Marcius, but I see no way to escape Clio…now. The Romans are too many and the roads well watched. You've seen the wretches nailed upside down to crosses outside the city walls?"

Cinnia nodded.

"Escaped slaves. Crucified as a warning to others."

"Sometimes death is better than life filled with pain, or a life with no honor or purpose." Cinnia's put her arm around Afra's waist. "You are my reason for being here."

"Not the gods?" Afra leaned into Cinnia.

"Yes…and no." Cinnia laid her head on Afra's shoulder. "I've pondered much since you pulled me back from the shadow world. You told me about the god-sent dream that foretold your journey. My gods abandoned me…or so I thought. My family, my queen dead; yet I live. For what purpose? To serve a spiteful, cheap woman? The gods brought us together, but you're the reason I stay. Without you to hold me in this world, I would leave it."

Afra shuddered and sought Cinnia's hand. "We might choose death or it might choose us. But today we live. Today we love. Do not give up that life or love easily today or tomorrow or the next day. Everything changes."

"Sometimes, at night, I feel the pull of the shadow world. Not death, but endless wandering." She squeezed Afra's hand. "Then I wake up and touch you; your solid flesh and strong arms. This is the world I belong in, the one with you in it."

Afra sat still, listening to her lover's breathing. Cinnia looked so strong in the flesh, yet she carried unhealed wounds in her heart.

As the funeral pyre started to die, Afra took off her necklace with the small carved figure of Isis, and put it around Cinnia's neck. "This has nestled between my breasts, lifted with my breath, and listened to my heart. Now I give it to you. May the Mother protect you and give you good dreams."

"I can't…" Cinnia tried to give it back.

"This is my promise to you. The gods brought us together. With this, a part of me will always be with you to ward off the shadows."

"But I have nothing…" Cinnia's face broke into a grin. She yanked several long blond hairs from her head and deftly braided them into a thin band which she tied around Afra's wrist. "There! Now you have part of me as well."

They beamed at each other until a shadow blocked the lowering sun.

Clio.

"A fine pair you are, grinning like children at play when we're here to bury my husband." She poked Cinnia with her foot. "Get up, lazy mule.

It's time to sing for your supper. I couldn't afford the professionals, but you'll do. Marcius may have been a no-good, shit-for-brains, son of a diseased whore, but he was my husband, and deserves some beauty at his leave-taking."

Afra was surprised to see a tear well in the corner of Clio's kohled eyes, and track down her cheek to her bitter mouth. Maybe the snake woman did have some affection for Marcius. Or maybe she was maudlin drunk on the sour wine.

Seeing Afra's glance, Clio dashed the tears from her eyes and stomped off to oversee the assistant ladling Marcius' hot ashes out of the dying fire into a plain crockery wine jug. *Another fitting symbol.*

The small party of four walked to a line of shallow holes, dug into the rich soil. At the first open hole, Clio handed the assistant a plain wooden plank with Marcius' name, age, and occupation carved in it. He hammered it into the soil to mark the spot, deposited the jug in the hole, and stood awkwardly to the side with a spade.

Clio knelt by the grave and threw in something Afra couldn't see. The widow rose. Cinnia broke into a haunting song. Afra didn't understand the words, but the dirge-like tune seemed appropriate.

Afra approached the grave and whispered. "Good-by, my friend. May your soul find peace in the Roman afterlife." She nearly choked as a sob turned to a coughing laugh. Four dice sat in the cooling ashes showing I, III, IV and VI—the luckiest of all throws, the Venus.

"Thank the gods that's over." Clio pulled the veil from her hair with a sigh after the purification ritual at Juno's altar. "Now I can do business again. To the magistrate."

The nine days of mourning hadn't prevented Clio from renting out Afra and Cinnia as members of the slave gangs employed in cleaning up the city. After hours of hauling baskets of rubble to carts, they came home each night exhausted and coughing from the dust—too tired to do more than fall asleep in each other's arms. The grueling work and little food left Afra feeling drained, dull. Today had been their first day off since Marcius' funeral.

Afra and Cinnia followed Clio, from the temporary altar to Juno, down the line of people in need of the purification services. Most had buried family, but there was a woman comforting an older man with vacant eyes. Lost souls like him frequented the streets, walking unseeing or raving, until someone came to lead them home. Afra shook her head. If Clio wasn't in such a hurry she would have sent the woman to the old herbalist next to the Temple of Isis…if she survived.

They walked through the destroyed Forum toward the basilica. Reconstruction was starting on the more important buildings: the Temples to Jupiter and Apollo. Scaffolding surrounded the basilica. Sail-cloth flapped over a hole in the roof. They walked up cracked steps, into the echoing building.

Clio stopped a couple of clerks to ask directions and they found themselves in front of a young man with large sad eyes. "Your business?"

"Magistrate, I am a poor widow," Clio bowed, "come to register my husband's will and take possession of these slaves as my property." A tear formed at the corner of her left eye and tracked unheeded down her cheek.

"Papers?"

Clio pulled out two scraps of papyrus and a formal looking scroll sealed with wax. "My husband's will as witnessed by and sealed with the sign of the Vestal Virgins. These are receipts for the purchase of these two slaves."

"Do you have proof of your relationship with," the magistrate squinted at the will, "Lucius Marcius?"

Clio pulled out two more pieces of papyrus. "The testimony of Julia Felix, our landlady that we lived as husband and wife in her inn for the time we resided in Pompeii and the receipt from the undertaker for my husband's burial nine days ago."

The magistrate broke the seal on the will with a knife, read quickly, and looked up. "Which one is Afra?"

"The tall Ethiopian."

"Of course." The magistrate's lips twitched at the corners. "It says here, she is to have her freedom and be known as Marcia Afra. Any transfer fees are to come from his estate."

"What?" Clio screeched and grabbed the will from the magistrate's hands. "That lying, no-good son of a raddled whore. How can he leave me destitute like this?" This time the tears were real. "May his shade wander the earth in torment until the world's end."

"I'm free?" Afra blinked in incomprehension.

"And a Roman citizen. All freed slaves of Roman citizens are accorded citizenship at manumission." The magistrate nodded at Clio. "As soon as she pays the fee, I'll make out your paperwork."

Free! Marcius kept his word! Afra saw the anguished look on Cinnia's face.

"And Cinnia?"

"The slave known as Cinnia and," he squinted closely at the will again, "a pair of trained cheetahs, plus all his clothes, and money go to the widow." He glanced at the furious Clio. "The transfer fee for Marcia Afra is two bronzes."

"I'll not pay to lose my own slave."

The magistrate frowned.

"I can pay." Afra fished two coins from her own slender *peculium*.

The magistrate scribbled on a blank piece of papyrus and imprinted it with a signet ring. "Here is your manumission. Guard it well, citizen." He nodded toward Cinnia and addressed Clio. "Does she have any skills?"

"None that are useful," Clio mumbled. "She can't even sew a good seam."

"You can always register her as a prostitute." He pointed at another table. "Over there."

"Thank you, Your Honor." Clio bowed out of the magistrate's presence and snapped her fingers at Cinnia.

Afra loomed over Clio. "You're not going to register Cinnia as a prostitute."

"I'll do as I please." She glared up at Afra. "My gods-cursed husband liked playing the bones. Besides her, I've nothing but Astarte, a broken contract with the *procurator,* and the threats of moneylenders. You," she poked a long-nailed finger in Afra's chest, "will deliver those cheetahs. I *might* be able to convince the procurator to take them in your stead for the games. She," pointing her finger at Cinnia, "is worth more on her back than on her feet."

"I have a little money. I can earn more."

Clio's mouth compressed into a thin line. She hissed between clenched teeth. "He paid you far too much."

"Marcius was an honorable man. He promised me my freedom, if I worked for him willingly."

Clio turned her back.

"Please!" Afra grabbed her arm holding out the *peculium.* "You can have it all now. I'll work for you to buy Cinnia."

"I'll think on it." Clio looked at the slim purse then sniffed. "Not much. Have those cheetahs ready tomorrow morning. We'll talk then." She dragged a dazed Cinnia away to the inn.

"I'll come for you!" Afra shouted to Cinnia. "Stay strong!"

Chapter Sixteen

I won't do it," Cinnia raged.

"You bloody bitch." Clio raised a rod to beat her, but Cinnia caught her wrist and twisted until the rod fell. Clio pulled back rubbing her wrist. "Do you know the penalty for a slave attacking her mistress?"

"Death?" Cinnia laughed, a note of hysteria tingeing her voice. "I'll kill myself before I let another Roman man touch me like that!"

"Roman men, is it?" A calculating look came over Clio's face. "Are you a tribade? Do you like to poke or be poked?" At Cinnia's confused look, Clio rolled her eyes. "Do you play the man or the woman?"

"I'm a woman."

"By all the gods, you are a dense barbarian." Clio stroked her chin. "But that does explain a lot. You and Afra?"

Blood rose in a tide to burn Cinnia's cheeks.

"Why the blush? Don't you look at the pictures at the baths?"

"It is not forbidden here?"

"Romans don't care about such provincial attitudes. A few philosophers rail against 'unnatural' women, but what goes on in private homes and brothels is ignored." Clio raised an eyebrow. "But that doesn't mean you can do as you please. I need money. Better it is earned on your back than on mine."

I'll come for you.

Cinnia closed her eyes and prayed.

"Wake up." Clio shook Cinnia, slapping her when she didn't respond. Cinnia stood up without speaking.

Clio looked at her closely. "So that's the way of it? Well don't think feigning madness will get you out of work." She rummaged through her wooden trunk, pulled out a string knitted tunic, and held it up for the light to shine through. "Alexandrian. The Egyptians know how to show off their women. Put it on." Clio tossed it Cinnia.

The tunic dropped to the floor. Blood rushed into Clio's face. "Stupid mule." She grabbed her rod and beat Cinnia on the shoulders and buttocks.

Pain lanced across her back.

I'll come for you.

But until then?

Everything changes.

Cinnia grabbed the rod. "Enough."

"Speaking again are you?" Clio put her hands on her hips. "Pick up that tunic and put it on."

Cinnia obeyed, blushing to her hair roots. The thing showed more flesh than it concealed. She had only to get through this one day. She would deal with tomorrow, tomorrow.

"You won't have to wear it long." Clio laughed. "Come along."

They traveled the Via Stabia beyond the Via dell'Abbondanza, north of the Forum. Clio turned down an alley and stopped at an entrance to a two-story building on the corner. A crack streaking up one side wall and a tarp on the roof showed the earthquake had touched it lightly. Graffiti painted on the walls indicated they were in the right place. Cinnia looked at the rude drawings through eyes blurred with tears. Her vision darkened and narrowed.

No. I have to stay in this world. Afra will come for me.

Clio knocked on the door with her foot. An old man, blind by the cast in his eyes, opened the door.

"I wish to speak with the owner about renting a room."

"Around the corner. Take the stairs to the second floor." The old man pointed toward an intersecting alley.

Clio grumbled at the stairs, but put on a pleasant face when a short rotund man answered her knock at the top of the stairs.

"Do I have the pleasure of addressing the owner of this establishment?"

"I'm Varro. My partner is out at the moment." He stepped back, indicating they should enter. "Please have a seat."

Clio settled on a backless, but well-padded chair, while Cinnia stood behind her. Varro took a seat behind a table.

"I'm Clio, a poor widow. My husband was taken by the gods' scourge." Clio and Varro bowed their heads making the two-fingered sign to ward off bad luck. "He left me with nothing but this slave. I wish to rent one of your rooms and put her to work."

"Do you have papers? I run a legitimate business."

"I registered her yesterday." Clio reached into a fold of her tunic and pulled out the registration papers. "What are your terms?"

Cinnia's breath quickened.

Just one day. I can survive one day. Everything changes.

"The rent is two denarii a day and fifty percent of her take. Here are the fees we charge the customers for the various services. He indicated a wooden board hanging behind his head.

"Will I get a discount if I take the room for a week or more? And fifty percent? How can you cheat a poor widow so?" Clio wrung her hands. "Ten percent is fairer."

Varro leaned back in his chair, a smile tugging at his lips. They bargained for a few moments, settling on a lower weekly rate and twenty-five percent.

"Done!" Varro rose. "Let me show you the accommodations."

They went down stairs and entered the building. Cinnia wrinkled her nose at the faint stench from the latrine.

"We have five rooms down here. Each furnished with a bed, mattress, and oil lamp. Caecus," he clapped the blind man on the shoulder, "is our door man. He keeps the water clock. Customers pay for quarter-hours. The girls provide their own food and drink. A public fountain is down the alley and around the corner. The girls stand out here when not working so the customers can choose."

"When does the traffic pick up?"

"During the afternoon and again after dinner. We get mostly tradesmen, freedmen, and slaves. A few take a break from errands during the morning, but not many. This is your room." He indicated another of the wooden signs with pictures of sex acts and fees hung on a thin wooden door. "Turn this over when you're in use." The back of the sign had a word, but Cinnia couldn't read it. He turned the sign back and pushed open the door.

Cinnia stared in horror at the raised stone bed and graffiti filled walls. She pushed down a wave of nausea, clutching the amulet around her neck.

I will come for you.

I'm sorry Afra, I can't do this. I can't wait.

Clio slipped Caecus a coin and whispered in his ear as she left, "Make sure she stays busy and you'll have another coin tomorrow."

AFRA RETURNED FROM THE FALLOW FIELD with the cats by second hour and spent the next hour sitting in the straw of their box grooming them. She brushed the spotted coats till they shone, fighting back the tears. "I'll miss you, my sisters."

Mari butted her hand, purring, begging for a treat while she combed Cari.

Afra laughed and pushed her away.

"They look good." Clio peered through the bars.

Afra twitched and looked over her shoulder. "Where's Cinnia?"

"My business, not yours." A small smile picked up the corners of Clio's thin mouth. Her eyes glittered as they searched Afra's face for a reaction.

She knows, Afra thought. *The snake witch knows and is taunting me.* She turned back to the cats and gave them a large bone to gnaw. *I must find Cinnia…and soon.*

"When will they be ready?"

"They could use another six months growth and training on bigger prey." Afra stepped out of the box confronting Clio with her height. "Perhaps I could trade my skills for Cinnia's freedom? Marcius said they would be worth far more fully trained."

"They look ready enough for my purposes. As for you," Clio snorted through her hooked nose, "pack your things and leave. I no longer require your services. I won't pay for your food or lodging."

"I had hoped we could come to a business arrangement."

"My business with you is done." Clio snarled. "Marcius should have let you rot in that cell. You're gods' cursed and bring ill luck!"

"What of Cinnia?"

"She's earning her keep."

"How?" Blood started to pound in Afra's head.

"Using her cunt the way it was meant to be used."

Afra moved before she thought, punching Clio in the face. The smaller woman reeled back, holding her hand to her face, spitting blood. "You black demon's spawn, you broke my nose!"

Afra grabbed her arm, twisting it up her back. "Evil witch. Where did you take Cinnia?"

"Help! Murder!" Clio screeched. She kicked back connecting with Afra's knee.

Afra put her hand over Clio's mouth.

Clio bit down, sharp teeth cutting to the bone.

Afra grunted in pain and pulled the arm up tighter until she heard the shoulder joint pop. Clio screamed in pain and went limp.

Afra lowered the unconscious woman to the ground in one of the stalls; ripped a piece of cloth from her former *domina's* tunic and wrapped it around her bitten hand. She stood shaking. The cubs paced and hissed, disturbed by the smell of her blood.

"What have I done, sisters?" Afra breathed harshly, trying to focus.

Finally she tore several more strips from the Clio's clothes, bound her hand and foot, and gagged her mouth. "That should hold her for a while."

She soothed the cats, the beginnings of a plan forming in her mind. "I'll be back for you."

AFRA CONFRONTED THE BLIND OLD MAN who kept the time for the brothel. "Do you have a Briton named Cinnia working here?" This was the ninth brothel she had visited. No sign of Cinnia. "She's new. Just come today."

"We had a crazy new one."

" 'Had?' My Mistress Clio urgently needs the slave she rented to you. She has met with an accident and needs her attendance."

The old man's brows came together in a frown. "Your mistress lied to us. The mad girl scared her first customer nearly out of his wits with her screeching and babbling. He thought her possessed. My master had to give him a free ride with one of the other girls. He's not happy."

"Where is she?" Afra scanned the hall behind the door.

"She ran from the house. I sent for the guards, but they are busy with all this construction. If you want to find her, you'll have to look yourself." He shut the door in Afra's face.

Where would Cinnia go? Afra raced as fast as her bruised knee and wrenched ankle would take her back through the Forum.

CHAPTER SEVENTEEN

THE MIST LIFTED FROM HER MIND as Cinnia ran. Women stared. Men pointed. Children tried to follow her, as she raced through the streets, nearly naked, heading for the only safety she knew in this foreign land. *Afra. I must find Afra!*

She skidded to a stop at an intersection of angled alleys. *Which way?* She chose left, ran around a corner, and collided with two guards, armed with thick clubs. Knocking one to the ground, she staggered, and fell to her knees. The other grabbed her hair and forced her head back, exposing the iron slave collar.

"Where are going in such a hurry, slave? Where's your pass?"

"Pass?"

"No slave can be alone on the streets without papers from his master."

She waved her empty hands, heart thudding, breath rasping.

The second guard was back on his feet, puffing, red in the face. "Get up."

Cinnia rose, wincing at the pain in her scraped knees. "I won't go back."

"To your master?"

"That place, where men pay to…to…" She pushed the pictures from her mind. She couldn't find the words.

"Escaped from a brothel, most likely." The red-faced guard grabbed his crotch and leered.

The one holding her hair said, "How many times do I have to tell you? No raping the whores. The owners complain to the council."

"Fuck the council. I want a taste." He squeezed Cinnia's breast. His hot breath clogged her nostrils.

Cinnia exploded. She kicked the red-faced guard in the balls. He went down moaning. She whirled to slash the other one with her nails, grunting as a handful of hair ripped from her scalp.

This guard was faster than his partner. He backed up, pulled his club from his belt, and assumed a defensive crouch. They circled one another for a few moments then Cinnia turned and ran.

As she passed the downed guard, he extended his leg, sweeping her off her feet, sending her crashing full length on the stone street. Breath left her chest in a whoosh. She fought darkness. A body landed on her back and pulled her arms behind her. She felt leather cutting into her wrists.

"Vicious bitch." Pain exploded in her lower back as the red-faced guard kicked her again and again.

She closed her eyes, ground her teeth, trying not to cry out.

"Stop it!" Cinnia heard a scuffle. The kicks ended, but the pain continued. "You kill her and the owner will demand your hide in addition to her value."

"But the whore…"

"Serves you right for trying that shit on a barbarian woman. Look at her. She could probably gut you in a second, if she had a knife, or break your scrawny neck with her bare hands. Better stay back. Let me handle her."

Cinnia peeked through her screen of hair at a pair of dirty feet encased in hobnailed sandals. One of the feet nudged her arm. "Can you stand?"

She drew a breath, gasped at the pain, pulled her legs under her, and tried to rise—not easy with her arms tied tight behind. The guard put out a hand and helped her up, but kept his club ready in his other hand.

"Who's your master?"

"Mistress."

"Mistress." His voice was not unkind. "Where does she live?"

Cinnia felt a glimmer of hope. "Afra. My mistress' name is Marcia Afra. She's at a stable outside the city walls. Through the Stabian gate."

The guard attached a leather thong to her bound wrists and walked behind with his club free, giving directions when they came to intersections.

She had turned the wrong way.

The red-faced guard limped along and muttered oaths. The crowds generally ignored them, with the exception of a few curious children, who trailed for a while until they gave up, bored.

As they walked toward the stable, Cinnia's mind cleared. She began to formulate a plan. She'd identify Afra as her mistress and the guards would let her go. The two of them could escape the city into the wilderness on the slopes of the mountain, Vesuvius, looming to the north. They could take the cubs for hunting and live free! Maybe she could go home. She shook her head. No. Home was gone, destroyed by the Romans. Maybe they could go south to Afra's homeland?

They arrived at the stable. Cinnia found it strangely quiet. Usually it was filled with small noises; a hoof stamp, a breathy snort, the squeak of a mouse being caught by one of the cats, the creak of leather or rope as an animal pulled it across wood. All the horses and mules were out, being used to haul debris from the earthquake, and their attendants with them. But a muffled sound from one of the stalls caught their attention.

"Who's there?" Her guard cried out.

"Mmmmmf," came from the far stall, then a regular tattoo as someone kicked the boards. "Mmmmmf!"

They rushed over to find Clio trussed like a bird for roasting, a gag stuffed in her mouth. Her guard pulled the gag out. Clio screamed, "Untie me you ignorant clod. And be careful of my shoulder. It hurts worse than Hades' fires."

While her guard untied Clio, Cinnia edged toward the door. The red-faced guard grabbed her tether and poked her in the back with his club. "You're not going anywhere."

She froze, hopes dashed. There would be no escape. No living free. *Afra, where are you?*

AFRA STRODE DOWN the Via dell'Abbondanza weaving in and out of pedestrians, avoiding the constant stream of carts filled with rubble and the occasional stinking pile of manure left by the draft animals.

Where could she be? Not at Clio's. She'd never go back there. The Temple of Isis? Would she hide? Where? Try to escape? Which direction? Is she in her right mind?

Afra looked for signs of disturbance in the crowd, but detected nothing out of the ordinary. Like most crowds, it seemed chaotic, but under the surface was a purpose. People had a direction and followed one another.

This is useless.

If Cinnia kept her head, she was looking for her. The most likely place for her to look was in the stable. Afra groaned. She would have to go back. Maybe Clio was still unconscious.

She heard the voices before she came to the door: the high screech of Clio in a rage and the lower, soothing tones of a man trying to calm the angry woman.

"I told you, she's mine! I rented her to a brothel. The stupid, lazy, barbarian bitch costs me more money than she brings in."

Afra came around the corner to see Cinnia sitting on a pile of straw, arms bound behind, feet hobbled together, head bowed. Clio, with her torn clothes and left arm hanging limply by her side, screamed at two city guards. She spotted Afra over the shorter one's shoulder and raised her good arm to point.

"That's her! That's the murderous Ethiopian slave that attacked me! Get her."

Cinnia's head snapped up. A brief smile, followed by a look of horror, crossed her face. The guards turned, pulling their clubs. Afra put out her hands to show she carried no weapons. "Here are my papers."

She reached into a small pouch tied around her neck; pulled out a piece of papyrus. "I'm a free woman."

"Not after today, you're not!" A thin string of spittle hung from Clio's lips. Hectic red blood inflamed her cheeks at the sight of Afra. "The penalty for attempted murder is death."

"If I wanted you dead, you'd be dead."

The guards approached from both sides hemming her in. One moving with a limp, grabbed her paper and glanced at it. Afra thought he held it upside down. "The seal looks right, but you'll have to come with us to see the magistrate. Assaulting a citizen is also a crime."

She looked over the men's heads to Clio. "Cinnia?"

A smile pulled at the corners of the small woman's mouth, but didn't reach her eyes. "You'll never know, demon spawn."

Afra lunged for Clio. The guards hit her with their clubs. One blow to the back of the legs sent her stumbling to her knees; another aimed at her head, she ducked but the club landed with full force on her shoulder. Fire spread down her arm. She toppled sideways.

"Afra!" Cinnia's scream tore across her consciousness, accompanied by the eerie chirping distress of the cheetah cubs in the next stall. Cinnia struggled in her bonds.

The guards continued to rain blows on Afra's back and ribs. The red-faced one kicked her head, sending her thoughts whirling in a dizzy dance. She heaved, threw up, and the blows stopped. She lay on the straw strewn with her blood and vomit, broken ribs rubbing against each other with every shallow breath.

She could hear Cinnia cursing and crying, but couldn't see her through eyes beginning to swell. Clio's dainty feet came into blurry view. Afra heard her hawk and spit, but couldn't feel the gobbet.

"I told you she was dangerous. Best to strangle her now and save the Empire the expense of her trial."

"The trial will be short enough," one of the men said. "She'll make good arena fodder."

The guards hauled Afra to a low stone building, threw her into a small windowless room, and cuffed her leg to the wall. She heard the lock tumblers fall into place. When the footsteps receded, she finally let herself groan. Every muscle thrummed with pain, her face swelled with bruises. She lay on her side on the bare earth, letting tears course down her face.

Again, I failed to protect the one I love. She sobbed. *Cinnia, as long as I have breath, I'll try to find you, but my love, you must help yourself now. May Mother Isis give us both strength.*

Cinnia wrenched at her bonds. "You better kill me now, Clio, because when I'm free, you're dead."

"Big talk." Clio limped over to Cinnia, her arm hanging useless at her side. Pain fought with rage to control her face. "You're still worth more to me alive than dead. You can lay here in your filth, until I get rid of you." One of the cubs let out a blood curdling growl. "And those horrible animals, too."

"Marcius, I curse the day I met you." Clio sobbed. "May your shade never leave the land of torments. All I wanted was a little coin and a comfortable life, a little wine, a few laughs. This is what you leave me… trouble and debts!"

The sharp smell of a sweating animal reached Cinnia's nose, as she heard the clomp of hooves on the floor. An older boy, leading a lame mule into the stable, stopped short at the sight of the battered women.

"What are you looking at, fool?" Tears furrowed the dust on Clio's face. "Put that animal away and come help me."

The boy led the limping mule to a loose box and hurried back. "What can I do, Mistress?"

"There's a coin in it, if you guard this slave." Clio held out the dirty rag she had been gagged with. "She'll curse you with a barbarian hex, so stop her mouth with this."

The boy approached Cinnia, eyes wide and with hesitant steps. She glared at him through her tangled hair, muttering curses in her native tongue. The blood drained from the boy's face.

"Hurry! Grab her hair and stop her mouth!"

He stepped close and yanked her hair back. She clenched her teeth. She heard the straw rustle before feeling the sharp kick to her stomach. She gasped.

"Now!" Clio yelled.

The boy stuffed the rag in her mouth. Clio and the boy retreated as Cinnia curled up in pain.

"She's dangerous, so don't go near her. She'll gut you as soon as look at you."

Clio's voice faded as Cinnia turned inward.

Chapter Eighteen

THE GRAY MISTS WERE COMFORTING THIS TIME, *not frightening. Cinnia felt no pain. She wandered, thinking of nothing, feeling nothing. A faint sound caught her attention. The barest hint of a melody. She turned toward the sound. A grove of oaks rose from the mist.*

A flute. One of the sacred songs her father used to play.

She walked the grove, searching for something…someone?

The flute led her on.

The undergrowth thickened. Thorns grabbed at her clothes. Branches slapped at her face. The more she pushed, the thicker the vegetation. Vines trapped her feet.

The music grew more insistent as she struggled. A familiar feeling of panic and helplessness clogged her throat and hastened her heart.

She stopped struggling. The vines withdrew.

She breathed deeply. The thorns loosed their hold.

She closed her eyes and slowed her heart.

When she opened them, the grove stood clear of underbrush. Golden sunlight streamed in bright bands. The music changed from the familiar melody to one of eerie ululation she had heard once coming from the Isis temple. It was haunting and beautiful, but foreign.

She left the sacred grove of her people for the reed-covered bank of a mighty river, so wide the other side disappeared in the mist. A huge animal, all gray bumps and tiny ears, floated a short way from shore. It opened its enormous mouth to bellow, exposing large stumps of ivory teeth. Cinnia had seen painted pictures of the river horses, but the real animal was terrifying. She would never swim in that river!

A misshapen dwarf played the haunting melody to a baby in a reed basket. The child laughed and shook a rattle of metal…a sistrum, Afra had called it.

Afra! Pain twisted Cinnia's gut and she sobbed.

"How came you here, Daughter?" A voice more beautiful than any music lightened Cinnia's heart.

She turned to see the figure of a woman, shorter than she. A brilliant light blurred her features. She wore her dark hair in many braids, gathered with ribbons on both sides of her face. Her sheer linen dress showed her breasts, swollen with milk, and wide hips, made for childbirth.

"I don't know." Cinnia thought hard. "I needed rest, comfort."

"Many do," the woman sighed. "You are so unkind to one another in the world. My husband preached love and was slain for it. You are welcome to stay as long as you need." They glided toward the laughing child.

The dwarf stopped playing and bowed to the woman. "My Lady."

The child was a naked boy. His chubby fists waved in the air as he laughed, but his eyes were old and wise. The woman picked up the child, sat on a stone, unpinned her tunic at the shoulder, and put him to her breast. She sighed with satisfaction.

The tableau triggered a memory. "Are you Isis?"

"Some name me so." She smiled down at her son, her beaded braids falling around her face. "I've had many names through the ages. I am Mother."

"Your son?"

"The Light, destined to save the world from evil. He has, he does, he will. Time has no meaning here."

"How long have I been gone?"

She shrugged. "As long as you needed to be."

"Must I go back?"

"Only if you want to."

They sat quietly for a few minutes. Mother switched the baby to the other breast.

"Why can't I see your face?"

"Love is a powerful force. It blinds some and opens the eyes of others. It can bring great joy and terrible sorrow. Some use it to bind, others to free."

Cinnia's thoughts turned to Afra; her bravery, her wisdom, her kindness, her strength, her beauty. What was the nature of their love? A few moments of physical pleasure? No, much more. There was a tie, a connection beyond the physical, given by the gods. They were meant to be together.

"I must go." Cinnia stood up.

"Are you sure?" Mother reached up and touched her cheek. "Pain waits for you."

"Pain is an old friend and not to be feared."

Mother smiled.

Cinnia headed away from the river.

"Daughter!"

She looked over her shoulder. Mother stood much taller. The child had grown to a beautiful young man.

"Tell Afra, when you see her, that her Mother brings Love and Light to the world."

The two figures blazed so brightly, Cinnia had to cover her eyes.

When she opened them it was dark. She saw nothing, but she heard the cubs whimpering with hunger in their pen.

She groaned.

Pain throbbed in her bruised back and wrenched shoulders. Her hands and feet tingled and cramped. She tried to spit out the wad of filthy cloth gagging her mouth but it was bound around her head.

All she could do was wait and think about her dream.

I'll see Afra again!

WITH THE DAWN CAME A CACOPHONY of sounds. The stable hands fed and harnessed the animals for the day's work. The stench of animal manure and urine filled the stable. The mules brayed and balked, the men cursed; but eventually they left. Cinnia heard a couple of boys joking down the aisle as they mucked out the stalls.

"Where's that dangerous barbarian you're supposed to be watching?"

"In the last stall."

"Can I see her?"

"Nah. That Greek woman would have my ball sack for a purse."

"What's one look? We won't get close."

"Mebbe, but just one."

Cinnia heard footsteps and rolled onto her stomach, hiding her face.

"That's it? Not much." A pause. "Nice ass, though."

"Look at those scars. Definitely from swords. And those bruises! She fought four armed guards yesterday and almost got away. I could barely gag her all trussed up like that."

"I thought it was two guards."

"Nah, it was at least three…"

"You, boy!" Clio's voice cut through the chatter. "She still there?"

"Y-Yes, mistress!"

"Here's your coin, now go away."

Cinnia rolled to her side, pulled her knees to her chest, rolled again, and levered herself into a kneeling position. Clio stood clean and dressed in her finest clothes, left arm in a sling; next to a tall muscular man. His bald head gleamed and a gold earring flashed in the light.

He looked Cinnia over. "Hard to tell what you got in there."

"She's a Briton. Fought in the wars and sold as a slave. My husband, may his shade suffer the torments of the damned, gave her gladiator training. Now she's too dangerous for me to handle."

The bald man frowned at the curse and gave the horned warding sign, out of Clio's sight. He approached Cinnia with caution. "Does she understand Roman?"

"When she wants to."

"Stand up."

Cinnia mumbled into her gag. He pulled the binding down. She spat out the sodden cloth. "Can't," she croaked. "Feet bound."

The bald man took a knife out of his belt, cut the bindings, and easily lifted her to her feet. She swayed. It felt like standing on hot knives as feeling slowly returned to her feet.

"Careful, she's a tricky one."

"She's not going anywhere soon. She can barely stand, much less run. Those bindings were tight." He rubbed his jaw. "Gladiator training, you say? What kind?"

"Just the basics. Marcius had the fever-brained idea to match her with another female slave and do exhibitions. Entertainment only. I thought she could earn more money on her back."

Cinnia glared at Clio with loathing.

"She'd be wasted as a whore."

"Are you interested or not? Your master said you could make the deal. If not, I've got other possibilities."

"I'll give you two hundred-fifty *denarii* for her."

"Two hundred-fifty! A male is worth five hundred! How could cheat a poor widow so?"

He raised his hand to stop the tirade. "A widow who curses her dead husband's shade doesn't deserve the title. It's a fair price. Take it or leave it."

Clio shut her mouth and glared at both of them. "Done. Give me the money. I'll give you the paper. I want her out of my sight."

The bald man pulled a pouch from his tunic and counted out ten gold coins.

One of the cubs gave a piercing scream. Cinnia turned to Clio. "What of them?"

"None of your business, bitch."

"But Afra..."

"Afra will be executed by the end of the week."

"No..." *Tell Afra when you see her...*

Clio smiled and left with her coins.

CHAPTER NINETEEN

TWO DAYS LATER, Afra came before the magistrate, a gray-haired man with a stern face and upright posture. He sat at one end of the basilica on a wooden chair with no back, but low arms; scribes took notes as he settled cases. Most were property disputes, with occasional petty theft. The property owners were represented by lawyers who presented their clients' cases. As the morning wore on and nothing much happened, the crowd thinned. Finally, the scribe called Afra's case.

She could barely walk. Blood crusted her face and the front of her tunic. She couldn't see out of one swollen eye.

The scribe announced. "Marcia Afra, a freed woman from Kush, is charged with assaulting a citizen with intent to kill."

The surprised crowd settled. This was why they hung around the law courts.

"What do you say in your defense?"

Afra straightened, wincing from the bruises, and mumbled through swollen lips, "I did not intend to kill Clio. She was mad, a danger to herself and others. I had to subdue her. I left her tied up and returned to release her."

"Liar! She tried to kill me!" Clio called from the crowd.

The crowd laughed. Afra's blood rose. She took a deep breath. Responding with anger was how she had come to this pass.

"The city guards will testify." The magistrate motioned to the two men who brought her in. "Is this the woman you apprehended in the stable two days ago?"

The taller one stepped forward. "Yes, sir."

"Tell your story."

"We apprehended an escaped slave in the city and returned her to her mistress, a citizen named Clio. This woman," he pointed at Afra, "arrived shortly after we did. The two women argued. This great black one here, tried to strangle the other one, but we brought her down before she could."

"So say you?"

The red-faced one nodded. Both stepped back.

"I didn't touch Clio when I returned. Those two beat me down without cause."

"This case is clear," the magistrate said. "We have the testimony of two city guards against the word of an ex-slave."

"A woman freed by a Roman citizen and therefore a citizen!" Afra cried.

The crowd rustled in anticipation of the sentence.

"The punishment for attacking a citizen of Rome—by another citizen or non-citizen—is death in the arena. Take her away."

Afra swayed. She heard Clio's high-pitched hysterical laughter ring out over the crowd.

THIS TIME, they threw Afra into a high-walled, outdoor pen with a dozen other prisoners. Iron chains hobbled her feet but her wrists were free. She twisted the braided-hair bracelet, now blackened with dirt. *Stay strong!*

The first thing Afra noticed was the absence of healthy men. There were two other women: a middle-aged matron dressed better than anyone else and an old crone, who by her muttering and rocking had lost her wits. The old woman jogged a memory, but Afra couldn't place her. These two occupied a spot closest to the gate. The men ranged from a crippled boy sitting next to the women, to a blind ex-soldier proudly wearing his legion insignia, to an older man with a scholar's beard and ink-stained hands. A few looked up at her entrance, most sat in the dust with heads bowed.

Afra shuffled over to the women and the boy. The matron looked her over with a critical eye. "I can't do anything about the eyes, but I do have cloth bindings that might help with the ribs."

"Just want to rest." She indicated a spot in the sun next to the matron.

The woman nodded. Afra sat down.

"Need water?"

"Yes."

The woman rummaged in a leather pack for a clay cup, rose, and fetched water from a barrel set in the middle of the pen.

"One thing they do provide enough of, water. Food's scarce. No blankets. The toilet pit is in that corner." The matron settled beside Afra. "You'll smell it soon as the sun hits it. I'm Bassa, this is Corva, and the boy is Celer."

Afra sipped the stale water. "Thanks. I'm Afra."

Bassa snorted at the obviousness of it. "What's your real name?"

"Amanirenas." It felt strange saying it aloud after all these months.

"Afra it is." Bassa closed her eyes and leaned back. The sun climbed over the wall bringing welcome warmth. "Did you do it?"

"Not what I was convicted of."

"A philosopher?" Bassa laughed and pointed to the bearded scholar. "You should talk to Priscus. He insulted the wrong person with his poems one time, too many. He's here because the guards found a valuable gold plate in his room belonging to that powerful man. Poor Celer stole a shred of meat from his master to feed his pregnant sister. Most here are murderers and thieves. A few, like you and Priscus, claim innocence."

"Did you do it?"

"Yes."

Afra's swollen face almost made it into a smile. "What awful deed did you do?"

"Poisoned my pig of a second husband. When my daughter began to bleed, he started sniffing around her. She came to me in tears one day, after he trapped her in the garden and fondled her breasts. I knew it was a matter of time, so I sent her to my brother, and visited an herb seller." She patted the old woman on the arm. "Unfortunately, Corva is losing her wits. She gave me something that gave him fits rather than heart trouble. He foamed at the mouth. His oldest son became suspicious. They tortured my maid…the rest…" She spread her hands wide indicating her fate. "I tried to kill myself with a knife, but wasn't fast enough."

"An herb seller? Her?" Afra nodded toward the witless old woman.

"Corva had a small shop in the street next to the Temple of Isis."

Afra took a closer look at Corva. "I thought I recognized her. She helped me once."

"You're lucky you're alive."

"She seemed fine."

Bassa shrugged. Corva continued to mutter. Celer whimpered.

Afra dropped into a doze.

That evening, the guards opened the gate and slaves carried in an iron pot filled with a noxious stew and a basket of bread, stale enough to break teeth if not soaked in water or the rancid stew. Most of the prisoners were a sorry lot and acted more like animals than people, when the food arrived. Priscus led the blind soldier to the pot and ensured he got a portion. Bassa and her charges didn't join the fray. Afra raised an eyebrow.

"My daughter brings me food. I share with Corva and Celer. Sorry there's not enough for you."

Afra shrugged and winced as her ribs moved.

"I can help with that." Bassa rummaged in her bottomless leather satchel. She pulled out a length of cloth. "My daughter packed everything she thought I'd need…and more." She ripped the cloth with her teeth. "My first husband was kicked in the ribs by a mule. I had to do this for him after every bath. Let me bind you up, you'll breathe easier."

Afra raised her tunic, so Bassa could wind the lengths tightly around her chest. It did relieve the pressure. "Thanks."

Afra shuffled off to get her portion. She thought she saw a rat tail in the mix and almost gagged, but forced herself to eat the vile stuff to keep up her strength. She wasn't sure why she felt the need to live, but did it anyway.

The gate opened for the slaves to remove the pot. A senior officer in the guard strode in. "Listen up, *noxii*! Our beloved Emperor Nero Claudius Caesar Augustus Germanicus, in light of Pompeii's recent hardship, has generously lifted the restrictions on gladiator games. The esteemed Sextus Licinius Murena will be standing for *aedile* in the next election and will be editor of games to be held in two weeks' time." He gave a vicious smile. "Prepare to die."

He marched out of the pen. The guards shoved the gate shut on the muttering, wails, and moans of the condemned.

"The arena! Why don't they slit our throats or chop off our heads like civilized people?" Bassa paled. "I had hoped because the arena was closed several years ago after the riot, they would send us to the mines."

"I trained with a gladiator. Will they let us fight?"

"Not us. Able-bodied *noxii* sometimes fight each other to the death. We'll probably be fed to the beasts." Bassa sat, head in hands. "If I had only been faster with that knife."

Two weeks. Afra leaned against the wall, eyes closed. *Stay strong Cinnia. Everything changes.*

CHAPTER TWENTY

CINNIA DIDN'T REMEMBER MUCH about the exhausting two-day march to the *ludus*—the gladiator school—at Capua. Calvus, the bald man, added her to a string of twenty slaves he had culled from the prisons and slave markets. They trudged in a single line, chained neck-to-neck, hand-to-hand, up the paved Roman road. Occasionally the smell of new-turned earth or budding olive trees penetrated her fog and she looked out at the slaves toiling in the fields. They had to stand aside for the occasional Imperial courier on horseback or fast-trotting mule chaise.

Cinnia, the sole woman, got no special treatment during the day. When the line took a break they all drank stale water from the same leather flasks and squatted over the same trench to relieve themselves. They all ate a small hard loaf of bread and crumb of cheese at the end of the day. Calvus and the five guards ate little better, having a bit more food and a little sour wine.

Calvus did stake her away from the men at night and gave her a light blanket against the spring chill. The other prisoners huddled together for warmth. Cinnia's fear that Calvus might want to lie with her, faded when he chose the youngest, prettiest male slave to share his bed roll. When one of the guards grabbed her ass, she shouted. Calvus whipped him and ordered that no one touch her. She didn't know why he showed her such a kindness.

"There it is!" One of the guards pointed to a timber and stone fortress, sitting high on a bluff, well outside the Capua city walls. The sun glinted off the ubiquitous red tiles the Romans used for roofs. "That's the *ludus*. Hot food tonight." He poked a prisoner in the ribs with his spear butt and laughed. "At least for me."

Cinnia stifled a groan. It looked like a steep climb up the front of the bluff. Her empty stomach protested, her lower back ached from Clio's kicks, but she clung to her dream, *"When you see Afra again…"* Life at the *ludus* had to better than this dreary trek. She might even hear something of Afra's fate.

She stumbled up the steep slope, through heavy wooden gates, as the sun sat red above the sea to the west. The walls enclosed a patchwork brick and stone building built around a large central training area.

"Another batch," Calvus announced as he passed a scroll to a scribe.

"As sorry a looking bunch of filthy turds as I've ever seen," a voice boomed from the door.

"Better pickings this time, Silo" Calvus smiled. "Something special."

Cinnia looked up. A big man, once strong, but now going to fat, lounged in the door. His close-set eyes squatted in a face dominated by a knife-blade nose. He spat in the dust. "What's so special about these scrawny, broken-down, sorry-assed dogs." He walked down the row, punching slaves in the chest, pulling their arms out to inspect their biceps.

When he got to Cinnia, his eyes lit up. "A female! The Emperor pays well for women in the arena." He looked her over. "Gaulish bitch? Good fighters, the Gauls. One of their women nearly took my head." He put his face close to Cinnia's. "Before I ran her through with my sword and spit her baby on a spear."

"Iceni," Cinnia spat.

"Gaul. Iceni. No one cares in the games. You'll be what I say you are and be happy with it."

Cinnia kept her face impassive. Her brief anger, drowned by hunger and fatigue.

He turned back to the line of prisoners. "I'm Silo the *lanista* of this *ludus*—the best gladiator school in Italy. Until you've won in the arena, you're piles of shit. You got that?" He glared at the prisoners, jaw jutted forward.

He turned to their guards. "Take 'em inside."

They passed into the chill shade of the building's entrance; through two more rooms, and back into the sun in the rectangular practice area. There a blacksmith struck off the chains, but left on the leg cuffs. Cinnia could feel the last of her strength draining.

"This way." One of the ubiquitous guards waved them through another door. "Strip." He leered as Cinnia removed her filthy tunic.

"Here," one of three men called her over. His grizzled hair receded from a high forehead. Bushy brows sheltered large brown eyes. "Sit."

He felt Cinnia's head, smelled her breath, and checked her teeth. "Stand. Raise your arms over your head." He clucked to himself at her scars, smiled at her well-muscled arms and legs, and frowned at the lurid bruises on her back. "Blood in your piss?"

"You a healer?"

"Physician. Trained in Alexandria." He raised an eyebrow. "Ever heard of it?"

"A friend visited there once and told me of it."

He nodded and asked again, "Blood in your piss?"

"For two days, not now."

"What's this?" he reached for the small amulet of Isis hanging between her breasts.

Cinnia slapped his hand away. "Do you wish your manhood to shrivel and drop off? This is sacred to my goddess."

"Isis?" He squinted at the small figure. "Aren't you Gaulish?"

"Iceni, a Briton." She covered the amulet. "My friend gave it to me."

"Same friend?"

She nodded.

"She'll do," the physician said to one of the guards and tossed her a clean, but much patched tunic. "If you piss blood again, come back."

A guard prodded her toward a scribe with a bored look on his face. The scribe looked up. "Do you vow to follow all the rules of a gladiator;

to pledge your body and soul to your master; or, if you fail, to die by burning, beating or by the sword?"

"What?"

"Put your mark there." The scribe pointed to a list, probably names.

Cinnia wet her thumb in the ink and put it on the paper where the scribe pointed.

"Next!"

The guard took Cinnia and the other slaves out of the infirmary to a long row of small rooms, three steps wide and four deep. Each had two pallets on the stone floor and no pegs to hang clothes. The guard fastened a chain to one of her leg cuffs and grinned. "Be a good girl and you'll be allowed to sleep without the chain." He kicked a noisome bucket. "If you need it before morning."

"Food?"

"Tomorrow. Kitchen's closed tonight."

Cinnia slept clutching the amulet and had no dreams.

A BLARING HORN, more musical than the *carnyx*, woke Cinnia. Guards walked down the row, pounding on wooden doors and bellowing, "Out of there, maggots, if you want anything to eat!"

A different guard from the night before pushed Cinnia's door open and smiled. "They said you were a beauty." He looked her over. "A bit scrawny for my taste, but better on the eyes than most of those pathetic bastards."

Cinnia pulled her lips into a snarl, but held her tongue, when the guard stroked her leg before loosening her chain. She longed to kick him in the balls; crush his head between knee and fists, but until she knew of Afra, she would do nothing.

"This way." The guard pushed her out the door to join a line of people. She recognized several from the trek. They walked under a colonnade, heading for the far wall. The line quickened at the smell of food. A boy, with glossy black hair and crooked teeth, shoved a wooden bowl and spoon in her hands as she entered. Cinnia took her place in one of four lines where cooks stood at large crocks, ladling a thick soup of barley and beans into the bowls. She grabbed a mug of watered wine and looked over the room for a place to sit.

The men sat on rough benches pulled up to long wooden tables. Cinnia spied a seat on the end of a bench with an arm's length between her and the next person. There were occasional grunts and mutters, but, for the most part, the men remained silent, sending curious glances her way. Most bolted their food and went back for more.

Cinnia barely finished when another guard entered and bellowed, "Outside. Lineup, you dogs!" They all jumped up and headed toward the door.

Cinnia blinked at the strong sun radiating off the practice sand.

Silo, with a short leather whip, stood flanked by five other men. "Most of you are slaves, prisoners of war, or criminals condemned to the arena. A few of you are here by choice." He nodded to a handful of men, better dressed than the prisoners, and wearing no slave collar. "All of you have taken the oath to serve as gladiators or suffer an ignoble death. Unless you train hard and be the best, you *will* die. But a few, a lucky few, will triumph and earn their freedom. Until then, your ass is mine!

"These are your trainers." Silo waved his hand to the men at his side. "Each *doctore* teaches a specialty. Learn it well or…" He mimed a knife cutting his throat.

Each trainer stepped forward and read names off the list. "With me."

Finally, Cinnia stood alone, looking around, puzzled.

"Females have a special trainer. We work the men so hard you'd think they couldn't raise their eyelids much less their pricks." Silo shook his head. "But females cause trouble. I wouldn't have women here at all, if the Emperor hadn't become so fascinated with the novelty of it." He shrugged. "Money is money. Follow me."

The other new recruits were clustered around their trainers, learning the fine art of jabbing at a stake with a wooden sword. A few were lifting rocks or hauling logs with chains. Cinnia smiled to herself. At least she knew how to do that.

Silo led her to a large room at the far end of the complex, flooded with light from the windows high up on all sides. Most of the buildings Cinnia had been in had natural light from an interior colonnade and three blank walls. The floor was covered in sand. Dust motes danced in the sunbeams. Next to the ever-present wooden stake, three women stretched. Dressed in brief sleeveless tunics, sweat and oil gleamed on their muscular arms and legs.

"Barba?"

A burly man with ginger hair and a grizzled beard—unusual for a Roman—stepped out of the shadows.

Silo shoved Cinnia forward. "Here's your new recruit. Cinnia." He smiled at the other women. "Work them hard, Barba. They may be women, but they'll have to fight and die like men." He turned and stomped out.

"Turn around," Barba ordered. He looked at Cinnia in the same way Silo and the physician had, assessing, calculating; nothing sexual at all. "Did those idiot guards put you in the barracks last night?"

Cinnia shrugged.

"Anyone molest you?"

"No."

"Good. The women have special quarters." Barba scratched his bushy beard, an action that caught Cinnia's breath. *Dumnor!*

She shook her head. *Ghosts and shades.* Cinnia turned her attention back to the living.

"Meet your companions for the next several months. Gerta." Barba pointed to a tall blond, with the blunt features of a German, who towered over the other two by a head.

"Portia." A tall, but stocky, woman with auburn hair and green eyes, ignored Cinnia.

The last woman had a Roman cast to her face—long curved nose and small bowed mouth—and the build of a dancer. Dark curly hair escaped from a braid pinned tightly to her head. "Julia."

Julia looked up, with startling blue eyes, and smiled. "Welcome."

Cinnia smiled at Julia; nodded to the other two women.

"First we need to get you outfitted," Barba said. "Julia, take her to the blacksmith to get rid of those cuffs, then the quartermaster's."

"This way." Julia headed back toward the front of the *ludus*. "Which province are you from?"

"Britannia."

"I heard the crier in the town square tell of those wars. A mighty victory for the Romans."

"Aren't you Roman?"

"My mother claims my father was a senator, but…" Julia shrugged her shoulders. "She was a slave from northern Greece. My master needed money, so he sold me. Calvus spotted me and Gerta in the auction and bought us for Silo. It's better than a cheap brothel or one of the big farms. At least I have the chance to be free in a few years."

"My former mistress tried to rent me out to a brothel. I left."

"Calvus looks for more than height and muscle." Julia nodded. "You have to have spirit, as well. He picked us out of over two hundred women. Most were timid little mice."

The same blacksmith as yesterday removed Cinnia's leg cuffs.

"Better?" Julia asked on the walk to the quartermaster's

"Much!" Cinnia grinned. "My legs feel so light, I might jump the wall."

"Don't joke about escaping." Julia's eyes went round. "There are ears everywhere. Silo and the guards look to their backs. They sleep uneasy at the thought of the gladiators taking up arms and escaping. That's why we're locked in our cells at night and practice with wooden and blunted weapons."

"No one has ever tried?"

"I heard rumors of a few in years past." Julia shrugged. "None successful."

Cinnia had given no thought to escape. She didn't know where she would go or how she would live without Afra. *But everything changes.*

Julia stopped before a window that opened into a store room. Clothes, belts, shoes, blankets, and more graced open shelves in orderly mounds. "Fullo! You here?"

A skinny youth, with sallow skin and spots, came from a door set in the back. At the sight of the women, his face split into an inane grin. He stammered, "J-Julia!"

"Cinnia needs a kit."

He ducked his head and clucked to himself.

"He's shy," Julia whispered. "He came here as a boy and hasn't met many women."

Fullo turned to the various shelves, pulling things down, inspecting them. Some he returned to their places, others he put carefully in a pile on a small table under the window. When done, he shoved the pile into Julia's arms and, not looking at Cinnia, said, "J-Julia will explain."

"Thanks, Fullo." Julia smiled at the boy.

He beat a hasty retreat to his back room, blushing.

"Our quarters are over here."

Julia showed Cinnia a much bigger room than the tiny cell she inhabited the night before. Three narrow beds attached to the walls, reminded Cinnia of the brothel's arrangement. Here, each bed came with a niche and pegs for storage. A small table graced the middle of the room with two backless stools stored underneath. Brown wool blankets covered two of the beds on opposite sides of the door.

Julia set the pile on the empty bed at the back. "Let's see what Fullo gave you. Blanket, wooden comb, clay cup, tunic, loin cloth, belt, breast band, hair bands, sandals. Yes, these are the basics. Next winter you'll get socks and a cloak. If you bleed, we have cloths on that shelf." Julia indicated another recessed area next to the door, stacked with felted cloth.

"*If* I bleed?"

"Many women find they stop having their monthlies when they train as a gladiator."

"You?

"Sometimes. Not regular like before."

Cinnia looked at the pile. Since she had arrived in this foreign land, she had not had so many possessions: a tunic, a cord belt, a broken comb, no more. She felt almost rich. She fingered the thick blanket; admired the sturdy, but plain, leather belt and sandals. "Do we wash our own?"

"Launderers pick up our dirty things each night and leave clean for the morning."

Cinnia held up the triangular loincloth. "What's this?"

"*Subligaculum*. That, and the breast band, is what we wear in the arena. Actually these are to practice in. The ones we will wear in the arena will be much showier. The men's have tassels and bells." Julia took the cloth from her. "Here, I'll show you. Raise your tunic."

Cinnia pulled her tunic up to expose her lean belly and bare bottom.

Julia leaned in close to reach around her back. Her hair smelled of meadow flowers.

"You put the wide area at the back and tie two corners in front. Pull the third corner between your legs, under the knot and the extra fabric hangs down over the knot like this." She grabbed the wide leather belt. "This goes over the top of the whole thing to keep it from falling off and to cover the knots."

"Women wear these?" It felt strange. "I thought we'd fight in short tunics."

"Women and men. What do you normally wear?"

"Nothing. In cold weather we wear trousers, but nothing under them." Cinnia looked into Julia's blue eyes and smiled. "Thank you. Few have been so kind."

"I'm the best you'll get here." She laughed. "Gerta knows little Roman and speaks less. Portia is a stuck-up bitch and has her own room. I heard she came from a senatorial family and ran away to the gladiator school to avoid a hated marriage. She doesn't wear a slave collar. Personally, I think there are less dangerous ways to avoid marriage. Keep away from the men, especially the non-slaves. They think there's only one use for a woman. If Silo or Barba catches them, they'll be flogged, but the damage will already be done. Calvus is all right."

A horn sounded in the courtyard.

"Jupiter's balls! We need to get back to the practice room or Barba will have my hide for a belt."

Cinnia smiled. *Hacking at a wooden stake is much better than serving as a whore.*

Chapter Twenty-one

THE NIGHT BEFORE THE EXECUTIONS, Afra huddled with Bassa, Corva, and Celer, sharing their body warmth. After two weeks, her ribs felt better and the swelling was gone from her face, but hunger wracked her body and hopelessness blotched her soul.

Most of the condemned prisoners shared her misery. Afra listened to a steady murmur of prayers, curses, and ravings. Priscus wrote in the dirt, digging with his long fingernails.

Mother Isis warned of great pain and possible death. Is this my fate? Did I not honor the gods well enough? What choices did I have?

Afra shook her head. Everything she did—trying to save Asata, doing her best for Marcius, rescuing the cubs, loving Cinnia—was who she was. She could not have done differently without being a different person. Her mistake had been losing her temper with Clio. The woman had always been a goad. In her fatigue and fear, Afra had acted rashly. In most cases, that instinct for action played her fair, but this time it had betrayed her.

She sat twisting the braided hair around her wrist. *Cinnia, I'm sorry. I failed you. Live long and may happiness find you.*

"Afra?" Bassa put a hand on her shoulder. "You've worked with beasts. Do they kill quickly?"

"If you run from a great cat, it will land on your back and bite through your neck. That is fairly quick." She ran her hands over her head. Her hair grew longer and she twisted strands into tiny knots. "Wolves, dogs, hyenas will go for the throat or belly. The throat is fast. You can live for several minutes with your belly torn out."

"So we should run?"

A scene flashed from a half-forgotten hunt: a line of people beating drums and thrashing the bushes to drive all the animals before them.

"No." Afra sat up straighter; hope giving her a measure of strength. "I have a plan. I don't know if it will save us, but it is better than running."

THE NEXT MORNING THE GUARDS put them in irons and paraded them through the streets of Pompeii to the amphitheater. Everywhere they went the people jeered and pointed. A few threw dung or rotted food at the condemned.

The city looked different after nearly three weeks: most of the rubble cleared, unbroken statues put right. No builders scrambled on scaffolds surrounding the civic buildings. It was a public holiday. Almost the entire population wended its way to the arena.

Afra's stomach grumbled as they entered the open plaza surrounding the arena. The city fathers evidently hadn't wanted to waste even rat stew on the condemned criminals. The rich smell of roasting meat vied with the comforting smell of baked bread as the guards herded them through the plaza. Afra, standing taller than nearly everyone, noted the vendors selling food, wine, and trinkets from niches in the solid stone walls of the amphitheater.

A small boy ran past screaming with delight, waving a small clay figure of a gladiator. A slight smile tugged at her lips, until her thoughts turned to her own fate.

Mother Isis, give me—give us all—strength. Whatever my destiny, I put my life and fate in your hands.

The guards herded them into a dark cell, beneath the amphitheater seats, where they struck off the prisoners' shackles. They heard, muffled through the stone, the trumpets and crowd roar during the initial entrance of the *editor* and the parade of gladiators.

"The entertainers will be doing their fake fights now." Bassa listened to the crowd laugh. "They'll be coming for us soon."

Afra gathered Bassa, Corva, and Celer. "You remember what to do?"

"Stay together, flap our arms to look big, yell," Celer ticked off the points on his fingers. "Do you really think this will work?"

"I don't know, but it's our only hope." Afra looked over her little troop. Bassa tried to explain to Corva, again, what she should do, but the old woman looked at her blankly.

"I overheard your plan." Priscus joined them with the blind soldier. "Do you think two more bodies would help?"

"It couldn't hurt." Afra shrugged. "Keep your friend facing the right way. When we get out on the sand, stay close to me. Follow my directions."

The heavy door creaked open. "Out, you *noxii,* and give the audience a good show!"

Guards, armed with spears, laughed as they herded the condemned down a dark corridor. At the door to the arena, two slaves stood with buckets and brushes. As each prisoner passed, the slaves slathered them with red gore.

The iron tang of blood filled Afra's nostrils as the slave painted her limbs with the sticky stuff. She walked out the door onto the floor of the arena. The late morning sun sparkled on the sand, dazzling her eyes. She squinted, picked up a hand full of sand, and tried to clean the blood from her arms. She could do nothing about the stains already soaked into her tunic.

More and more condemned poured from the door. Afra gathered her small troop and moved away from the others, toward the end of the arena, where they could keep the animals from coming at them from behind.

"Take the blood off with the sand, if you can." All but Corva followed her example.

Trumpets sounded and the narrator of the games called out, "The esteemed Sextus Licinius Murena, giver of the games, now presents the execution of criminals by the beasts! These are murderous slaves, thieves, rebels condemned to an ignoble death! Let the sentence be done!"

Arena slaves dressed in bright red tunics, hauled several covered cages on wagons into the arena. One hauled back a tarp and opened the cage door with a lance. A huge male lion emerged, lean from hunger. He blinked in the bright light, roared, and tried to retreat back into the cage. The beast handlers prodded him in the hind quarters with iron-tipped spears until he ran onto the sand. The crowd shouted its approval.

Afra watched the big cat with sympathy. Male lions usually didn't hunt, particularly during the day. He was starved, stunned by the light, and confused by the noise of the crowd. If all the animals were in this shape, they might, *just might,* have a chance of survival.

Other doors opened. More hungry, confused animals lumbered onto the arena floor: another lion—a female, a couple of enormous dogs with slavering jaws, a leopard, and a huge shaggy animal she had seen as a pelt on a floor. Marcius called it a bear.

Some of the condemned men panicked and ran; attracting the attention of the predators. The bear brought down one man, breaking his back with a single swipe of his powerful paws. The lioness jumped another man, tearing out his throat. Chaos reigned as people ran screaming, chased and mauled by the animals. The stench of entrails wafted on the heat. The crowd shouted and pointed at particularly gruesome deaths.

"Line up!" Afra shouted to her charges. They lined up, except for Corva who sat in the sand behind them. The male lion was the first to approach them. "Step forward! Yell!"

As a group, they stepped toward the lion, flapped their arms, and shouted. He veered off in search of easier prey. Afra watched the animals closely, assessing their danger to her small troop. A pair of cheetahs streaked across the arena. The smaller cats avoided the other predators, looking to scavenge already-downed prey.

Afra's heart leaped. She shouted a wild ululation, scaring off the approaching leopard.

"Mari! Cari! To me!"

At the sound of Afra's voice, the cheetahs turned away from a pile of entrails and raced toward the small knot of people, chirping a greeting.

"They're mine," she shouted to her followers. "Stay behind me." Afra stepped out of the line. The cheetahs ran to her feet. She kneeled down and grabbed each, burying her face in their fur, laughing and sobbing. They rumbled with pleasure.

"My sisters! Mother Isis is indeed great!" She felt their ribs. "But you're so skinny!"

By now the crowd had noticed the unusual behavior. They started to shout, some encouraging, others in anger.

"Look! They're a bunch of women and cripples!" Someone shouted. Others started to mutter. "Mercy for the women and gray hairs!"

The *editor* called over an attendant and said something.

"Mari. Cari. Guard!" The cheetahs stationed themselves on either side of Afra, facing the other animals. Most of the other condemned were dead or dying. A row of beast handlers at the other end of the arena were prodding animals off their prey with their spears and leather whips, herding them toward the survivors.

With a hand signal, Afra sent Mari and Cari to head off the female lion trying to sneak around the end of the line. Lions killed cheetahs in the wild, but they usually hunted as a pride.

Afra held her breath, fear for her cheetahs, struggling with pride in their bravery. The strange situation was enough. The lioness snarled and turned back.

The bear came next. Afra had never seen such a creature. When it stood on its hind legs and roared, she thought they were dead. It dropped to its four legs and lumbered forward, shaking its head from side to side.

"It can't see well. Shout and flap!"

In the face of a wall of noise and movement the bear retreated. One of the beast handlers tried to prod it forward, but the bear grabbed the spear in his mouth and swiped at the man, opening his stomach with one pass of his paw. The beast handlers retreated carrying their downed colleague. The animals trailed after the fresh blood or left for easier prey.

Afra listened to the crowd as she watched the animals retreat. The mood seemed confused. She heard shouts for mercy and others complaining about the lack of a show. "Mari!" Afra shouted and pointed. The animal raced away. "Stop!" Mari skidded to a stop, sand flying. "Return!" The cat padded to her feet. "Down!" When the cat lay at her feet she reached down and rubbed her ears. The crowd roared its approval.

Afra picked up a bloody arm bone, dropped by one of the beasts. "Cari! Retrieve!" She threw the bone in front of the *editor's* box. The cheetah raced after it, grabbed it in her jaws, and returned. "Give!" The great cat put the bloody bit in Afra's hand. "Down! Over!" Cari rolled onto her back. Afra rubbed her lean belly. People were now whistling and shouting for more.

"Good girls," she whispered to both. "Up!" Both came to their feet. Afra gave another signal. Mari stood on her hind legs, facing Afra, front paws on her shoulders. A few in the crowd shrieked, thinking the cats were, at last, attacking. Mari gave Afra's face a good licking. The cat's rough tongue felt good on her sweaty skin, but Afra wrinkled her nose at the blast of rotten meat smell from Mari's breath.

A trumpet sounded. The crowd quieted.

Afra ordered Mari down and both cats to her heels. They stood still; tails twitching.

The *editor* stood in his box. The narrator announced, "Survivors of the beasts, come forward. Handlers, round up your animals."

Afra looked over her shoulder at her troop. Hope showed in their eyes. Flanked by the cheetahs, followed by her companions, she made her way to the editor's box. They were a pathetic bunch, covered in blood and dust; the hale helping the lame, blind, and mad. A high fence separated the sand from the stands. Guards, armed with bows, stood around the wall. No animal or human could escape or cause mayhem in the stands.

Afra looked up at the *editor,* recognizing the magistrate who condemned her to the arena. A lump formed in her stomach. Their fate would be determined by this man…and the crowd.

Sextus Licinius Murena held out his arm and addressed the crowd. "What say you?"

"*Missio! Missio!*" roared the crowd. Mari and Cari added their cries.

Reprieve! Afra gave the hand movement to the cats. They sat next to her, ears twitching at the noise. *But not freedom.*

"*Missio!*" declared the magistrate.

The crowd shouted its approval. Sextus Licinius Murena took his seat. The last of the animals disappeared into their cages. Guards came on the sand to escort the survivors through the Gate of the Living. They kept a good distance from the cheetahs. As they entered the dark passage, the water organ began a lively tune. Workers rushed out to carry off the bodies and prepare the sand for the afternoon gladiator games.

"You lot, in here," a guard ordered them into a holding cell. "Not you." He barred Afra's way with his spear. "Our esteemed *editor* wants to see you. The cats go back to their cages."

"They must be fed first."

"I'm sure the beast handlers have something for them."

"Not human flesh!"

He grunted and indicated stairs leading down another dark tunnel.

"To me." The cats stalked at her heels as she followed the guard into the underbelly of the arena. Oiled torches provided flickering light. The farther they went the more restless the cats became. The smell of blood, sweat, and fear permeated the air. Soon they were hissing and chirping in distress.

"How far?"

"Next corridor."

She smelled it before they came out into a large room filled with cages of wild cats. The dogs and bears must be kept separate. The smell of wet fur, blood, and cat musk hung in the air like a miasma. The female lion had blood on her muzzle. The leopard lay panting, lethargic, its belly filled with human flesh. A wiry man with claw scars across his left bicep and missing two fingers; jumped to his feet with a big smile. "Wonderful work with those cheetahs. Never saw anything like it. Can you teach me your training techniques?"

"Later, Naso. Murena wants to see her. We need to get these cats put away."

Naso's smile slipped. "Over there."

Afra inspected the cages. "I need clean straw, fresh water, and meat—not human."

Naso muttered, but did as she asked. Afra coaxed the animals into their cages with pats, murmurs, and large joints of beef. "Take good care of them. I'll be back."

The guard next led her to a suite of rooms under the seats, behind the editor's box, where the magistrate and his guests enjoyed a mid-day meal. A joint of ham, eels in garlic, salads, and dozens of dishes Afra couldn't identify covered the tables. A slave in blue livery served wine in delicate stemmed glasses.

Her stomach cramped and mouth watered.

The magistrate spied her and pointed to a side door. The guard took her into a small room painted bright yellow, with green vines twining around the walls. A chandelier of oil lamps lit the room, furnished with a couple of folding camp chairs.

Afra ignored the seats and prowled the perimeter of the room. She couldn't smell herself, but knew she must be stinking up the small room. She shook her head, three weeks of sweat, blood, and dust were the least of her worries.

The door opened. Sextus Licinius Murena entered with a guard. His nose twitched, but he didn't say anything until he took a seat. "Quite a performance you put on, Marcia Afra."

Afra started.

"That is your name?"

"Yes. I'm a free woman from Kush."

"*Were* a free woman."

Afra kept her face blank.

"I remember your case. You're a striking figure, even after a beating." He gave her a slight smile. "You claimed innocence if I remember right."

"Yes."

"Are you?"

"I did tie Clio up, but I never intended murder. I returned."

"And the others in your little band?"

"A mother who protected her child, a mad old woman, a crippled boy who stole to feed his family, a scholar who insulted the wrong man, a soldier who served Rome well and was turned out to beg when blinded."

"Sad stories, all, but you have some of the facts wrong. The mother murdered her husband. The mad old woman sold her the poison. It doesn't matter that Bassa thought she protected her daughter. She could have left her husband. Bassa and…" he consulted a list, "Corva, the poisoner will die. The soldier is a deserter blinded after he came home. His centurion saw him on the street begging and turned him in. We must retain discipline in the ranks. Desertion is punished by death. The arena was the appropriate fate for those three, but now they will have a more merciful death."

Afra had to admit the justice of his statements. Bassa freely admitted her murder and had accepted her punishment of death…just not in the arena. Corva, whether in her right mind or not, did wrong. The soldier? She didn't know one way or the other, but Murena seemed well-informed.

"The other two are trickier cases." He consulted the list again. "The slave boy Celer stole food. He admitted it, but it's a slight infraction; more worthy of a beating than beasts. It's illegal for a master to condemn a criminal slave to the beasts without a hearing before the urban prefect. However, I suspect his master gave a small gift to the prefect, because he didn't want the expense of a crippled slave and couldn't sell him. I'll see what I can do to finding another household for him to serve in."

"Thank you, sir. And Priscus?"

"Our mouthy poet, condemned for stealing gold from Gnaeus Cornelius Arvina."

Afra was startled by the huge smile on the magistrate's face. He seemed about to laugh out loud, but controlled it.

"Arvina happens to be my rival for *aedile* in the upcoming elections. Priscus skewered him in several, clever, humorous poems. I doubt the old man gained access to Arvina's household to steal the plate. However, I have no proof. I can commute his sentence, not set him free. He'll have the option of suicide or slavery. I'm currently in need of a good secretary. Perhaps he'll consider that position over self-destruction." He looked closely at Afra. "And that leaves you."

"You have my fate in your hands, Excellency. You have shown yourself merciful and fair in your judgments."

"The appropriate fates for all the others were clear to me, but yours?"

Afra gazed steadily into his eyes. She would not argue or beg for mercy.

"Whether or not you intended murder, you did assault a Roman citizen. Roman law demands your enslavement and condemns you to the arena. However, the crowd commuted your sentence from death by beasts with their cries for *missio*."

He paused. She held her breath.

"You're wasted as a *noxii*. I'm sending you to a gladiator school. I happen to have part ownership in a good one outside the city. You'll be a slave, but if you work hard, you could buy your freedom with your winnings or earn it from the crowd. They seem to like you."

Afra bowed her head. *Still a slave, but I have a chance. Praise to you, Mother Isis.* "May I ask a favor, Excellency?"

"I believe I've done enough."

"The cheetahs…?" She wouldn't plead for herself, but would for them.

"Ah, yes, remarkable animals."

"Please sir, would you take them? I trained them to be game hunters, not executioners."

"I have a country estate where they can be installed. They should be happy there. I'll be most pleased to have them. I'll send my huntsman to you to learn your secrets."

"May the gods smile on you, sir."

He motioned to the guard. "Take her directly to the *ludus*. I'll write orders for the disposal of the others."

Afra bowed.

Chapter Twenty-two

Cinnia sat at their small table staring at the bowl brimming with cooked barley—filling, but unsatisfying. She longed for a dollop of honey to sweeten the mix. Six months of hard work and good, but bland, food put more muscle on her frame. She was quicker than the lumbering Gerta and could outlast the dancing Julia. Portia was a better match, but the Roman woman didn't have Cinnia's drive.

Julia rushed in, "Have you heard?"

"What?"

"Silo's in a towering rage. That group of Parthians that came in yesterday. The ones he had such high hopes for? All dead!"

"Not the plague!"

"They strangled one another. The last one bashed his head against the wall. The noise brought the guards, but it was too late. He died in the infirmary during the night."

"I wouldn't want to be the guards on that watch!" Suicide wasn't common, but did happen among the fighters. Their training was harsh, the arena brutal. Not a few gave in to despair. They were guarded night and day to prevent such losses. The guards that lost those men would be lucky to escape the arena themselves.

"Any other news?"

"About what?" Julia teased.

"Afra, who else?" Cinnia sometimes grew tired of Julia's light ways, but the Roman woman seemed to have friends everywhere who passed on gossip and news. She had offered to inquire, as best she could, about Afra.

The blue eyes sparkled. "Yes!"

"Yes?" Cinnia jumped up and shook Julia by the shoulders. "And you told me of the Parthians first? What? What news?"

Julia brushed her hands away, pouting. "I'm not sure I should tell you. After all, it might not be Afra."

"Please, Julia." Cinnia tamped down her impatience. "For friendship's sake?"

"Fine." Julia plopped onto her bed. Her eyes drifted shut; a slight smile played on her lips.

Cinnia kept quiet, knowing she would get the news faster with silence, but itching to strangle the woman.

"The carter who brings the vegetables had an interesting story. It seems that several months ago an Ethiopian woman, condemned to death by beasts in the arena at Pompeii, saved herself and a handful of others. She's evidently a sorceress with power over animals. She commanded two devil cats to guard her. The other beasts turned on their handlers. The crowd cried '*Missio*' and they were reprieved."

"It has to be Afra! And the cubs." Cinnia leaned over and kissed Julia on the lips. Her friend's eyes flew wide. "What luck! No one else could do such a thing!"

Afra's alive! Blessings on you, Mother Isis!

Cinnia danced around the small room then stopped. "What happened after the arena?"

"The *editor* sent her to his *ludus* outside Pompeii." Julia folded her arms over her breast band. "Personally, I don't see why the crowd cried '*Missio*.' Such a powerful sorceress should be put to death."

"Julia!" Cinnia gave a sharp glance at the woman. "There was no magic. Afra trained those cats—they're called cheetahs—from infancy. They would die for her." She took Julia's hands in hers. "Afra is a woman, like you, and the gods made her for me."

"We should go." Julia withdrew her hands and rose.

The other woman's coldness couldn't spoil Cinnia's high spirits. *Afra's alive!*

They strode down the peristyle, past the men assembled in the practice area, doing morning exercises with their heavy wooden swords. The men rarely missed an opportunity to hoot and taunt the women, but Silo and Barba made it clear they were not to be touched. Besides the men had other ways to satisfy themselves. Cinnia frequently saw prostitutes delivered to the male barracks. Once she saw a well-dressed woman wrapped in an expensive cloak escorted to a special room outfitted with a large soft bed.

Cinnia bit her thumb at one gladiator who shouted a particularly rude comment and lengthened her stride.

Gerta occupied the women's practice room, hacking at the wooden stake. When they entered, she stopped, wiped the sweat from her brow and smiled. Over the past months the massive German had become friendlier. Julia tried to help her with the language. Cinnia suspected she understood nearly everything, but she spoke little. Portia was late, but she probably wouldn't be punished. Cinnia had seen coins pass between her and Barba.

Their trainer, sorting equipment in a corner, looked up. "Full kit today, including helmets."

The three women groaned in unison. It was high summer and, though early morning, sweat already soaked Cinnia's breast band. The room, cut off from the breezes outside, would soon become stifling. Barba claimed it helped prepare them for the heat of the arena.

Julia picked up the blunted trident, lead-weighted net, and shoulder guard of the *retiarius*. The lightly-armed gladiator style suited her quick feet. In the ring she'd have a sharp knife to cut away her net if her opponent caught it, but that wasn't allowed in practice.

Gerta hefted the full-sized rectangular shield, greaves, arm guard, and stifling helmet of the *secutor*. Heavily armored, the *secutor* style was good for defense, but the helmet enclosed the whole head; the tiny eye holes allowed limited vision.

Cinnia took up the smaller rectangular shield, curved sword, and crested helmet of the Thracian. Greaves for both legs and articulated full right arm guard, gave the Thracian style gladiator more protection than the *retiarius* and more flexibility than the *secutor*. The faceplate on the helmet had grills that allowed good forward vision. That left Portia's *myrmilla* equipment; similar to Cinnia's, but with a full-sized shield, short straight *gladius*, leather arm guard, and one greave.

The women helped each other tie on the quilted material that protected their legs and arms; buckled on the greaves and guards. They were nearly finished when Portia showed up.

"I see our princess deigned to join us this morning." Barba stalked over to the auburn-haired woman. "An extra hour of practice for being late."

Portia sputtered, "How dare…"

Barba back-handed her across the face. "You took an oath, like these others, but you had a choice. This is not a game! A bigger room and better food is one thing. Training is another. You train or you die. Now get your equipment."

Portia scowled, wiping blood from her nose, but donned her equipment without further complaint.

They stood in a line, helmets at their feet, while Barba inspected them, tugging on a knot here, tightening a buckle there.

"You'll have to do." He sighed. "We're contracted for the Apollo games in Nuceria. That's a week away. You'll fight as *tirones* with other women from another *ludus*. I expect you all to come back."

Cinnia nodded. *Tirones*—new recruit—was the most dangerous level. The crowds wanted sport and skill. The awkward fights of the *tirones* usually resulted in death for the loser. Barba explained this is where the *lanista* took the most losses. Once a gladiator reached the highest level of *primus palus*, it was rare the crowd asked for death, although the loser might die of the wounds he—or she—sustained in the fight.

Cinnia trained harder, staying for Portia's extra punishment hour to practice. She needed to survive these games.

*****

CINNIA DRAGGED HER ACHING BODY to the baths. She sniffed at the heavy musk of male sweat lingering in the rooms. Portia had a servant to tend her needs. There was no sign of Gerta, but Julia scraped the last of the oil from her body with a curved *strigil*. Cinnia found this Roman practice of cleansing by rubbing oil over the body and scraping off the oil, sweat, and dirt strange. The Romans knew about soap from the Gauls, but preferred their own ways. Cinnia had to admit it left her skin baby soft and sweet-smelling. Plus, the masseuses did a brisk business selling the scrapings of champion gladiators. Evidently, rich Roman women used it as an aphrodisiac. Did they drink it or rub it on their bodies? Cinnia wrinkled her nose at the thought of either and gave a slight shudder.

Julia looked up, smiling. "Tired?"

"I barely have the strength to lift a cup of water." Cinnia groaned and sat down next to her. The cool stone felt good on her bare bottom. "I swear by the triple goddess that my hair aches."

Julia pushed her onto her stomach. "The massage slaves have left for the afternoon rest, but I know a few of their tricks."

Cinnia moaned with pleasure as Julia rubbed in the oil and kneaded her knotted shoulders.

"Better?"

"Much!" Cinnia sat up and began scraping the oil from her limbs. The brass *strigil* pulled at the few hairs left on her legs. "Ouch."

The barbers had removed all the hair from under her arms and the bush between her legs in a painful process of tweezing and pulling out the hairs. The *strigil* served the same purpose for her legs.

Cinnia grumbled, "Why do the Romans hate body hair?"

"If you haven't noticed, it gets hot in this part of the world." Julia fanned herself with her hands. "Besides bugs like to live in hair." She wrinkled her mouth in distaste.

Cinnia scratched her shorn pubic area. "It's as itchy without hair as with bugs."

Julia rolled her eyes. "Let's bathe."

They skipped the hot room, having sweated enough, and went for the cold plunge. Cinnia relaxed on the edge of the tiny, but deep, pool. Most people came from the steam room and walked into the water up to their necks, then came right out. Cinnia liked to linger a bit. In this heat, it wasn't cold enough to raise gooseflesh. The cool water refreshed her.

Julia seemed to like it less. She quickly moved onto the warm pool. During the winter, fires heated the water as it moved through the pipes, but during the summer, the water sat in a stone tank outside the walls, warmed by the sun. This pool wasn't big enough to swim in, like the public baths in Pompeii.

Cinnia found Julia floating in the warm pool, on her back, eyes closed, smiling. Her hair floated loose like a dark cloud around her head and shoulders. Cinnia's breath caught in her chest at the sight of Julia's small mounded breasts. Heat built in her groin—a feeling she hadn't had since she and Afra made love, how many months ago? The thought that her body betrayed her brought unwanted color to her cheeks. She had seen Julia naked every day for months, why today, did Julia's body call to her own?

Julia's eyes opened in a lazy, half-lidded way, showing flashes of blue.

Cinnia jumped into the pool, splashing her friend, trying to cover her own insistent feelings.

"I thought you were too tired to lift a cup." Julia stood, laughter echoing off the stone walls. Water streamed from her hair down her breasts and belly. She splashed back and dove underwater to pull Cinnia off her feet.

Cinnia went under, spluttering.

They both came up grinning.

Julia grabbed Cinnia by her braid. She thought she was in for another dunking, when Julia pulled her close and kissed her fiercely.

Cinnia's lips parted as Julia's tongue probed. Cinnia tasted echoes of honeyed wine.

Julia pulled her closer. Cinnia reached round and cupped Julia's tight buttocks, grinding her hips between the other woman's legs.

Julia moaned.

With a sob, Cinnia pushed her away. "I can't!"

Julia stumbled and sat down in the water. She came up gasping and choking.

"I'm so sorry." Cinnia offered her hand. "I never meant for this to happen."

"What?" Julia pulled herself up. "Almost drowning me?"

"No." Cinnia dropped Julia's hand, standing, arms outstretched. "This. Us. I love another."

"Afra."

Cinnia nodded.

Julia pulled her eyebrows together in a frown. "She may be alive… or not. If alive, do you think she would deny you the comfort of my friendship?"

"This…coupling…is more than friendship."

"I say it is less." Julia touched Cinnia's shoulder; ran her hands lightly down her arm. "This is release, taking pleasure in each other's bodies. Friendship is much more."

Cinnia's skin thrilled to her touch, but she stepped away. "One or both of us may die in a week. We may face each other in the arena someday."

"All the more reason for us to take pleasure now." Julia followed. "We don't know what tomorrow will bring."

Cinnia had no retort. Julia spoke truth, but did that make it right? If she took pleasure with Julia, did she betray Afra?

"Come, Cinnia." Julia stepped out of the water. "I know a place we can be together…and dry."

Cinnia took her hand and followed.

Chapter Twenty-three

MOTHER ISIS, GIVE ME PROTECTION. Hercules, give me strength," Cinnia prayed. She had become fond of the heavily muscled, bearded god that many of the male gladiators honored. The people of Nuceria paraded his statue as Hercules Victor, along with Apollo's, during the games' opening parade of the gladiators. She reached out with the others to touch the painted wooden statue as it passed, hoping for good luck in the arena.

Now she stood with the other women, fully equipped, helmets under their arms, ready to go onto the sands at Nuceria. Her opponent from the other *ludus*, chosen by lot, fought as a *myrmilla*. She stood half a hand shorter than Cinnia and several pounds lighter; sweat gathered on her brow and trickled between her breasts. Cinnia felt a momentary stab of pity for the smaller woman then forced it away. She didn't want to underestimate her opponent. The *myrmilla* would fight to win and kill her if she could.

Trumpets blared and the narrator announced, "A special exhibition of female gladiators to honor the people of Nuceria from the esteemed *editor* of the games."

They marched out to stand before the *editor's* box and shouted the traditional greeting, "We who are about to die salute you!"

The crowd roared. The narrator announced the match ups and the pairs took up their spots around the amphitheater. Each pair had a *summa rudis*—a man armed with a stout wooden rod to call fouls, breaks, and beat any reluctant fighter.

The early afternoon sun shimmered off the sand. The *velarium* of close-woven white wool, pulled over masts at the top of the amphitheater, shaded the spectators in the stands. Cinnia's feet were well-calloused from months of bare-foot practice, otherwise she would have hopped from foot to foot on the hot sands. She sent grateful praise to Barba for his insistence on practice in full gear in their overheated room.

The two women saluted one another and took their stances.

The narrator, the crowd, the music, all faded into the background as Cinnia narrowed her focus to one thing: her opponent.

The *summa rudis* lifted his rod, signaling the beginning of the fight. The two women circled each other looking for weaknesses. Cinnia thought she had stamina and agility on her side. She was more lightly armed and larger. The *myrmilla* made a sudden jab with her *gladius*. Cinnia blocked it with her smaller shield, and parried. The two traded thrusts and feints for several minutes, doing an intricate dance on the hot sand. Cinnia knew the better the show, the more likely they were to survive.

After several minutes, Cinnia's mouth clogged with dust; thirst nagged her. They exchanged several more blows. Her heavy breath filled her helmet with moist air. Sweat soaked the wool band she wore across her forehead under her helmet. She could sense the *myrmilla* beginning to tire. The heavy shield dropped a trifle lower, the other woman was a half-beat slower to parry. Their helmets obscured their faces, so Cinnia couldn't see her opponent's eyes. Did they show fear? Anger? Resignation?

Her opponent's shield slumped. Cinnia thrust over the edge with her curved blade, scoring a deep wound on the woman's unprotected shoulder.

The *summa rudis* dropped his rod between them, giving the *myrmilla* a chance to recover, but she bled heavily. Cinnia took the brief rest to slow and deepen her breathing.

The rod came up. The *myrmilla* rushed Cinnia. It was a desperate move to bowl her over with the heavy shield before the wounded woman became too weak to hold it. Cinnia stepped to the side and sliced the woman's exposed flank, a fatal wound. The *myrmilla* cried out, falling to her knees. She dropped her shield and sword, clutched her side, head bowed, unable to raise her arm in the traditional gesture to ask for mercy.

The *summa rudis* lowered his rod, to back Cinnia off. He turned to the *editor*. Only then, did Cinnia notice they were the last pair to finish. The crowd cried, "*Perit*—she's finished," and the *editor* gave the sign for death. The *summa rudis* motioned Cinnia forward.

"Do your duty," the woman whispered and lifted her head.

Cinnia raised her sword and brought it down swiftly, piercing the breast and heart as she had been taught…a clean death blow.

The crowd roared its approval.

Cinnia looked around the arena. All four of the women from her *ludus* survived as victors. One of the losers also stood, spared, but two other bodies littered the sand.

"Victors approach the *editor!*" the narrator of the games called.

Cinnia doffed her helmet and approached, with Julia on her left, Portia and Gerta on her right. A quick glance showed that Julia seemed unharmed, but blood dripped down Gerta's leg from a shallow wound.

The *editor*, a handsome middle-age man, launched into a speech. Cinnia lost the thread of it as fatigue, heat, and thirst sapped her strength. The crowd hissed and whistled as the speech grew longer. A hard-faced matron wearing an elaborate blond wig sat in the box with the *editor*. She tugged discreetly on his tunic and he brought his speech to a close by presenting each of them with a victory frond and a small purse.

The cheers of the crowd lifted Cinnia's spirits as they circled the arena and left through the Gate of Life. She…and Julia…had survived.

In the cell under the stands where they disarmed, Cinnia sought a corner and threw up.

"Are you all right?" Julia put a hand on her back. It was warm, comforting, but not the hand she wanted.

"I'm fine. Just the heat." Cinnia took a gulp of water, swished it around her mouth, and spat it out.

She reached for the talisman of Isis usually hanging on her breast and grasped air. Of course, she couldn't wear it in the arena, but she missed its slight weight.

Afra, where are you?

AFRA STRIPPED OFF HER GREAVES and blood-spattered padding. Not her own blood. Not this time.

How long before I'm the one dragged out in the death cart. Six months, four fights and three dead.

The woman today had been a good fighter, a *retiaria* with the pitiless black eyes of a deadly snake. She reminded Afra of Clio. She had nearly caught Afra in her net, but…Afra shrugged…not today.

Slaves took the gear away to be cleaned. She sat on a wooden bench, shoulders drooping, hands dangling between her knees.

"Good work in there, Afra. Here are your winnings. I'll have Caepio add these to your account." Sextus Licinius Murena handed her a bag of coins. "As I predicted, the crowd likes you and are generous. You're exotic, skilled, and know how to put on a show. I've seen your name and form drawn on the walls outside the arena. An enterprising young man is selling a figure of you." He tossed her a small fired clay figure. The only resemblance to her was the little knobs all over her head representing her hair.

"I don't do this for the money or the crowd." She respected Murena. He did right by her. But she did not have the easy confiding relationship with the patrician magistrate as with the plebian Marcius. She rarely saw him except before and after the games.

"For what? The good name of the *ludus*? Your honor?"

"As you wish." Afra kept her face blank. He would never understand her need to survive and escape. The Roman aristocracy put much store on their honor and good names.

His lips pursed in puzzlement, but he didn't pursue the discussion.

"Too bad you're the last female from your cohort. The new lot doesn't give you much competition."

"Caepio has me training with the men now. I grow stronger fighting them."

"Any…uh…problems?"

"Only when I beat one of them. They sulk."

"Good, but I meant do any of the men try to get in your bed?" Murena frowned. "I'll let it be known that anyone who touches you will be sent to the mines."

"No need." She smiled briefly. "They think me a witch with power over beasts. I let it be known any man who comes to my bed will be swarmed by rats which will eat off his cock."

"A fitting punishment. Speaking of beasts…" Murena snapped his fingers. A slave brought him a goblet of wine.

"How *are* the cubs?" A bit of passion entered her voice.

"Cubs no longer."

Afra thought back to that day on the docks of Alexandria. "Yes, they are two years old; full grown now. They will have lost the last of their baby ruff."

"My huntsman says they are doing well. I'm the envy of all my neighbors. Everyone wants a brace of hunting cats."

"I could serve you better training animals than butchering people for entertainment."

"You're a condemned criminal, Afra. Until you win or buy your freedom, this is your fate."

She hefted the bag of coins. "How many of these before I *can* buy my freedom?"

"The more you earn for the *ludus*, the more valuable you become, the higher your price."

"There must be a price at which a gladiator can buy her freedom, else I'm trapped." Afra raised an eyebrow. "I thought you an honorable man."

"You don't belong to me. You belong to the *ludus*. I have partners."

"Are *they* not honorable men?"

"Afra, be patient. You have been fighting just six months. Most gladiators fight at least three years before…"

"Dying?"

"Some." Murena shrugged. "If you survive the early years, you will most likely buy or earn your freedom within five years. Please the crowd, bring honor to the giver of the games. That's the way out of the trap. That or death."

Five years! Would Cinnia wait that long? Could she survive that long? She shook her head. Death was not an option.

"I came to give you news, as well as your purse." He took another drink of wine. "Our beloved Emperor Nero will be coming to Pompeii next month to inspect the progress of rebuilding after the earthquake. There will be celebratory games. Two other *ludi* will provide a number of female gladiators. The one from Capua is reported to have several good female fighters, but I hear one in particular is fearsome. They call her Britannia."

Afra's heart sped up. Could that be a coincidence, that this woman bears the same name Marcius gave Cinnia?

"Do you know what she looks like?"

"I've never seen her." He shook his head. "She fights as a Thracian. A good match for you."

"Will we be matched ahead of time?"

"The men will, but Fortuna will decide the women's fates with lots."

Now her heart raced. Could it be Cinnia? This was the first inkling she had of her lover's fate.

Murena put a hand on her shoulder. "Do me honor, Afra. Please the Emperor. That's the way to freedom."

She stood, topping him by half a head. "As I said, I have my own reasons to survive. They are not in conflict with yours."

"Good! I'll see you before the games next month. The Emperor's presence means I'll be busy." Murena quaffed the last of his wine and left.

Afra twisted the thin braided bracelet on her wrist. Cinnia's pledge. She never took it off…for practice, bathing, or fighting. Afra felt in her heart Cinnia survived. Whether her love survived was another question.

Afra thought back to her long-ago dream. *Honor the gods, serve them well...Isis will reward you.*

Will you Mother Isis, Queen of All Gods and Goddesses? Have I sacrificed enough? If not, tell me what more you require.

Chapter Twenty-four

Cinnia entered the feasting hall with sweating palms and a dry throat, Julia chattering by her side and Gerta looming behind. Portia had disappeared with a lover to a private room. Cinnia scanned the room for Afra. *Where is she?*

She had attended several of these traditional pre-game feasts given in honor of the gladiatorial combatants, but none as elaborate as this. The tables groaned with food: roast joints and fowls; baked, fried and sauced fish, eels, oysters; boiled pulses; chopped vegetables and salads; fresh fruits and tarts; cheeses and bread. Slaves filled empty goblets with fine wine. A small band of flute and lyre players provided music. Only the best for the emperor's party.

The gladiators, dressed in their best tunics, enjoyed the food provided by the sponsors of the games and women, as well. The most famous of the gladiators, from all three *ludi*, had more than one woman serving them—in more than one capacity. Spectators circulated through the hall, observing the fighters who might die tomorrow. A few shrewd ones no doubt took notes on which ones overindulged in food, drink, and women, making last minute changes in bets. Cinnia noted that most of the more experienced fighters ate in moderation; drank well-watered wine. A few, given bad omens by their gods, lamented their fates or gorged on their last meal.

"There!" Julia pointed at a door. "I saw three other women—fighters by the looks of them—go in that room." She grabbed Cinnia's hand, pulling her toward the door.

Cinnia followed; hope spurring her forward; fear slowing her pace. She knew Afra was to fight the next day, as was she. *Afra should be here. But what if she had changed? What if she had a new lover? What if Afra blamed her for her loss of freedom?*

They passed through to a much smaller space than the men occupied, but as sumptuously furnished with food and drink. Traditional Roman couches, able to accommodate reclining diners, lined the walls. A bright fresco showing a hunting scene adorned the walls. Small three-legged tables served as repositories for plates and wine glasses. Half a dozen women already occupied the first three couches. There would be seven pairs of women fighters tomorrow; an auspicious number.

Afra wasn't there.

"These should do." Julia herded them to the couches opposite the occupied ones. The women eyed one another across the room. Tomorrow they would fight. Some would die.

"Wine!" Cinnia ordered, as soon as she reclined. Disappointment soured her stomach.

"With water!" Julia amended. "You don't want to go into the arena with a sore head."

Cinnia grumbled but took the watered wine. "If we're matched tomorrow, you'll wish I'd drunk myself into a stupor."

"There's no honor in killing a sot." Julia nibbled on a roasted chicken leg redolent of garlic. "If you don't make me look good, the winner's take will be paltry. I need a fat purse."

Gerta grunted assent and took up a savory beef pie. "Better than barley soup."

Cinnia smiled. The food at the *ludus* did get monotonous. The ubiquitous barley and beans diet was filling, but designed to fatten the men. The extra layer was protection from shallow sword cuts. Gerta had put on several pounds. Julia seemed able to eat anything and stay trim.

Cinnia didn't want to carry the extra weight or risk being slower, so she ate in moderation.

A gust of music blew in as a stern-looking Roman dressed in a blue wool tunic with gold embroidery opened the door. Over his shoulder, Cinnia spied a tall black woman.

Cinnia froze.

Afra's eyes searched the room and landed on Cinnia.

White teeth showed in a dazzling smile.

Before Cinnia knew what she did, she was in Afra's arms, whispering, "Mother Isis told me we would see each other again!"

Afra held her love tightly, joy racing through her veins with each rapid beat of her heart. The moment seemed to last forever, until she looked over Cinnia's head at Murena's astonished face.

She untangled their arms, holding Cinnia away from her. "Let me see you. Are you well? You have more scars!"

"And you a broken nose. Did the guards do that to you?"

"That and more." She unconsciously put her hand to her side where her broken ribs ached occasionally.

"Julia told me of your reprieve in the arena. Mari and Cari?"

Afra nodded.

Murena gave a discrete cough.

Afra stiffened, turning to the Roman. "My apologies, Magistrate. Cinnia and I are…" She stumbled to a halt, trying to find the words.

"Is she the escaped slave the guards returned to your mistress?" Murena nodded at Cinnia.

"Clio was not my mistress." Afra's face hardened. "I was freed."

"But she was hers?" He nodded at Cinnia.

"Clio sold me to Silo's *ludus*." Cinnia's lifted her chin. "She has no claim on me."

"I wasn't suggesting she did. Just trying to get the facts straight. I'm a magistrate. I always want the facts."

Cinnia's shoulders relaxed. She bowed her head slightly. "Many pardons, Magistrate. Afra and I have been separated since that day. There is much we'd like to say…"

He looked around at the crowded room, a slight smile flickered across his face. "Afra, you're my best hope of impressing the Emperor tomorrow. I expect you in your bed by midnight."

"That will not be a problem, Sir."

The Roman snorted and left.

"So you're the one who troubles Cinnia's dreams and gladdens her heart."

Afra turned to see a tall Roman woman with black curly hair and startlingly blue eyes assessing her.

"Afra, this is Julia of the *ludus* Silo." Cinnia pointed to a large blonde eating lustily. "And that's Gerta. We have another comrade, a free woman, but she's too proud to eat with us lowly slaves."

"We had a flock of free women join our *ludus* a couple of months ago, several from the noble classes." Afra shook her head. "There must be madness among the aristocratic Roman women, that they choose such a fate. Murena is alarmed. He fears their influence on his own two daughters, who are of an impressionable age."

Julia opened her mouth to reply, but Cinnia broke in. "Please excuse us, Julia. I need to talk to Afra." Cinnia twined her arm around Afra's waist. "It's been nearly a year."

"Of course." The Roman's mouth hardened.

Afra saw something flicker in the Roman woman's eyes. Fear? Jealousy?

Julia looked over her shoulder. "I'll take the couch with Gerta."

Cinnia led Afra to the corner couch where they reclined, legs entwined, hands tracing the outlines of breasts and hips. A slow heat built in Afra's loins, but she didn't want to put on a show for these women. She grabbed a glass of wine from a serving slave and took a long drink.

"I didn't know what happened to you. I feared…" She looked into Cinnia's eyes and traced her full lips with her thumb.

Cinnia blushed; her eyes slid away. She took Afra's hand and softly kissed the palm. "Clio told me you were dead, but I dreamed different. Months later Julia brought me word of your escape from the beasts. Now your name is legend at the *ludus*. Even the men talk of your prowess in the arena."

"It's a matter of pride for Murena, but none for me. I trained and fought to survive. I survived to find you."

"And now?"

Tears threatened to well, and Afra swallowed the lump in her throat. "I don't know. I thought only of finding you. Now…here…tomorrow we both face death."

"Mother Isis gave me a message for you."

"Mother Isis spoke to you?" Afra whispered. "At the temple?"

"In my dreams, when I was most low. She said, 'When you see Afra again, tell her that her Mother brings Love and Light to the world.' That's when I knew I'd see you again."

"The gods are cruel to bring us together in this spectacle of death."

"Mother Isis said that it is people who are unkind to one another." Cinnia gazed over the room. "The gods demand sacrifice, but it's the Romans who demand death in the arena."

"How many have you killed?"

"After my six months training, seven fights, six kills." Cinnia took a gulp of wine. "The men scratch their opponents' names in their cells, keep track of their wins. They boast of their prizes, and how many noble Roman women want to lie with them. I remember each face in life and death and pray their shades find rest." She shook her head. "And you, how many?"

"Nine fights, seven kills."

Cinnia's eyebrows went up. "Nine fights in six months?"

"Five months. It took me several weeks to recover from my injuries."

"That's too many chances for death. You can't be expected to keep that up. The top gladiators fight only twice or three times a year!"

"I am not a top gladiator. I'm little more than the novelty act Marcius trained us for."

"You—we—are so much more than that!" Cinnia ran her hand over Afra's face, tracing the sideways slope of her broken nose. "Oh, my love, what are we to do?"

Afra sat up. "Leave here."

"Escape?" Cinnia whispered. "How?"

"No, my love, there is no escape but death." She held out her hand. "But we have tonight. Come with me."

Afra grabbed a pitcher of wine, sought a private room, she paid a guard to turn away other entrants. It was furnished with a plain pallet, chair, small table, and oil lamp; but Afra had eyes only for Cinnia.

The lamp light shone on her golden hair, tightly plaited, pinned in a bun at the nape of her brown neck. Afra reached up and removed a pin to let the braid fall down Cinnia's back. "May I?" she asked.

Cinnia's eyes glowed. "Of course."

Afra unplaited the braid, running her hand through the silky strands, separating them, taking a deep sniff. "How I've missed the smell of fresh air and warm sunshine in your hair."

Cinnia groaned, stiffening in her arms. "I must tell you something. About me and…and…"

"Julia?" Afra guessed, her chest tightening in fear.

Cinnia nodded.

Afra dropped her hands, a pain stabbed deep in her gut. She turned her face away, so Cinnia couldn't see the hurt.

"We are friends. Sisters-in-arms." Cinnia reached up to cup Afra's face and turned it back to hers. "We pleasure each other when we are not too tired. No more than that."

"Is that what this is? Pleasure?" Afra tried to keep the pain from her voice.

"Of course." Cinnia smiled. "And much more. Do I not touch your heart as well as your body? Did not the Great Goddess herself bless our love? Did we not both fight and strive to survive on the hope we might one day find each other again?" She clasped Afra's hand, guiding it to her breast to cover the small wooden amulet.

She still had it! Thanks to you, Queen of all the Gods and Goddesses, for returning my love to me. Afra took a deep breath to stifle a sob and dropped her head in shame. She should never have doubted Isis' promise. A tear leaked from under closed lids.

Cinnia's soft lips kissed it away.

Afra pulled Cinnia into a tight embrace, kissing her with all her pent-up longing and loneliness.

LATER, CINNIA STROKED AFRA'S lean flank, fighting tears.

Her lover caught her chin and lifted her face to stare into her eyes. "The Romans can't take our memories. Keep this night in your heart when you're lonely or afraid. Remember, you are loved."

"I don't fear pain or loneliness." She pulled Afra close, whispering. "Don't tell me you haven't thought about it. The lots. What if we are paired? If not tomorrow, some day it will happen. There are too few of us women. I couldn't fight you!"

Afra stroked her hair, but it didn't soothe Cinnia's fears.

"I have thought about it. If we refuse to fight, we will be slaughtered immediately, as an example to the others and entertainment for the crowd."

"Is death our only choice?" Cinnia lightly ran her hand over Afra's wrist, searching for the pulse of life, finding a thin braid of hair. Her heart cried at this further sign of devotion. "We could beg a knife from the guard, open veins, die in each other's arms."

"I will accept death, if need be, but I choose life. If we fight each other tomorrow, we should fight with all our strength and skill. Perhaps the crowd will grant the loser a reprieve." Afra's gaze became unfocussed. "Two of my opponents have won reprieves. Alive, we have the chance, a slim one, to buy ourselves free. I might persuade Murena to buy you from Silo for his *ludus*. We might be together."

"If there's no *missio*?" Cinnia shuddered at the thought.

"The winner kills the other with love in her heart, and—only then— takes her own life." Afra clasped her tightly. "Better we chose our deaths than a Roman does."

"A pact. We will follow one another in death." Cinnia frowned. "I don't fear death, but I do fear what follows. What if my gods claim me and yours claim you? Will we be separated again for all of time?"

"I don't know." Afra loosened her grip "But I don't believe so. Mother Isis brought us together. Why would she separate us after death?"

"But…"

Afra stopped the question with a kiss. "Aren't you the one who said all goddesses are The Mother? Leave the gods to their realm. Let's enjoy ours. We have a couple of hours before we have to be back in our cells. Surely we can think of something to do with the time except talk of death and the gods?"

Cinnia smiled, but it didn't reach her eyes. Afra was right, but she couldn't shake her sense of foreboding.

CHAPTER TWENTY-FIVE

AFRA WOKE EARLY THE NEXT DAY, alone in her bed. The night past, more dream than reality. She bowed before the clay figures that she kept in the niche in her room: Isis, seated with Horus on her lap, and jackal-headed Anubis, judge of the dead. "Mother Isis, give me strength to do what must be done. Dreaded Anubis, if my soul is sent to you, I pray you find me worthy."

She broke her fast with bread, beans, and olive oil brought to her room by a slave she paid. Her winnings added up, allowing her these small luxuries. The main eating hall would be full of men boasting about their coming fights, nursing a sore head, or nervously preparing for the arena. She wanted peace for a few moments to marshal her thoughts and feelings. Nothing must distract her.

A clanging bell and insistent shouts warned her that the time had come. She donned her yellow breast band, her matching yellow loin cloth fringed with blue tassels, and her thick leather belt studded with brass. Afra ducked out of her cell, joining the men of her *ludus* for the trek to the arena. Many gave the horned sign to ward off evil as she walked by, but she ignored them.

Afra remembered little of the trek to the amphitheater: flashes of color, cheers from the crowd. Some called her name, one woman boldly tossed her a transparent veil weighted with a coin. Afra plucked it from the air, sniffed at the scent of roses, tucked it in her belt and nodded. The woman, a red-head with crooked teeth, smiled and blew her a kiss. The men grumbled next to her, but she didn't hear what they said.

At last they paraded through the plaza, redolent with the smell of cooked food and sweating bodies, and into the bowels of the amphitheater. Fighters from different schools were placed in different holding rooms at the arena to prevent any riot or mischief. Afra took her usual seat on a bench in the corner in the back. No man challenged her for the place.

Sextus Licinius Murena stepped through the door and surveyed his fighters. All quieted.

"You are the best fighters in the best *ludus* in Campania. Do me and the Emperor honor today and I will double your winnings. Fail me and I'll have you killed even if the crowd cries, '*missio.*' These are a special gift for today's games to honor our emperor." Caepio, their *lanista*, handed out beautiful blue-dyed capes with a snarling wolf embroidered in gold on the back. "Wear them with pride."

The room erupted in a roar as the men shouted, spurring each other on to greater feats.

Afra looked at the wolf, wondering if it was a bad omen. She shrugged. She'd be fighting neither wolf nor cat, but a human today. She prayed again it wouldn't be Cinnia. Murena caught her eye before he left, giving her the briefest of smiles.

"Alright, you sons of whores, it's time for the parade. Look pretty for the crowd." Caepio lined them up from least prestigious—Afra—to most popular—an ugly ex-soldier who wasn't the biggest man in the pack, but wickedly skilled with his *gladius*. The masseuse made a lucrative trade off his sweat and oil scrapings. They trooped out of the holding room onto a series of chariots, preceded by slaves carrying statues of Mars and Hercules, followed by slaves carrying their weapons and armor.

They entered the arena through the Gate of Life to the roar of the crowd. Over 20,000 people stood cheering as the gladiators progressed around the perimeter and exited their chariots before the Imperial box.

Afra scoured the arena for a glimpse of Cinnia, finally spotting her among the red-caped gladiators from Capua, following behind her own companions. The final entrants were caped in vivid green.

All the gladiators assembled before the Imperial Box. The narrator announced. "All hail Emperor Nero Claudius Caesar Augustus Germanicus, *Pontifex Maximus, Pater Patriae*, four times Consul and nine times Imperator; and his noble wife Poppaea Sabina Augusta. The Emperor gives these games, in the name of Mars and Hercules *Victus*, to the good people of Pompeii in this, his eighth year of rule."

The crowd shouted, stamping their feet on the stone floor to create a rolling wall of sound that washed over the gladiators, the emperor, and his guests. Afra thought the noise might deafen her. She searched the box for the face of the man who commanded these games, the man who entertained his people with spectacles of death.

Nero rose to acknowledge the crowd. He was a slight man of medium height, with a broad face; his golden hair arranged in elaborate rows of curls. A woman of startling beauty stood by his side, staring out over the crowd. She looked bored, until Nero whispered something in her ear, then she laughed. Afra spotted Murena in the box next to the Emperor's. The crowd chanted, "Nero! Nero! Long life!" for several minutes until the trumpets blared. They gave a final shout and took their seats.

In the relative quiet, the narrator gave a signal. The gladiators extended their right hands and intoned, "We who are about to die salute you."

Nero nodded his acceptance. The crowd roared again.

"And now for the lots!" The narrator shouted. Usually the second class male fighters drew lots to determine who they would fight, but today it was the women. The men on display were all champions; paired earlier in the week according to their skills and the opportunity for most the exciting performance.

Afra held her breath and prayed. The narrator announced the first pair, the second. He pulled out two markers. "Afra, of Pompeii, fights as *myrmilla* against Amazonia, of Capua, a *secutor*." She let out her breath with a long sigh. *Thanks to Fortuna. Not today.* She wouldn't have to fight Cinnia. The narrator announced, "Britannia, of Capua, fights as a Thracian with Atalanta, of Capua, a *retiaria*."

The gladiators bowed and trooped out the Gate of Life back to their holding rooms. They wouldn't be back until the midafternoon. Afra tried to catch Cinnia's eye, but now she was ahead of her in the pack. She disappeared behind a door.

CINNIA WAS STRICKEN. She didn't have to fight Afra, but she was paired with Julia who fought under the name Atalanta, swift of foot. Before, they had always fought against women from another *ludus*. In her anxiety over her possible match with Afra, she hadn't thought about fighting one of her companions. Relief struggled with remorse and fear. Afra would fight the immense Gerta as Amazonia, no easy win.

She took several deep breaths. They had several hours before the women fought. She needed to be calm, focused, or she would be the one carried out on the death cart.

Julia approached and sat beside her. "I'm sorry, my friend."

"As am I." Cinnia bowed her head briefly. "I will give no quarter."

"I understand. We will both fight to win."

"As we should."

"Why couldn't it have been Portia?" Julia looked across the room at the haughty Roman woman. "I'd have gladly speared her liver."

Cinnia smiled; clasping Julia's extended arm. "The Mother's blessings on us both."

Julia stood and retreated to another bench. Three male champions played dice in a corner. Another took a nap. Cinnia didn't know how anyone could sleep their last possible hours away.

She closed her eyes to make it easier to see Julia's moves in her mind. Barba had them practice against each other frequently, so they would know the weaknesses and strengths of the various fighting styles. But it also made them aware of their own particular strengths and weaknesses. Julia was quick. She could dance out of her sight, send her spinning, but her net work lacked finesse. She tossed the net at a person like she would toss it at the practice stake, not allowing for movement. If she did catch you, her trident was deadly. Cinnia pictured the best defensive and offensive moves, seeing herself in her mind execute each one perfectly.

The sounds of the crowd echoed faintly through the stone of the arena. Cinnia listened to keep track of the program: laughter for the mock entertainers, cries of fear and delight for the beast hunt, roars of approval as the *noxii* fought each other to death. At mid-day, slaves brought water and offered food, but few ate. The air wafting in held the stench of warm bodies, rotting meat, and a hint of the perfume sprayed in the stands to keep the smell from being unendurable. When the water organ struck up a lively tune, Barba walked through the door with the dressing slaves carrying the women's armor.

Cinnia's dresser wrapped quilted fabric around her legs, securing it with greaves tied at the back of her calves. A roll of the fabric provided a cushion on the top of her bare feet for the greaves to rest. This was the fanciest equipment she had worn. The greaves sported silver embossed figures of Victory on one and Nemesis on the other. A Medusa head decorated the knee guards. Next he tied quilted fabric onto her right arm and attached an articulated arm guard that protected her from shoulder to wrist. A narrow leather strap attached at the shoulder, reached across her chest, under her left arm and across her back to hold the guard in place. She put her helmet under her arm. The high crest of alternate stiff black and white horse hairs tickled a bit and she readjusted it. She carried her small square shield. Cinnia's stomach clenched and she fought down nausea.

"It's time. Do our *ludus* honor."

She narrowed her focus to Barba and his words, shutting out all other sounds. At his direction, she trooped out the door and stood at the gate, waiting for the narrator to announce her name. Julia stood beside her, black hair plaited, tightly pinned to her head; a colored wool band tied around her head kept the sweat from her eyes. She wore quilted fabric to protect her legs and left arm; a short shoulder guard strapped to her left shoulder was her only armor. The lead-weighted net was tied to her protected arm. Their edged weapons would be given to them in the arena, after they had been tested for sharpness.

"Britannia, Thracian and Atalanta, *retiaria*!" the narrator bellowed. They stepped onto the gold-colored sand, made their way to the front of the Imperial box, bowed, and received their weapons: Julia's trident and sharp belt knife, Cinnia's deadly curved *sica*. Their *summa rudis* led them to the left, positioning them with space between them and the other fighters. The crowd sounds retreated. Cinnia watched Julia as she unwound her net, positioned her trident. The *retiaria* was no longer her friend. Julia would kill her, if she could.

The trumpets sounded. The narrator cried. "At the order of our most esteemed and beloved Emperor, the women will fight without helmets!"

Cinnia had heard that the emperor sometimes ordered changes in the equipment on his whim. Once the men lost their shields; another time they fought blindfolded. But the lack of a helmet was to her advantage. Cinnia's helmet was protection against swords, but more hindrance than help against the lightly armed *retiaria*; it blocked her peripheral vision.

She saw fear flicker in Julia's eyes. With clear vision, Julia's fast feet were not as much of an advantage. Cinnia tossed her helmet to the perimeter. Slaves raced around picking up the discarded equipment.

The trumpets sounded again.

Their *summa rudis* put his wooden stick between them.

The women took up their stances.

"Begin!"

The rod rose.

Julia began her dance. She feinted with the trident. Cinnia stepped away.

Julia whirled her net. Cinnia waited to the last moment and slipped to the side, blocking a couple of the lead weights with her shield. She jabbed at Julia's exposed side.

Julia danced away and whipped her net back. Cinnia pursued, before she could get her net redeployed. Julia defended herself with the trident.

They circled each other, heat shimmered from the sand.

Cinnia stopped with her back to the lowering sun, forcing Julia to squint. She rushed the *retiaria* again. Julia retreated and flicked the net at Cinnia's legs, almost taking her down.

Cinnia recovered, barely escaping another jab with the trident, by twisting to the right. She ducked under the net, rolling in the sand to come up on Julia's unprotected left. She slashed, but missed.

Both women gasped for breath.

The *summa rudis* brought down the wooden rod to give both a chance to recover. Cinnia hear the crowd shouting, "Atalanta!" and "Britannia!"

The rod went up. The women started their deadly dance anew. After several minutes, Cinnia finally saw her chance. Julia moved to her left, whirling her net. When she released it, Cinnia stepped back, caught it with her shield, and yanked.

Julia staggered, but pulled out her belt knife to cut herself free of the net.

Cinnia rushed in, abandoning her entangled shield, slashing at Julia's exposed shoulder. She scored a deep cut. Julia's trident wobbled as blood flowed.

Cinnia saw shock in Julia's eyes and fell back, feigning a twisted knee.

Julia recognized Cinnia's hesitation, shook her head, and cried, "No quarter, my friend."

The blood pulsed from Julia's shoulder. With each beat of her heart, she weakened. With a last effort Julia danced to the left, jabbed at Cinnia's legs with her trident, and whirled away, slashing at her face with the small knife.

Cinnia ducked and stabbed. Julia seemed to jump into the sword's path, impaling herself through the stomach. Cinnia let go and stepped back, her face a rigid mask, while her gut clenched and roiled.

A trumpet blasted and the crowd shouted, "Got her! She's had it!"

The *summa rudis* waved Cinnia back.

Julia went to her knees, right hand clutching the sword, left extended for mercy. Before the Emperor could ask the crowd's wishes, Julia toppled, blood soaking the sand.

An official dressed as Charon, ferryman to the land of the dead, turned her over and checked her pulse. Her beautiful blue eyes filmed in death. He shook his head at the *summa rudis*, and slit her throat to make sure she was dead.

Cinnia's knees nearly gave way. The feeling that fired her during battle, ebbed, leaving ashes and fatigue. The fact of killing Julia—her friend—had yet to register. The crowd chanted, "Britannia! Britannia!" She lifted her bloody fists into the air to cheers and cries of "well done!"

For the first time she became aware of the rest of the fighters. All but Afra and Gerta were done. Five bodies littered the arena floor, one defeated woman held out her hand. The crowd cried, "*Missio!*"

Afra stalked Gerta like a cat would a lumbering beast; quick strikes, fast footwork. The lack of the all-encompassing helmet, with its limited vision, gave the *secutor* an advantage in this match. They both had large oblong shields and short stabbing swords—the *gladius*—of the Roman legionnaires; but Gerta was better armored with greaves and articulated arm shield. Afra fought with quilted padding on legs and sword arm, plus one greave on her left leg.

But the big woman was rapidly tiring. She stumbled. Afra scored her thigh. A twist and Gerta's shield went spinning. Two more moves and Gerta was on the ground with her hand in the air. Reprieve.

Cinnia expelled the breath she didn't realize she was holding. It was over. They both survived.

The narrator announced the winners. They approached the Imperial box, after handing over their bloody weapons. Cinnia stood next to Afra, brushing her hand. A thrill shot up her arm. A temporary set of wooden steps was moved into place. The winners climbed, to be greeted at the top with the palm frond of victory and acclamation from the crowd.

Nero smiled at them, "Good sport! Wonderful moves! You've been trained well. I'll be recruiting many more women into the imperial gladiator school."

They trooped down the steps and progressed around the arena waving their victory fronds at the crowd. Afra was clearly a local favorite. The crowd chanted her name, but there was also a large portion shouting "Britannia!" They finished in front of the Imperial box and bowed.

The trumpet blasted.

Cinnia looked forward to stealing a glance as they left, maybe a kiss in the darkness of the passage. Afra seemed to have a little influence with her Roman master. Maybe she could talk him into buying her. They could be together again.

The narrator announced, "Our beloved Emperor Nero has decided to add a special pair to the champions this afternoon."

The crowd quieted.

"Afra and Britannia will fight after the male champions!"

No! Cinnia's mind went numb.

CHAPTER TWENTY-SIX

WHAT IS THIS TRICKERY?" Afra towered over Murena, hands clenched, jaw set. "I fought once today!"

The guard on the door stepped forward, but the Roman motioned him back.

"Sit, Afra." He brushed his hand through his hair in a weary gesture. "Have some water."

A slave thrust a goblet into Afra's hands. She drank it down.

"The Emperor can do as he pleases with his own games. At least you have time to recover before you fight again. The champions will take at least two hours fighting one pair at time."

"No one else has to fight twice."

"One of our esteemed emperors had a victorious gladiator fight a second time—right after he won. When he took that match, as well, the emperor ordered a third fight. He lost that one, but the emperor gave him a magnificent funeral."

"Kind of him," Afra mumbled.

"You fought well." He jingled a heavy purse. "I and many others made a lot of money betting on you."

"Money! Is that what this is about?"

"Some." He shrugged. "Women gladiators are a novelty. People didn't think you could fight at all, much less put on as good a show as the men. The crowd recognizes skill. That's why they shouted your name."

"Why Cinnia?"

"She was the second favorite. Nero loves a show. He writes his own poetry and music, performs in public, much to the people's delight and the noble's chagrin. He is attuned to the audience and saw the interest that you two generated in the crowd. He needs the people, because the Senate is a constant threat."

Afra dropped her head into her hands, weary to the bone. Every time she thought she spied a track through the Roman thicket, it disappeared in thorns. She had experience with the intricacies of a court, the jostling for place, but the vast and intricate Roman politics eluded her.

She looked up at Murena. "May I beg a favor?"

"If I can."

"I want to see Cinnia before we fight."

"I'll see what I can do. Meanwhile, have a massage, drink water, eat a little if you can; but not much. Rest."

CINNIA CHAFED UNDER THE MASSEUSE'S HANDS. Why? She had done her best. Killed a friend for the howling jackals. Why did the emperor demand she fight her lover, as well? The black mist swirled at the edge of her mind.

The sting of a leather strap across her shoulders brought her back. "Are you listening to me?" Barba glared at her.

She sat up rubbing her shoulder. "I am now."

"That black bitch is as tough as old sandal leather. She moves like a cat. She's taller, has a longer reach, but you're heavier and your sword is longer. You'll also be better armored, but don't go shield to shield. The weight of her shield will push you back. The only weakness I spotted was she tends to feint to the left. Watch for it."

"What of Julia?"

"What?"

"What of her body? Did she have enough money on account for a burial?"

"We can claim her body after the games, if we want. If not, it will be tossed away with the *noxii* and dead beasts. I think she had enough for a burial, but no tombstone."

"She had no family but us. I have plenty on account. Claim her body. I'll pay for the marker. Make sure it has her name, age, fighting style, and number of wins. She'd like that. If I die, burn my body. Bury the ashes under an oak tree."

"Cinnia, it isn't good to dwell on death right before a fight."

"When better to think of death?" A smile curved her lips, but her heart was heavy with loss. Julia, that bright spirit, would walk the earth no more, her blue eyes never again see the sun. The shock of her upcoming fight with Afra, had driven all thoughts of Julia from her mind till now. When she died in the arena with Afra, none of them would be properly mourned.

"None of us escape death, but you have a little control over your life. Get out there. Fight for it!" Barba hissed between clinched teeth. "You're good. Better than the male *tirones*. Have some pride, girl!"

Cinnia fought back the darkness.

The faint shouts of, "He's had it!" came through the walls. Another fighter met his fate.

She straightened her shoulders. She had to be sharp if she and Afra were to survive.

"Sorry, Afra. Silo wouldn't hear of you two meeting alone before the match. He suspected mischief." Murena led Afra and her entourage to the armoring room.

"Thanks for trying."

"Fortuna bless you." He clasped her hand. "I must get back to my box."

She ducked through the low door.

Cinnia stood in a far corner.

They gazed at each other across the room as their dressers put on fresh quilted padding and cleaned armor. No helmets; no swords. They picked up their shields.

Their *lanistae*, trainers, and dressing slaves surrounded them, so they couldn't touch.

They progressed to the Gate of Life. The trumpet sounded. The narrator called out, "Afra of Pompeii!"

Caepio handed her the *gladius*.

Afra stepped onto the cooling sand. The raking couldn't remove the smell of death. The *velarium* was furled and the shadows deepened in the corners. She strode across the arena, sword and shield held high, to stand in front of the Imperial box. The crowd exploded.

"Afra! Afra! Afra!"

Another trumpet blast.

"Britannia of Capua!"

Another round of chanting. Fewer people shouted for Cinnia, but just as enthusiastically as for her. Afra caught the faint cries of the odds makers. She was favored, but not by much.

Cinnia joined her in front of the box.

"Remember our pact, my love," Afra said as they bowed to Nero and his wife. "Fight your best. If one dies, so does the other."

They took their places. The arena quieted. The narrator announced, "Begin!" The *summa rudis* lifted his wooden wand.

A rush of energy flooded Afra's limbs. They circled.

Fighting without helmets made it both easier and harder. Easier because they could watch each other's eyes for next moves; harder to face a lover across the shield and see every flicker of pain and weariness.

Afra feinted left. Cinnia parried.

Cinnia moved right and thrust her shield. Afra jabbed at her legs.

The moves felt familiar.

Cinnia grinned.

They fell into the routine they learned from Paetus: thrust, parry, whirl, and dance away; stumble, slip, drop the shield a hair, recover. Variations they made up on the spot.

But the swords were sharp and both drew blood. They had to, the crowd wanted it. The wounds weren't deep, but would be draining. Their lives dripped slowly into the sand.

After several minutes of furious action, they both stood panting. The *summa rudis* dropped his wooden rod between them, a trumpet sounded and they stepped back. Afra leaned on her shield. Cinnia hunched, hands on knees, blowing like a hippo.

The crowd quieted except for bets shouted back and forth.

The *summa rudis* signaled the fight to resume.

They parried and thrust for several more steps then Cinnia stumbled for real. Afra knocked her shield aside and sent it spinning across the sand. Cinnia crouched in a defensive position.

Afra threw her shield away. "It's too heavy. Slows me down."

The crowd screamed its approval.

Cinnia laughed, and wiped at a tendril of hair plastered to her forehead.

Sword on sword, they were an even match. Afra thrilled at the artistry. Evidently the crowd did, too. The dull roar seeped into her mind as they matched step to step and thrust to thrust. The iron swords sang through the air, sending shuddering vibrations down her arms with every clash.

Inevitably, thirst distracted her mind; fatigue slowed her movements. She spat dust, licked dry lips. She could walk for hours in the desert— with water—but this furious, demanding action drained her reserves. Her lungs seared and muscles ached.

Cinnia was in no better shape.

The *summa rudis* called another halt.

The women swayed in their spots. *How much longer can we fight?* The crowds watched in silence. Afra could hear Cinnia's raspy gasps for breath, echoing her own fight to take in enough life-giving air.

When their breathing calmed, the fight resumed for the third time. Cinnia, with a sudden burst of energy, struck several times with her deadly curved *sica,* driving Afra back.

Afra dug deep for the strength to parry. She pushed back locking their swords hilt to hilt between their straining bodies.

They both pushed, digging their feet into the sand, panting face to face, a static tableau.

A trumpet sounded. The *summa rudis* separated them again. They fell back gasping for breath, sweat and blood streaming down their arms and legs. They had to have fought for well over half an hour—longer than any fight she had to endure or witness. She shook out her burning muscles; licked salty sweat from her upper lip—glad for the moisture. Afra wasn't sure she could raise her sword for another round.

Cinnia's eyes grew round and she turned her head to the stands. It was only then that Afra heard the crowd chanting *"stans missus"*—a draw!

Nero was on his feet looking over the crowd. He called over the narrator. A trumpet called for attention.

The narrator bellowed, "Our esteemed and beloved Emperor Nero has declared the contest a draw! Both Afra of Pompeii and Britannia of Capua win the victor's frond!"

The crowd shouted its approval.

"In addition, our most generous Emperor awards both the wooden sword!"

Afra stood dazed by the noise and the news. The wooden sword! Freedom! Life for them both! *Mother Isis be praised.*

Afra approached the wooden steps with renewed vigor. She wanted to hug Cinnia, but did no more than clasp her hand, raising it, trembling, over their heads as they ascended to where Nero and his empress sat. She bowed her head as she and Cinnia fell to her knees.

"Wonderful fighting. Never saw anything like it. It's inspired me to write a poem." Nero handed them both a victory frond and a wooden sword. He straightened and declaimed:

> *"Afra and Britannia fought in equal strife;*
> *Long time in level balance hung their life;*
> *At last the struggle found an issue fair,*
> *And equal victory and defeat they share.*
> *To both were freedom and the palm assigned;*
> *Such recompense did skill and valor find.*

"Not a bad effort, don't you think?" Nero turned to his audience in the box. Everyone nodded, smiled and exclaimed on the excellence of the emperor's efforts for several minutes.

Afra began to wonder how long they would be required to kneel while the emperor basked in glory. She heard some darker tones to the wider audience waiting for the final ceremony, hinting at some impatience

"Most wondrous, my love, a magnificent effort worthy of a victor's palm as well." Poppaea Sabina Augusta rose, kissed her husband on the brow. "When we go to Greece you must enter it in the competition."

He turned back to the kneeling women. "Get up! Get up! You have to take your turn around the arena."

They both rose, murmuring thanks, eyes averted.

"You're free by my grace, but I expect you both to work for me. I'll be stocking my imperial gladiator school with more women. I want you to train them. My steward will be in touch. Here are your winnings." Nero handed each a heavy purse.

Afra heard the words, but couldn't take in their import. She bowed again and retreated down the steps with Cinnia.

They raised their wooden swords and victory fronds aloft, weariness forgotten.

"Afra! Britannia! Afra! Britannia!"

Afra thought her heart would burst with love and relief as they processed around the arena to the shouts of Romans. They made one last bow and exited through the Gate of Life, hands clasped and smiling into each other's eyes.

EPILOG

THE GODS MUST BE LAUGHING.

I prepared to die in the arena today, by my lover's hand, or my own. Instead, I lay here in Cinnia's arms, her sweet face turned to mine in peaceful sleep. We have money and freedom, but do we have choice?

The Roman Emperor holds our lives in his hands. We could live in luxury and security, training others to risk their lives as we have. Murena believes that is an honorable thing to do. But he is a Roman, rich from my effort, and the favor of the Emperor.

We could run to the ends of the earth beyond the reach of Rome. I would like to see Cinnia's northern land of rivers and misty forests, but to get beyond the legions we would have to travel even further north. Is that part of the journey Isis saw for me, or is this sunny land my fate?

We could go south. Perhaps my queen would take me back into her service if I paid a blood price for Asata and her child.

But would Cinnia's tribe—or mine—accept us? At least the Romans do not scorn us for our love.

I have heard rumors of a tribe of women warriors in the East who live on the banks of a vast sea beyond the Roman one. Perhaps we should search in that direction.

We will decide tomorrow, or the next day, or the next.

Whatever we do, we do it together. We are goddess-blessed; promised to each other. We will not be separated again.

AUTHOR'S NOTE

WHENEVER I PITCHED THIS BOOK as my "lesbian gladiator novel," I encountered raised eyebrows and skeptical snorts. The first question everyone asked: "Were there really lesbian gladiators?" My answer: "Of course!" We know there were female gladiators fighting in arenas for a couple of centuries, although far fewer than men. Some had to be lesbian.

What really surprised people was the fact of *female* gladiators. They rarely appear in popular culture. Despite the popularity of *Xena Warrior Princess* and the myths of the Amazons, they don't come to mind in the media-soaked imaginings of brutal, bloody, gladiatorial games. Women warriors? Maybe. Women gladiators? No. Yet they are there in classical literature, art, grave markers, and archaeology. All you have to do is look.

One organizer in Ostia brags on his tombstone that he was the first person to put women in the arena as fighters. Tacitus in his *Annals* not only tells of Boudica, but also mentions that Emperor Nero regularly had female gladiators in his shows. Suetonius tells us in his *Life of Domitian* that the Emperor once staged a performance at night where women fought either other women or dwarves by torchlight. These women fighters weren't all captives, slaves, or from the lower classes. Tacitus says, "Many distinguished women and senators were disgraced in the arena." Juvenal in his *Satires* mocks women from the senatorial class who chose to join the gladiatorial ranks: "…and look how their little heads strain under such weighty helmets and how thick bandages of coarse bark support their knees."

This book was inspired by a stone relief found in Halicarnassus (modern Bodrum, Turkey) showing two women equipped as gladiators and fighting without helmets (which may be represented on the ground). The Greek inscription says Amazon and Achillia (obviously stage names) fought bravely to an honorable draw. The relief is dated to the first or second century AD and can be found in the British Museum. I had my ending. I just needed to figure out who my characters were and how they got there.

One of the non-fiction authors I consulted felt Nero encouraged the expansion of women in the games, so I looked closely at his reign and found two remarkable events that happened, in the same timeframe, at opposite ends of the Empire: the expedition to Kush and the British revolt. Both involved cultures where women were valued as more equal partners in life and government than in Rome, and both had powerful queens who defied Roman power—one in battle, one with guile. These cultures could provide plausibly strong (both in body and character) women protagonists. Afra and Cinnia were born. Now to send them on their journey

Although most of my characters are fictional, I placed them at historical events and researched those events and cultures to the best of my ability. I included as much detail from recent archaeology in Kush, Britain, Portus (Rome's seaport), and Pompeii as seemed necessary to enhance the story. Kush is the Egyptian name for the land along the Nile from the first to sixth cataracts (roughly equivalent to modern Sudan). The Romans and Greeks called it Ethiopia. Kush is referred to frequently in Egyptian literature as a source of gold, ivory, timber, and other exotic trade. Egypt occasionally conquered and lost parts of Kush over the millennia only to have Kush conquer Egypt about 760 BC and hold it until 623 BC. I named most of my fictional Kushite characters after Kushite pharaohs and their consorts.

Kushite queens, traditionally, were powerful rulers in their own right. They appear in stone carvings smiting their enemies, and in literature defeating a Roman force. Strabo (in his *Geography*, Vol. II, Book XVII) reports that in 24 BC, a one-eyed warrior queen named Candace (a corruption of *Kandake*, the Kushite title for their queens) "invaded the Thebaïs, and attacked the garrison, consisting of three cohorts, near Syene; surprised and took Syene, Elephantina, and Philae, by a sudden inroad; enslaved the inhabitants, and threw down the statues of Caesar." The bronze head from a statue of Augustus was recently excavated from beneath the doorway of a temple in Meroe and is thought to be from this attack. A great *stela* from south of Meroe commemorates the ruler Amanirenas and her military activities against the Romans. Since she ruled in late first century BC, the timing is right for Amanirenas to be Strabo's warrior queen—and provide a suitable name for my main character, Afra.

Nero sent at least one expedition to Kush possibly in AD 61 or 62 and possibly a second in 66 or 67. Both Pliny and Seneca write of an expedition but with conflicting details. Pliny says the group met a queen, their purpose was to assess whether Kush was worth the effort of invading, and that they surveyed the land south to a drowned land (believed to be the Great Sudd swamp of modern Southern Sudan, approximately 600 miles south of Meroe). Seneca writes the group met a king, they were on a scientific mission to find the source of the Nile, and they surveyed the land south to a great swamp on the White Nile (again the Great Sudd). Some historians believe this means there were two expeditions; others don't. For the purposes of my story, I've combined the two narratives and pushed back the time to AD 60 (since the exact dates are unknown): the Romans meet a royal couple and survey the land under the pretense of "science/exploration," but with the intent of invasion. Afra saves Marcius' life in the Great Swamp and their journey begins.

The British revolt of AD 60-61 was another exercise in choosing between contradictory primary sources. Since I first heard of Boudica, I've been fascinated by her tragic story: wronged queen, vengeful mother, freedom fighter for her people, warrior queen who came *this close* to throwing the mighty Roman Empire off the island of Britain. I was excited about using her story in my book. Over the years, I had collected books and articles about Boudica—many useful and some fanciful. However, once I got into the research I discovered how little we know about Boudica the woman and leader. There are no proven coins linking Boudica or her husband to the Iceni people (or any Celtic tribe). Although the archaeology is rich with detail on the people living in the three towns likely destroyed by the rebellious tribes, again there is nothing directly linking a female ruler named Boudica to the destruction. We're not even sure of her name. In the same way Pliny thought the Kushite title Kandake was a name, Boudica meaning "Victoria" or "Victory" might be a title (or chant) rather than the name of the woman who lead the British rebellion.

Our sole sources for the story are three classical pieces written years after the events, by two men with their own political agendas. Two of those sources are by Tacitus, who wrote after Boudica's death, but within living memory. His two accounts contain contradictory and different details. In *Agricola* (the earlier book), "the whole island rose under the leadership of Boudica, a lady of royal descent—for Britain makes no distinction of sex in their leaders." Later he mentions she rules the Brigantes tribe. In the *Annals* (written later) she rules the Iceni and enlists the help of the Trinovantes tribe. Tacitus adds the details of her husband Prasutagus' death and Roman-style will, Boudica's flogging, and the rape of her daughters to this later narrative. These details— not included in his earlier version—are our sole source for the modern popular story of Boudica.

Cassius Dio wrote one hundred-fifty years after Boudica's death, and his *Roman History* contains details not in Tacitus' accounts, including our only narrative on Claudius' invasion of Britain in AD 43 and the recall of loans, in Nero's time, that Claudius gave to the British nobles, which might have stirred up resentment. Dio's account is similar to Tacitus' earlier *Agricola* version: the whole island rises in rebellion under Boudica; there is no mention of the Iceni or Trinovantes, or the assault on Boudica or her daughters. Dio provides a physical description of Boudica, a lot of gruesome details on the barbarity of the Britons toward their Roman captives, and long inspirational speeches that Boudica and the Roman generals give to their armies—all of which we can accept only with a large helping of salt.

So our two primary sources contradict one another and one contradicts himself. Plus we have to remember these were two Roman elite men writing for other Roman elite men. Richard Hingley and Christina Unwin point out in their excellent book *Boudica: Iron Age Warrior Queen*, that classical writers use a formula when talking about barbarians (anyone not Roman) in general, and barbarian women of power, in particular. The Romans seemed to be deathly afraid of any powerful woman—they did not fit in their social constructs. Whenever barbarian women leaders show up in Roman histories they are disparaged, denigrated, and described in a similar manner. As Stacy Schiff says in her biography of Cleopatra, "Cleopatra ceases to exist without a Roman in the room." These women seldom have their own voices.

So what's an author to do? I decided to go with the popular narrative as described in Tacitus' *Annals* and explain the possible alternative scenarios in this *Note*. Boudica (or a queen by another name given the title "Victoria") almost certainly lived and led a rebellion against the Romans in AD 60-61, destroying three cities and defeating the IXth Legion. But the true motivations and details (including the location of the final battle) are impossible to tease out. In making my choices, I followed Tacitus and Dio closely (including a modernized version of Boudica's apocryphal speech) with a slight difference. Tacitus has Boudica rebelling while Paulinus is subduing the druids of Mona. I wanted Cinnia to be at both events, so I put a little time between the two and added the destruction of Mona as a contributing factor for the rebellion. Tacitus doesn't mention the fate of Boudica's daughters, so I chose to have them escape and provide a way for Cinnia to survive. Who knows? Maybe I got it right.

Once I put my characters on their journey, the next big event was the earthquake in Pompeii in February 62. This event is sometimes referred to as "the first destruction of Pompeii" because of the devastation it caused. Seventeen years later when Vesuvius erupted, there were still buildings under reconstruction and much evidence of repair. It also allowed Nero to reopen the Pompeii arena to gladiator games. The Senate had closed it in AD 59 after deadly riots broke out at the games between the citizens of Pompeii and Nuceria. There's no evidence that Nero ever attended the games in Pompeii, but I put him there to further my plot and set up my next book.

Which brings us back to the beginning: gladiators. One of the major myths about gladiators is that they always fought to the death. This is rooted in the origin of the gladiators where slaves were ordered to fight to the death at funeral games as a sacrifice to the gods. Gladiatorial games evolved over the years from a primarily religious rite to political theater. There are many primary resources on gladiators: classic literature, mosaics, frescos, graffiti, souvenirs, burials, and much more. All the evidence points to the conclusion that at the time I'm writing about, gladiators—especially the top ranked ones—were highly valued property.

Much like modern athletes, the best gladiators commanded top money for their performances and numerous women wanted to have sex with them. Vendors sold souvenirs with their names and likenesses and fans covered the walls of buildings with graffiti extolling the skills (both fighting and sexual) of their favorites. It was rare for a crowd to demand the death of a favorite, even in defeat, if they fought well. *Editors* had to reimburse owners for the value of gladiators who died or were freed during their games, so it was in their economic interest to allow a defeated gladiator to live, unless the crowd was totally disappointed in the performance.

I researched what is known about gladiatorial combat during this time period: the training, equipment, arenas, other entertainments (including executions), rituals, and rules. Some scenes from my book inspired by documented events include: the mass suicide of gladiator trainees, Afra's cheetahs protecting their former trainer in the arena, the outcome of Afra and Cinnia's fight, and Nero's poetic speech at the end. My apologies to Martial, who wrote the original poem in AD 80, about

Priscus and Verus, two male gladiators, who fought to a draw during the inauguration of the great Flavian Amphitheater (now known as the Coliseum). Emperor Vespasian gave them both victory and freedom.

Throughout this book, although a work of fiction, I tried to be as accurate as possible in my details, and make clear in this *Note* where and why I made choices between what is disputed or unknown. But, I'm sure I screwed up somewhere and my readers will let me know. If you have questions or comments, I'd love to hear them. You can contact me through my website at faithljustice.com.

Glossary

- *aedile*—city office responsible for maintaining public buildings, regulating public festivals, and enforcing public order
- Ammit (also known as Ammut and Ahemait)—ancient Egyptian goddess of divine retribution
- Andraste (also known as Andrasta, Adraste, Andred)—patron goddess of the Iceni tribe, the goddess of victory, of ravens and of battles. Her name is thought to mean "the invincible one" or "she who has not fallen"
- ankh—key of life, the key of the Nile or *crux ansata* (Latin meaning "cross with a handle"), was the ancient Egyptian hieroglyphic character for "life"
- *as* (singular) *asses* (plural)—bronze (later copper) coin, smallest denomination minted by Rome, four made a *sestertius* and sixteen made a *denarius*
- Atalanta—a character in Greek mythology, a virgin huntress known for her fleetness
- *aureus* (singular) *aurei* (plural)—gold coin valued at 25 silver *denarii* or 100 *sestertii*
- *ba*—one of five parts of the soul believed by Egyptians to be everything that makes an individual unique; lives on after the body dies; sometimes depicted as a human-headed bird flying out of the tomb to join with the *ka* (another aspect of the soul, its vital essence) in the afterlife
- *beastiarius* (singular) *beastiarii* (plural)—animal fighters (as opposed to *venetorii* who were animal hunters) in the Roman games
- *beneficiarii*—retired legionnaires used for tax collecting and general policing by civil government
- Brigantes—Celtic tribe located in what is now northern England, ruled by Queen Cartimandua possibly from the time of the Claudian Roman invasion until her death about AD 69

- *buccinae*—curved horns used by the Roman military
- *Campus Martius*—"Field of Mars" a low-lying plain enclosed on the west by a bend of the Tiber River near Tiber Island, on the east by the Quirinal Hill, and on the southeast by the Capitoline Hill, originally used for pasturing horses and sheep, and for military training
- Camulodunum—town (modern day Colchester) established on Trinovante land for retired Roman legionaries and their families, destroyed in Boudica's rebellion
- *carnyx*—curved Celtic war horn
- Cartimandua—queen of the Brigantes, possibly from the time of the Roman invasion until her death about AD 69
- Cerealia—major Roman festival celebrated for the grain goddess Ceres, held for seven days from mid- to late April
- Cernunnos—"The Horned One" a Celtic god of fertility, life, animals, wealth, and the underworld
- *collegia*—numerous private associations with specialized functions such as craft or trade guilds, burial societies, and societies dedicated to special religious worship
- *colonia*—towns founded for Roman citizens; in Britain, those who had completed their military service in the Legions and were owed a grant of land
- consul—the highest elected political office of the Roman Republic; after the establishment of the Empire, the consuls were merely a figurative representative of Rome's republican heritage and held very little power or authority, with the Emperor acting as the supreme leader
- Coritani (also Corieltauvi/Corieltavi)—Celtic tribe who lived in what is now the English East Midlands, in the counties of Lincolnshire and Leicestershire
- Cornovii—Celtic tribe who lived principally in the modern English counties of Cheshire, Shropshire, north Staffordshire, north Herefordshire and eastern parts of the Welsh counties of Flintshire, Powys and Wrexham

- *denarius* (single) *denarii* (plural)—a small silver coin worth sixteen *asses* or four *sestertii*
- *doctore*—gladiator fight instructor
- *Domina/Dominus*—mistress/master
- *editor*—Roman noble who sponsored/gave gladiatorial games
- faience—a quartz ceramic with a bright luster, usually blue-green that can be cast in molds and widely used for small objects from beads to statues
- *fascinum*—the embodiment of the divine phallus; refers to the deity himself (Fascinus), to phallus effigies and amulets, and to the spells used to invoke his divine protection against the evil eye
- *fibula* (singular) *fibulae* (plural)—an ornamental clasp designed to hold clothing together; usually made of silver or gold but sometimes bronze or some other material; used by Greeks, Romans, and Celts
- Fortuna—Roman goddess of fortune and personification of luck both good and bad; sometimes veiled and blind, as in modern depictions of Justice; also represented life's capriciousness or fate
- *Forum Romanum*—a rectangular plaza located in a small valley between the Palatine and Capitoline Hills, surrounded by government buildings at the center of the city; the site of triumphal processions and elections; the venue for public speeches, criminal trials, and gladiatorial matches; the nucleus of commercial affairs in Rome
- *gladius* (singular) *gladii* (plural)—the primary sword of Roman foot soldiers; *gladii* were two-edged for cutting with a tapered point for stabbing during thrusting and a knobbed hilt; root for the term *gladiator* (swordsman)
- greave—metal leg guard used by soldiers and gladiators, extending from ankle to knee and tied at the back; ceremonial ones are highly decorated with images, sometimes gilded
- *hasta* (singular) *hastii* (plural)—Roman thrusting spear with a leaf-shaped blade
- Iceni (also known as Eceni)—a Celtic tribe inhabiting roughly the modern-day county of Norfolk; according to Tacitus, the tribe ruled

by King Prasutagus and rebelled against the Romans under their Queen Boudica in AD 60 or 61

- *Imbolc*—a Celtic seasonal festival marking the beginning of spring; associated with the goddess Brigid; generally celebrated on February 1
- *insula* (singular) *insulae* (plural)—"island"; an apartment building that housed most of the lower- or middle-class urban citizen population of Rome; ground-level floors housed taverns, shops and businesses, with living space upstairs; could be up to six or seven stories
- Isis—Egyptian goddess worshipped as the ideal mother and wife as well as the patroness of slaves, sinners, artisans, and the downtrodden; often depicted as the mother of Horus, the falcon-headed deity associated with king and kingship
- Juno—major Roman goddess, protector and special counselor of the state, sister and wife of the chief god Jupiter, patron goddess of the women of Rome
- Jupiter (Jove)—the chief deity of Roman state religion; king of the gods and the god of sky and thunder; personified the divine authority of Rome's highest offices, internal organization, and external relations; presided over oaths and justice
- *Kandake*—Kushite title for queen
- kohl—black eye makeup made by grinding lead sulfide with other ingredients, used in Egypt and the Middle East for cosmetic purposes and to protect from the sun
- Kush—an ancient African kingdom situated on the confluences of the Blue Nile, White Nile and River Atbara in what is now the Republic of Sudan
- *lanista* (singular) *lanistae* (plural)—owner of a gladiator school
- *lar* (singular) *lares* (plural)—guardian deities who may have been hero-ancestors, guardians of the hearth, fields, boundaries or fruitfulness; they observed, protected and influenced all that happened within the boundaries of their location or function
- *Legio IX Hispana*—(Spanish Ninth Legion) was one of four legions used by Aulus Plautius and Claudius in the Roman invasion of Britain in 43; Boudica's forces destroyed its infantry as the legion moved

to support Camulodunum; the cavalry and commander Quintus Petillius Cerialis retreated

- *Legio XIV Gemina Martia Victrix*–(Fourteenth Victorious Twin Legion of the God Mars) was one of four legions used by Aulus Plautius and Claudius in the Roman invasion of Britain in 43, and took part in the defeat of Boudica in 60 or 61
- *Legio XX Valeria Victrix*—(Twentieth Victorious Valerian Legion) was one of four legions used by Aulus Plautius and Claudius in the Roman invasion of Britain in 43, and took part in the defeat of Boudicca in 60 or 61
- Londinium—trading town established by the Romans (modern day London) and destroyed in Boudica's rebellion
- *ludus* (singular) *ludi* (plural)—training school for gladiators; also elementary or primary school attended by boys and girls up to age eleven
- *marcellum*—market building usually covered
- Mercury—a major Roman god, patron of financial gain, commerce, poetry, divination, travelers, boundaries, luck, trickery, and thieves; also the guide of souls to the underworld
- *missio*—reprieve; the loser in a gladiator contest is allowed to live
- mole—a massive structure, usually of stone, used as a pier, breakwater, or causeway between places separated by water; but, unlike a true pier, water cannot freely flow underneath it
- *myrmillo* (masculine) *myrmilla* (feminine)—(from *mormylos* or sea fish) style of gladiator using full helmet (usually crested with a fish), full-sized rectangular shield, *gladius*, leather articulated arm shield, and one greave
- Nuceria—Roman city in Campania, Italy; a riot between the citizens of Pompeii and Nuceria at the Pompeii Amphitheater in AD 59 resulted in a ten-year ban on gladiator games in Pompeii
- *noxii*—"noxious ones"—convicts condemned to death in the arena in various ways: executed in mythological reenactments, forced to fight each other to the death, fed to wild beasts, etc.

- *oppidum* (singular) *oppida* (plural)—"enclosed space"—large defended settlement associated with Celtic culture, common in the second century BC through first century AD; important economic sites, places where goods were produced, stored and traded; also political centers, the seat of authorities taking decisions that affected large numbers of people
- *palaestra*—open area used for sports training, usually a square or rectangle enclosed by colonnades along four sides creating porticoes and rooms for storage and bathing; in imperial Rome these were frequently attached to baths
- *palla*—outermost rectangular woman's mantle/shawl worn over the shoulders and hair
- *Pater Patriae*—"Father of the Country" an honorific conferred by the Roman Senate since 386 BC; not all emperors were offered it and not all those who were offered it, accepted; Nero first declined the honor because of his youth, but accepted later
- *peculium*—any property held by a slave with permission from the slave's owner; slave's purse and contents
- *peristyle*—a columned porch or open colonnade in a building surrounding a court that may contain an internal garden
- *perit*—"He's finished!" Cry from the arena crowds urging the death blow for a surviving losing gladiator
- *pilum* (single), *pila* (plural)—javelin used by the Roman army with a shank made of soft iron which bent after impact (rendering the weapon useless to the enemy who might throw it back) and entangling any shield it might penetrate making the shield useless
- Portus—Rome's primary sea port, built by Claudius to handle large merchant ships including the grain fleet
- *primus palus*—"first pole"—elite gladiator, first in the company
- *procurator munerum*—administrator responsible for organizing the games on the emperor's behalf
- *Pontifex Maximus*—"greatest pontiff"—the high priest of the College of Pontiffs, the most important position in the ancient

Roman religion; it gradually became politicized until, beginning with Augustus, it was subsumed into the Imperial office

- *Qore*—Kushite title for king

- *retiarius* (masculine) *retiaria* (feminine)—"net fighter"—gladiator fighting style featuring a lightly-armored (shoulder guard, padding on arm and legs) fighter with a leaded net, trident, and knife; usually paired with a *secutor*, but sometimes fought a *myrmillo*

- Rhakotis—a poor district in Alexandria mostly inhabited by native Egyptians; the name of the village where Alexander the Great built his city

- *rostra*—a large platform in Rome where speakers would deliver orations; named for the six *rostra* (warship's rams) which were captured during the victory at Antium in 338 BC and mounted to its side

- *secutor*—"pursuer"—gladiator fighting style developed to pair with the *retiarius*, similar to *myrmillo* with full shield, gladius, greaves, and articulated arm shield, but the smooth helmet encloses the whole head with only two eye holes as protection against the *retiarius'* trident

- *sestertius* (singular) *sestertii* (plural)—large brass coin worth four *asses* and the standard unit of account (for most of the first century AD an ordinary legionary earned 900 sestertii a year)

- *sica*—curved sword used by gladiators fighting as Thracians

- Silures—a powerful and warlike tribe or tribal confederation of ancient Britain, occupying what is now south east Wales; they fiercely resisted Roman conquest and waged effective guerilla warfare against Roman forces until about AD 78

- *sistrum* (singular) *sistra* (plural)—a musical instrument of the percussion family; it has a handle and a U-shaped metal frame, made of brass or bronze with small rings or loops of thin metal on movable crossbars that produce a sound from a soft clank to a loud jangling; from the Greek "that which is being shaken"

- *stans missus*—a draw in a gladiator game

- *stoa*—an open covered walkway supported by columns, lining the side of a building, or surrounding the marketplace, open to the public; merchants and artists could sell their goods, and religious gatherings took place
- *stola*—long, pleated dress, worn over a tunic, generally sleeveless, fastened by clasps at the shoulder called *fibulae*, usually made of fabrics like linen or wool, worn as a symbol representing a Roman woman's marital status
- *strigil*—curved brass instrument used to scrape oil off skin
- *subligaculum*—Roman undergarment/loincloth wrapped around the lower body; worn by both men and women; part of the dress of gladiators, athletes, and stage actors
- *summa rudis*—referee for gladiator games; a man armed with a stout wooden rod to call fouls, breaks, and beat any reluctant fighter
- Taharqa—a pharaoh of the Ancient Egyptian 25th dynasty and king of Kush from 690 BC to 664 BC; buried at modern-day Nuri in Sudan in a pyramid tomb measuring over 50 meters high
- *tali*—"knucklebones"—popular Roman gambling game using four rectangular shaped dice (originally made of sheep or goat knucklebones, later were made from metals, wood, terracotta, precious gems, etc. but the original shape of the knucklebones was preserved); the four sides of the dice were marked with symbols or numbers (1, 3, 4, 6); the Venus throw where each die showed a different value was the best outcome
- Taranis—Celtic god of thunder worshipped essentially in Gaul, Gallaecia, Britain, and Ireland to whom human sacrificial offerings were made; associated with the wheel
- Thracian—gladiator fighting style using a curved Thracian sword (*sica*), small round or square-shaped shield, full shin greaves, articulated arm guard, and crested broad-rimmed helmet with face grill; frequently paired with *myrmillo*
- *tirones*—new recruits in gladiator schools and the Roman army
- *tribade*—lesbian

- Trinovantes—Celtic tribe inhabiting the north side of the Thames estuary in current Essex and Suffolk, and included lands now located in Greater London; fought in Boudica's rebellion according to Tacitus
- *velarium*—canvas awning deployed over the seats of the amphitheater to provide shade and to create a ventilation updraft to encourage circulation and a cool breeze
- *venatore* (singular) *venatorii* (plural)—animal hunter in gladiatorial games
- Verulamium—a Roman settlement located in the southwest of the modern city of St Albans in Hertfordshire; destroyed in Boudica's rebellion

About the Author

FAITH L. JUSTICE is a science geek and history junkie, which is reflected in her writing. Her short stories and poems have appeared in such publications as *The Copperfield Review*, *Beyond Science Fiction and Fantasy*, and the *Circles in the Hair* anthology. Her historical novel *Selene of Alexandria* was a finalist in the 2011 Global eBook Awards. Faith has published in venues such as *Salon.com*, *Writer's Digest*, *The Writer*, and *Bygone Days*. She's an Associate Editor for *Space & Time Magazine*, a frequent contributor to *Strange Horizons*, and co-founded a writer's workshop more years ago than she cares to admit. To read her essays and interviews, get a sneak preview of her historical novels, or ask a question or leave a comment, contact Faith online:

Website/Blog: faithljustice.com
LinkedIn: linkedin.com/profile/view?id=64543293
Twitter: @faithljustice
Facebook: facebook.com/faith.justice.7

OTHER BOOKS BY FAITH L. JUSTICE

SELENE OF ALEXANDRIA

"…readers will be captivated."—Historical Novel Society

"…does what historical fiction does best—weave historical fact, real-life historical figures, and attention to detail with page-turning, plot-driven fiction."—The Copperfield Review

This story of ambition, love and political intrigue brings to life colorful characters and an exotic time and place. In A.D. 412 Alexandria, against the backdrop of a city torn by religious and political strife, Selene struggles to achieve her dream of becoming a physician—an unlikely goal for an upper class Christian girl. Hypatia, the famed Lady Philosopher of Alexandria and the Augustal Prefect Orestes offer their patronage and protection. But will it be enough to save Selene from murderous riots, the machinations of a charismatic Bishop and—most dangerous of all—her own impulsive nature?

HYPATIA: HER LIFE AND TIMES

Who was Hypatia of Alexandria? A brilliant young mathematician murdered by a religious mob? An aging academic eliminated by a rival political party? A sorceress who enthralled the Prefect of Alexandria through satanic wiles? Did she discover the earth circled the sun a thousand years before Copernicus or was she merely a gifted geometry teacher? Discover the answers to these questions and more in these essays on Hypatia's life and times.

AVAILABLE IN PRINT AND EBOOKS IN ALL THE USUAL PLACES.

TIME AGAIN AND OTHER FANTASTIC STORIES

What would you do with an extra hour of life? Kiss your sweetheart? Eat ice cream? Graffiti your workplace? Find out how one man uses his bonus hour in the award-winning story "Time Again." Then check out how a young woman deals with a transforming experience, business consultant Alice overhauls Wonderland, a fierce mother takes on the devil who wants to marry her daughter, and more, in this collection of the author's best fantasy stories.

SLOW DEATH AND OTHER DARK TALES

Looking for sparkly vampires or heroic werewolves? Sorry, humans—and the occasional ghost—intent on murder, revenge, and righting wrongs take center stage in these tales. Meet a grieving mother witnessing a death-row execution, a wronged bureaucrat condemned to a future drug rehabilitation center, an Alzheimer's patient trapped in his own deteriorating mind, a ghost on a mission of justice, and more in this collection of the author's best dark fiction.

COMING IN 2015:

TWILIGHT EMPRESS: A NOVEL OF IMPERIAL ROME

Twilight Empress tells the little-known story of a remarkable woman—Galla Placidia, sister to one of the last Roman Emperors. Roman princess, Gothic captive and queen—Galla Placidia does the unthinkable—she rules the failing Western Roman Empire—a life of ambition, power and intrigue she doesn't seek, but can't refuse. Her actions shape the face of Western Europe for centuries. A woman as well as an Empress, Galla Placidia suffers love, loss, and betrayal. Can her strength, tenacity, and ambition help her triumph over scheming generals, rebellious children, and Attila the Hun?

RAGGEDY MOON BOOKS

raggedymoonbooks.com

www.ingramcontent.com/pod-product-compliance
Lightning Source LLC
Chambersburg PA
CBHW070553120726
47909CB00007B/2333